I0639023

STOLEN MEMORIES

A LUCKY TOWN NOVEL

BOOK 3

AMANDA SIEGRIST

ALSO BY AMANDA SIEGRIST

A happy ending is all I need.

Consequences Novel

Dark Consequences

Cruel Consequences

Fatal Consequences

Haunting Love Novel

Third Time's the Charm

Thirteen Days Gone

One Mistake Too Late

Holiday Romance Novel

Merry Me

Mistletoe Magic

Christmas Wish

Snowed in Love

Snowflakes and Shots

Holiday Hope

Sleigh All the Way

Lucky Town Novel

Escaping Memories

Dangerous Memories

Stolen Memories

Deadly Memories

Forgotten Memories

McCord Family Novel

Protecting You

Trust in Love

Deserving You

Always Kind of Love

Finding You

Dare You to Love

Mona & Mason

The Paranormal Chronicles, Volume I

Perfect For You Novel

The Wrong Brother

The Right Time

The Easy Part

The Hard Choice

Psychic Love Novel

Exploding Love

Captured Love

Slaying Love Novel

Won't Let You Go

Doomed Love

Deadly Crazy

Evidence of Sin

Finding Redemption

Obsessed Hope

Short Stories

Paint By Murder

Follow Me, Sweet Darling

Sleighville Novel

Dashing Through the Fear

Here Comes Chaos

The Last Noel

Standalone Novel

The Danger with Love

Conquering Fear Novel

CO-WRITTEN WITH JANE BLYTHE

Drowning in You

Out of the Darkness

Closing In

SOME SECRETS ARE WORTH KILLING FOR...

1

SETH SLAMMED his truck door shut and jogged toward the gas station, wanting to get from one warmth to the next. The temperature was brutal out, only single digits. He would've loved to take the day off work and finish redoing the cabinets in his house, but his bills had to be paid. Being a carpenter—and the local handyman of the town—he had plenty to do. It was rare when he took a day off. There was always someone needing his assistance.

In the past two months, he might've taken on more work than was necessary. He needed to occupy his mind with something other than his best friend, Evan—*former* best friend.

Pulling open the door, attempting to erase any damaging thoughts that would lower his mood, he headed to grab an energy drink. He stayed up late last night sanding his kitchen cupboards—too late—and he needed a little pick-me-up before work.

As he rounded the aisle, he knocked right into a woman. The bottle she was holding slipped from her fingers and hit the floor, shattering and spilling the contents everywhere.

"Shit! I'm so sorry." Seth steadied her by grabbing her shoulders, glanced at the floor and the mess between them, then his gaze landed on her.

All the air rushed out of his body, like a sucker punch to the gut. Oh, he'd been hit hard in the gut before. Grasping for air. Pain radiating everywhere. One look at this woman, and he was feeling the same effects.

Long blonde hair past her shoulders—at least, that's what he figured considering how long her ponytail was. Not the curly kind that Stacy, his ex-girlfriend, had but straight, perfect hair. It looked silky soft. He wanted to run his hands through it to see how soft it truly was.

Exquisite hazel eyes, so expressive and dynamic. Right now, they looked to be vibrating with irritation. He hadn't meant to bump into her, but he wasn't *that* sorry. He could stand here all day and drown in her amber depths.

He had green eyes. Dull, in his opinion, but on the rare occasion he wore a particular shade of green, people would comment on how it made his eyes pop and look pretty. Not that he liked being described as pretty. But *her eyes*...oh, her eyes were pretty.

No.

Gorgeous.

Utterly gorgeous.

Beyond gorgeous.

"You can remove your hands from my shoulders."

Her stern tone and the harshness in her eyes snapped him out of his gawking. Shit. He was gawking and acting like a man who had never seen a woman before. Letting go of her shoulders, he pulled his best smile out, hoping to ease one out of her. Oh, he knew a smile would only enhance her beauty. He wanted to see her smile.

"I'm sorry. I didn't mean to run into you."

He honestly hadn't. His mind was everywhere these days. Trying hard to forget about his best friend and how much he wanted their friendship back but still so hurt that Evan had lied to him. Trying hard to forget how his sister Kat had been hurt and how he should've been able to protect her. But he'd failed. Trying hard to forget how useless he was in helping Aubrey when it seemed like Kat and Logan could help her with ease.

Yeah, his mind tended to wander a lot. That's why he worked all the time or found different projects in his house. He needed to keep occupied with something.

She backed up, her expression still unyielding, then stepped around him. "I'll go find someone to clean up this mess."

He watched her walk down the aisle. Her attitude was a little odd, especially since he apologized, but hey, maybe she wasn't a morning person. He wasn't that much of one until he had his coffee. And he usually had two cups. One at home and one at work.

What was he doing?

He shouldn't just be gawking and letting such perfection —beautiful perfection—walk away from him without getting her number. Instead of working himself to the bone every day, all day, he could release his frustrations in another way. A beautiful woman would be a nice distraction for once.

Damn, even from behind she was something. She had on a snug winter coat just past her hips, so he saw a hint of her ass. Her tight jeans gave him enough of a picture that she had a perfect round ass meant for his hands.

"Hey!"

Her steps slowed. She swiveled in his direction. The

expression she wore displayed a bit of annoyance, and irritation still lingered in her eyes.

"Let me buy you another drink." His hand pointed to the floor at what looked like a Frappuccino flavored drink. "To replace the one I broke."

Then, like the sun rising for a brand-new day, a hint of a smile appeared. "Oh, you'll be paying for that bottle you broke. But that's it." She pivoted around and kept walking as if she hadn't just broken his heart.

And damn. Seth was pretty sure she did.

That was definitely a brush-off.

He was just cold-shouldered by the most beautiful woman he'd ever seen. He thought about following her, but didn't want to seem stalkerish. He had already made a fool of himself by running into her. She said she'd find someone to clean up the mess, so he walked past the spilled drink to grab his own from the cooler, and he decided it was for the best. His life at the moment was a mess. Asking a woman out should be the furthest thing from his mind.

Sure, life was back to normal after everything that happened two months ago. It appeared normal, but it was far from it. His sister was shot—with him standing right next to her. He almost watched his sister die. Some nights, he dreamt of running through the woods with her slung over his shoulder as he ran hard to get her help. Sometimes, it turned into a horrifying nightmare where he never stopped running, blood running down his chest as his sister's life slowly withered away. Some nights, he made it to the cabin as he had in real life, but she died before he reached the cabin. He hated dreaming about it at all.

Aubrey was doing much better, her fear of the dark improving. Not one hundred percent, but better than two months ago. As far as he knew, anyway. He didn't visit her and Logan as often as he should. Being around Logan showed him he'd never be as good a man as Logan was. Some days, he hated himself and didn't understand why Logan didn't shut him out of his life. He hit him. He hurt his brother. He should've never been forgiven for doing something so malicious. He still hadn't forgiven himself for it. But he tried to ignore it since it appeared Logan had moved on. Because if he didn't, Logan would get on his case about what was wrong, and he didn't want to talk about it.

Aubrey and his brother Logan were planning their wedding for this summer. Logan was distracted with that, and so was Aubrey, which was good for her. It was better than the bad memories of her abduction.

His sister Kat was happy living with Danny, Aubrey's brother. Danny had yet to ask her to marry him, but their relationship was solid and moving along great. He had never seen his sister as happy as she was with Danny. After being shot, she deserved happiness.

And him...

His life sucked.

He had no girlfriend, which was okay. He didn't need one. He and Stacy weren't meant to be. It was for the best they ended their relationship four months ago.

He had no best friend. Although Evan called two months ago—after everything went down with Evan's half-brother Joshua—hoping to make amends. At the time, surrounded by his family, he thought, sure, why not. But when it came to actually meet Evan for drinks, he never showed. He didn't want to forgive the asshole for the things he'd done. For the things he should've confessed when Aubrey was first found. Maybe Kat never would've been hurt if he had.

Evan never tried contacting him again. Seth was okay with that.

He worked, slept, worked, slept, and so on. Day in and day out. That's what his life consisted of. He would occasionally pop in with his family; otherwise, they'd be at his door wondering why he was ignoring them.

No matter how many times he ruminated about how to fix his life, how to feel an ounce of happiness for once, he couldn't find a solution.

He needed to get the gorgeous woman out of his mind. He knew meeting some random woman wasn't the answer to his problems.

Grabbing a drink, he noticed the woman had told Greg, a nice, laidback guy who worked the gas station every morning, about the spill.

"Sorry about the mess, man. I can get it."

Greg waved him off with a friendly grin. "Nah, I got it. Did you see that chick?" He blew out a breath and lifted his brows in amusement. "So hot."

Yeah, Seth saw her, all right. Made a complete jackass of himself.

"I'll be paying for the drink on the floor." Seth looked back to where he could grab a Frappuccino drink. "I should grab her a new one. I feel bad."

"She left. Told me about the mess and stalked out of here. She's hot, but with a 'tude." Obviously. He didn't mean to knock into her and ruin her morning. He probably dodged a bullet with her.

Greg had the mess cleaned quickly and then rang up his drink and the drink that splattered all over the floor.

Seth stepped outside into the brutal cold and raced back to his truck.

He turned on the heat and rubbed his hands—trying to

get his mind back on track and into work mode. He needed to try harder and not think about the past but focus on his future.

Just as he was putting his truck in drive, his phone rang.

He pulled it out of his pocket, debating for a second whether he wanted to answer Logan's phone call. It wouldn't be the first time he ignored one of his brother's calls. Immature, yeah. Did he care? Well...yeah. But sometimes, he wanted to be left alone. He didn't want people in his space, bugging him, making sure he was okay.

But he was trying to act better. He was trying to act like... a grownup. Because, although he might not admit it out loud, he had acted like a spoiled, rotten child the past few months. He needed to grow up and start acting like he was twenty-five and not sixteen. His birthday was coming up in a few weeks. He was inching closer and closer to thirty. It was way past time he started acting his age.

"Hey, Logan, what's up?"

A heavy sigh sounded in his ear. "I need you to come down to Barry's Garage. Right now, if you can."

Barry's Garage...

Evan worked there.

Why would his brother want him to go there? Was this a sort of it's-time-to-make-up-with-Evan sort of thing? He wasn't interested.

"Please, Seth." Another heavy sigh sounded. "I wouldn't ask if it wasn't important."

"Yeah, okay." He slowly put his foot on the gas. "What's going on? Why do I need to come?"

"I...just come right away. I don't want to talk about it over the phone."

Seth's heart raced at all the possible scenarios.

The only scenario that had his heart speeding double time was...Evan was dead.

He couldn't even say why his thoughts immediately went in that direction, but they did.

As he drove to the place his best friend had worked since he was eighteen years old, he only had one regret.

Not showing up to meet him and make amends when he had the chance.

TRYING to find a calm within the brewing storm, she took several deep breaths before opening her car door and stepping outside before she changed her mind.

It was a done deal. She was here, and she had to follow through. There was no backing out now, especially since it had been her idea.

Forcing herself not to give the impression she was nervous—because, oh, boy, she was nervous—she made the quick distance from the parking lot to the sheriff's building in a lot fewer steps than she anticipated.

She shouldn't be nervous. Her job was the one thing she excelled at. She had no reason to be nervous. Of course, that didn't stop the nerves from pulsating through her veins.

As she walked inside, she started to smile, but then stopped right before it punctured her features.

No smiling. She had no reason to smile.

She had to be professional and in control at all times. Because if she lost control, she'd lose her mind and her grip on sanity.

And when it came to her job, she was always in control.

"Hi, can I help you?" the woman behind a very clean desk asked as she stood. She had a friendly smile, and her black hair was tied in a loose ponytail. She wore minimal makeup, but she was very pretty. Not that any of that mattered. Only her mission mattered.

Showtime.

She could do this.

"I'm Deputy Pepper Wilson. It's my first day." Then she lifted her arm and pushed back her jacket sleeve to look at her watch. "I'm a bit early. I hope that's okay."

She was always punctual. She hated being late for anything.

The woman's brows rose. Her smile remained, yet it wavered a fraction. "Of course. I was expecting you in about an hour. You're very early."

"I like to be prompt. It's my first day, and I didn't want to be late." And she couldn't take the nervous energy creating chaos in her body. Pacing back and forth in her house had finally driven her nuts, and she had to come.

"I'm Charlotte. If you need anything, I'm your girl. I run the front desk and all the calls that come through the office." Charlotte rounded the desk and held out her hand. "It's nice to meet you. Welcome to Lucky. It's a great town." Then she rolled her eyes and laughed. "But it has its moments of gossip."

She shook her hand, as required, so she didn't look like a complete bitch because she knew she was sounding like one. Her tone didn't alter once from a brisk, business-like manner. Strict and rigid in everything. By the book. Focus and determined.

Because she had to be all those things.

She could not fail in her mission.

"Thank you. When I spoke to Sheriff Caldwell over the phone, he said there would be a uniform waiting for me."

"Yes, and you need to change quickly. I'll show you

everything you need and out the door you go." Charlotte waved her to follow.

"Out the door...already? Is the sheriff in? I thought...maybe...he'd show me around."

Damn. That didn't sound confident. She needed to rein in her nerves. The last thing she needed was the people in this town to turn suspicious.

Charlotte stopped and turned, her smile disappearing. "The sheriff's not here. You'll be joining him soon, though... at a crime scene. We have a dead body."

Then Charlotte continued walking.

She just stood there.

A dead body?

The last dead body she had looked at—

Nope. She couldn't go there right now because, if she did, she'd lose her mind.

She could do this. A dead body was nothing. She only had to put her game face on and do her job like she always did.

Inhaling sharply, removing the moment of insecurity, she steeled her shoulders and caught up to Charlotte before she realized she'd even hesitated.

A uniform, which surprisingly fit her to perfection, was waiting for her in a small locker room. Charlotte was waiting for her in the room when she stepped out of the bathroom all dressed and ready to go.

Lying on the table before her was a badge and gun.

"Here are your things. I'm very sorry that your first day isn't laid-back with a nice tour around town. We don't get many dead bodies around here, if ever. Although, the past few months have been rough." Charlotte's features dimmed into sadness before vanishing in a flash. "But Sheriff Caldwell is the best. If there's a problem, he fixes it. Bolt—

Deputy Bolten, but everyone calls him Bolt—is very nice and will show you the ropes as well. With your background in law enforcement, you'll fit right in as if you've been here forever."

She sure hoped so, but unfortunately, she didn't hold that same belief. She never made friends easily. Not in school. Not at work. Not even in her own family. People usually couldn't handle her stern demeanor. One coworker had even described her as a "force of nature," and he hadn't meant it in a nice, pleasant way.

Her entire life was a lie.

If Charlotte knew everything...

Well, she didn't. Neither did the sheriff or anyone else. As long as she played her part right, no one would know. She could do what she came here to do and then leave. Try to be happy for once. Something that had been elusive and out of her reach for as long as she could remember.

"Location of the crime scene?"

Charlotte blinked, twitching in surprise as if expecting her to say something else. Like, thank you? She wasn't going to say anything else. Straight and to the point. She was here to work, not play around with pleasantries.

She couldn't afford to let these people in.

Plus, she didn't know who she could trust.

And until she got a handle on things and met everyone, she wouldn't trust a soul. Her gut usually didn't steer her wrong. Right now, it said she could trust Charlotte, but one simple encounter wasn't enough to make a clear decision.

"Umm...well, do you have GPS on your phone? I can give you the address to Barry's Garage. That's where you need to go."

Oh, she didn't need her GPS. She did her research. She knew this town from top to bottom. She could walk it with her eyes closed. Well, hopefully. Her research had been a little rushed. There could be times when she would need to use the GPS. She couldn't start to act overconfident. That's when mistakes happened.

"I know where it is."

Charlotte nodded, her brows dipping. "Okay, good. It's good to have you here. It's been rough the past two weeks with just Sheriff Caldwell and Bolt. I'm happy you're here."

"Thank you."

There. That thank you would have to suffice for her lack of the other one.

Then, with no smile or offering any pleasant words of her own—because she *was* appreciative to Charlotte for welcoming her to the department—she grabbed her badge and gun. Double-checking the weapon was loaded and working sufficiently, she added it to her utility belt.

Hopefully, she didn't have to fire it at all. The last time she fired her weapon…

Yeah, she didn't want to think about that either.

"Is there anything else you need or I can help you with?" Charlotte asked, all sense of friendliness gone.

"No."

With her back ramrod straight, her face expressionless, she walked out of the room and to something she hadn't expected on her first day in town.

A dead body.

What was she getting herself into?

2

—————

Seth pulled up behind Logan's vehicle and put his truck in park. He saw Dr. Matthews walk inside the garage, disappearing from his view, and his brother standing right outside looking in his direction.

He had an intense urge to put his truck back into drive and get as far away from this place as possible. Knowing he couldn't ignore his brother, he turned the truck off and stepped outside into the brutal cold.

Logan met him halfway.

Was it to shield him from seeing his best friend's dead body?

Was he dead?

What was going on?

"Thanks for coming." Logan ran a gloved hand down his face. "It's…"

"He's dead, isn't he?" Seth blurted when his brother couldn't seem to finish his sentence.

Logan's eyes rounded in disbelief and then shame lit his expression. "Shit, Seth. I'm sorry, I didn't mean to make you think...it's not Evan. It's Barry. He's...he was crushed by a car."

"Crushed?"

It didn't make sense. A freak accident? Barry was the best mechanic around these parts. He knew cars inside and out. A person could throw him a question and he always knew the answer. Evan aspired to be just as good, working hard every day, learning and absorbing so many things from Barry.

Logan looked down at the ground, rubbing another hand over his face, then he met his gaze. "Yeah, it looks like he was working underneath a vehicle and it fell on him somehow. A quick check of the system showed it was working properly, so..." Logan shrugged. "Could've been an accident."

Silence lingered in the air.

"Or could've not been..." Seth said, wanting to get the reason why he had to show up out in the open. It was freezing out and he had to get to work. "What did Evan say happened?"

Logan sighed heavily. "You know I love you, right?" Logan laughed and shook his head. "No matter how I say this, you're going to get pissed like you did last time I said anything about Evan."

"Yeah, well, I learned my lesson, didn't I? My best friend is a damn liar. So if he gave you a version of events that you don't believe, I'd say don't believe them."

His brother was wrong this time. He had no intention of getting upset over his former best friend. And he had a lot of making up to do with his actions in the past. He had to start giving his brother the benefit of the doubt and let him do his job without acting like a crybaby. His brother was damn good at his job, and Seth knew this. He knew, even though he didn't act like it, that his brother never meant to disrespect him when he was doing what he had to do.

"Well, that's the thing. I haven't spoken to Evan. He hasn't been by the garage yet, and he should be here by now. He's always at work at seven, like Barry. Stan found Barry and called it in. He was here early this morning to pick up his car before work. I had Bolt go to Evan's house, and he's not there either. His car isn't here, and it's not at home. Right now, I have no idea where Evan is. He's not answering his phone."

Seth's entire stomach dropped. A nasty, churning sensation filled him to the point he wanted to throw up.

"What are you saying, Logan?"

Logan's expression softened, yet the hard glint in his eyes didn't waver. "I'm saying I have a dead body and a missing employee. There could be a few reasons for him not showing, but the big glaring one is...because...he killed Barry."

Seth staggered back as if Logan sucker punched him in the gut. And he wouldn't fight back if his brother decided to take a swing. Seth still hadn't forgiven himself for punching Logan in the face two months ago. He hit Logan so hard that Logan fell and was knocked out.

Irresponsible.

Inconsiderate.

Spoiled.

A screw-up.

That's what he was. And he had no idea how to change to be a better man. A man just like his big brother.

But Logan was wrong.

Evan might be a liar and no longer his best friend, but he would never hurt anybody, let alone murder them. And Barry? Forget it. Evan looked up to him as if he were his father. Those two were close. Tight-knit. He'd never lay a finger on Barry.

His expression hardened. "You're wrong."

Logan nodded. "I sure hope I am."

Seth crossed his arms, the anger swelling and expanding in his veins. He didn't want to take the chance he'd hit his brother again. "Why am I here? Other than you pissing me off."

"I thought he wasn't your friend anymore."

Seth threw his hands in the air, exasperated. Why wouldn't Logan tell him what he was here for? "I'm not, but he's not a damn murderer. He'd never hurt Barry."

"Again, I hope not, but I have to look at everything before me and work the case no matter what I might personally think."

Seth turned around and waved a hand in the air. "Good. You go do that. I have to get to work."

Yeah, he was acting like a petulant child again. Damn, he didn't know how to shut that part of himself off.

"I need your help, Seth."

He paused, his face starting to burn from the cold air.

"I don't know where Evan would go. Where he might hide..." Logan sighed again. "You do, though."

Logan had to be kidding. Seriously?

He turned back around and met Logan's melancholy expression. He shouldn't be so hard on his brother. The town was lucky to have such a great sheriff, always doing his job, no matter how difficult it might be.

"Fine."

There. That was a step in the right direction to becoming a better brother.

"Thank you." Logan averted his eyes, looking behind his shoulder. "Wait right here."

Logan walked past him to a patrol vehicle that had pulled next to his truck.

He inhaled a harsh, brutal breath when the woman from the gas station stepped out of the vehicle and shook hands with Logan.

Holy. Shit.

The new deputy Logan hired was her. The most gorgeous creature on the planet who'd barely given him the time of day. Was he really that pathetic?

He probably was. In the past few months, he'd kept to himself, trying to work through his emotions. He wasn't always approachable, although that never stopped his family.

Logan told him not to move, so he didn't. He needed to prepare himself and what he would say to her. If he even got a chance to say a word to her. Logan wanted him to find Evan, so he'd be leaving soon. But, oh, man, he would love another chance to speak with her. Buy her a drink. Ask her out on a date. Anything.

After about two minutes, Logan and the woman walked his way, stopping right in front of him.

"Seth, this is Deputy Pepper Wilson. This is her first day. She hails from the Cities with an excellent background in law enforcement." Logan glanced at her with a smile. "We're lucky to have you."

She nodded at his compliment but didn't say anything or even smile in acknowledgment. Hmm...well, maybe it wasn't just him she wasn't friendly with. That made him feel better but also concerned. Did he want to ask out a woman who didn't even smile?

"Deputy Wilson—"

"Pepper is fine," she said, cutting him off.

Logan blinked in surprise, then increased his smile. "Of course. Pepper, this is my brother, Seth. Evan is his best—"

"Was," he interjected, also cutting off his brother. "He *was* my best friend."

Logan ran a hand down his face as he inhaled a deep breath. "Right. Evan was his best friend, but they only stopped being friends a few months ago. Seth is the best person to be able to find him right now. And that's what I need. I need you two to find him."

"What?"

"Excuse me?"

Seth shared a look with Pepper, shocked by the venom in her tone. The way she said "excuse me," as if his accidentally bumping into her had been deliberate.

He was confused. Why did she have to tag along? Because he'd find Evan on his own much faster. He didn't need a damn babysitter.

"I can do this on my own," Seth said when she didn't add anything to her disgusted words.

"I'm sure you can, but..." His brother ran another ragged hand down his face. "If he's involved in this in any way, I need a deputy there. I'm sorry—"

"Don't," Seth interrupted. Boy, his attitude a few months ago put a dent in what his brother thought of him. Seth knew he had to start acting better and like an actual adult. "Don't apologize. There's no way in hell I think Evan hurt Barry in any form, but I get it. You're doing your job. I'm not going to get upset about it."

A slow smile emerged on Logan's face. "Really?"

Seth shrugged as he chuckled. "Okay, not too upset."

Logan laughed as well, then directed his attention to Pepper. "Seth knows these parts like the back of his hand. He also knows Evan very well. You two should find him soon. He's not to be treated as a suspect, but he needs to come in for questioning. I need to know why he didn't show up for work today."

Pepper offered a brisk nod. "Understood." Then she turned in his direction. "I'll drive."

Then she walked away toward her vehicle.

Seth shared a look with Logan and then said in a dry tone, "She's pleasant." And so very beautiful, but he'd keep that little tidbit to himself.

She may be gorgeous as hell, but she had the largest stick up her ass he'd ever seen. He was starting to rethink the whole asking her out thing. He'd admire her beauty, but her disposition could use some work.

"She's good at her job, Seth. That's all I need, especially with Derek gone."

Logan walked away before he could offer any sort of consoling.

He lost his best friend two months ago.

His brother lost his best friend two weeks ago.

Guess it was that time of the year to be losing best friends.

SHE RUBBED her hands together to stave off the chill, then grabbed the steering wheel and steeled her spine when the passenger door opened.

The man from the gas station, the same man she completely embarrassed herself in front of, shut the door and buckled up.

She could do this. She could be pleasant and professional and pretend he wasn't the most handsome man she'd ever met.

And kind, too.

He might think he ran into her, but she wasn't paying attention and made the mistake of running into him. Her mind had wandered, fretting and worrying at what she had to do, and she simply hadn't been paying attention. Nothing that happened had been his fault. He even offered to pay for a new drink.

What had she done? Acted like nothing but a bitch.

Snapping her eyes in his direction, she raised her brows as if she were annoyed. She wasn't, really, but she needed to keep him at a distance. She had to keep everyone in this town at a distance. There was no way she could afford to let anyone in or become friends. It didn't matter how handsome or nice he was.

His light brown hair swooped back gracefully, not a strand out of place. It looked soft to the touch as if he had no hair products holding it back, yet she wondered how it stayed combed so perfectly. There was a slight wind in the air, but not one piece of hair had moved. And his eyes. So expressive. So vibrantly green, like an emerald sparkling in the sunlight. Every time he looked at her, she swore he looked straight at her heart, seeing the damaged parts and all. Of course, she couldn't discredit his smile either. Sweet with a hint of cockiness. She didn't want to keep him at a distance, but it didn't matter what she wanted. It didn't matter it had been so long since she had a man in her life. It didn't matter she ached for a man's touch, even something as simple as holding hands. It didn't matter that she'd never find a man who could love her for her.

Nothing mattered but her mission.

"Where are we going?" Brisk and to the point. She had to remember to keep everything to the point. She was here to do her job.

"I have to call my work and tell them I won't be coming in today. I usually grab a cup of coffee in the break room and then get started. I really need a cup of coffee."

Her brows pleated in confusion. "Didn't you buy a drink at the gas station? We don't have time for this."

"I bought an energy drink, but I always have coffee. I need my coffee." Then he smirked. "You didn't get a drink. You could use one."

Oh, he said that in a way that insinuated she got out of bed on the wrong side. A nasty retort sat on the tip of her tongue, but she bit it back and turned her attention back to the road. She would not let him get a rise out of her.

"Fine. We'll get *you* a coffee. You can tell me where to go while I drive."

"Fine. Although, I can buy you a drink to replace the one I broke."

He sounded sincere; odd, considering his attitude from a moment ago. She decided to ignore his comment. He shifted in his seat as she pulled away from the garage.

"So, Deputy Wil—"

"Pepper. You can call me Pepper." She cut him off just as she had cut off the sheriff when he tried to call her Deputy Wilson. Normally, she would never stop anyone from using her title, but she had her reasons this time.

"Sorry...Pepper," he said with a slight cockiness to his tone. "Are you sure I can't buy you a coffee? I honestly feel bad."

Ignoring his comment again, she took a right, heading back to the same gas station where they met. It wasn't too far away from the mechanics.

She didn't want him to feel bad. And she certainly didn't want him to be nice to her, especially when she kept acting like a colossal bitch.

It was time for work mode. Enough of this small talk and circling around the fact he wanted to replace a coffee when she'd been the cause of the mess in the first place.

"Where would your friend go? I saw tread marks as if someone sped away."

"You did?" Seth asked, shocked. "You barely looked around."

Glancing at him, she couldn't hold in a tiny smile. She was damn good at her job. She had zoned in on that piece of evidence the second she exited her car. She'd been proud she spotted it, as had the sheriff when she pointed it out. Maybe that's why he suggested she look for Evan because she had a keen eye for things. And she couldn't have been happier.

It'd upset her when she heard who they were looking for. Evan had been one of the first people on her list to interrogate, to find some answers. And now he was missing. It wasn't looking like a promising start. But this small obstacle wouldn't deter her from her mission.

"Yes, I did. Sheriff Caldwell gave me a brief rundown. He said there didn't appear to be any signs of a struggle. So, if someone did hurt Barry intentionally, they probably caught him unaware. However, that doesn't tell us why someone sped away. Maybe your friend did."

"He's not my friend anymore."

She had a hard time staying silent at his comment. He sounded so...lost and hurt. Oh, she knew those two emotions so well. But she didn't know what to say. She couldn't even repair her own broken heart.

But again, she was not here to connect with anyone, especially this cocky, know-it-all...ugh! Okay, he was a nice guy. She still couldn't forget how he smiled at her and offered to buy her a new drink...twice.

"Where would he go?"

Seth huffed, running his hands over his jeans a few times. "If he was in trouble..." A soft sigh escaped. "A few months ago...me. Now, I'm thinking..."

She pulled into the gas station and put the car in park, then turned his way when he didn't finish his sentence. "Yes?"

He met her gaze. "Stacy Cotton. She's my ex-girlfriend. They've grown close in the past few months."

"Your best friend is now dating your ex-girlfriend?" Ouch. That was harsh; even she could admit that.

"Former best friend." Then Seth opened his door and slammed it shut.

More pain filtered from his tone. Even the way he slammed the door spoke of all the anger and hurt that filled him.

She placed her hands on her lap and stared out the windshield, watching Seth as he went straight for the coffee. She reminded herself to not feel a thing. No making attachments.

In and out.

Do what she came to do, and that was it.

Not to mention, she had no idea who she could trust in this small town.

But her gut was screaming she could trust Seth. Just like it screamed she could trust the sheriff. Her gut had never let her down.

Seth returned a few minutes later with the largest cup of coffee he could purchase.

"Where does your ex live?"

"Not far from here, but she works at the local diner. She's usually at work by now."

She nodded, backed up out of the parking spot and

headed for the diner first. She couldn't wait to get there. One step closer to her objective.

And she was also curious what Seth's former girlfriend looked like. Not that she cared too much. Just curiosity for the case. That was all.

When they arrived at the diner, Seth didn't wait for her to get out of the vehicle. He jumped out so fast, she almost had to wonder if he was excited to see his ex-girlfriend. Why did they break up in the first place?

Not her business.

Of course, not wanting to be outdone by anyone, she moved fast and grabbed the handle of the door to the diner first.

His brow rose, a tiny smirk emerging, but he didn't say anything as she opened the door and stepped inside first.

She stopped at the counter, but before she could say anything, Seth smiled at the woman behind the counter.

Oh, yeah. He still had a thing for his ex-girlfriend, if his smile was any indication.

"Hey, Callie. How's it going?"

Callie's—not his girlfriend—smile back at Seth said plenty. She couldn't blame Callie. Seth was a sexy guy with his trendy hair, smooth smile, and tender eyes. "Just fine. It's a cold day, but it hasn't been too busy this morning."

Seth turned to her and kind of smiled. More so a dangerous smirk that spoke volumes. She wasn't sure why it unnerved her so much, but it did.

Her gut was screaming a lot of things at her right now, one being how much she found this man so attractive and alluring.

No. No. No.

She couldn't let this man get under her skin and her defenses.

"This is the newest deputy in town. She likes to be called Pepper." His wily grin widened at her. "Pepper, please meet Callie, the sweetest girl who works here."

"Oh, stop. It's nice to meet you," Callie said, as she extended her hand to shake.

She shook hands with the woman, but it was so brief and rushed, Callie looked at her with confusion.

"We're looking for Stacy. Can we speak to her?"

Callie glanced between them, retreated her hand, then settled her attention on Seth. "She left about thirty minutes ago after she received a phone call. She didn't mention what was wrong or anything, but it didn't look good."

Seth's jaw clenched as he leaned over the counter, lowering his voice. "Did she mention who called?"

Callie shook her head. "She didn't say much, but she didn't look happy. Is everything okay?"

"We need to know where she went," Pepper interjected before Seth could say anything. She was the deputy here, not him.

"I don't know where she went. Like I said, she didn't say much other than she had an emergency and needed to leave."

"Have you seen Evan Barten this morning?" she asked, her tone of voice brisk and firm. She could've used a bit more patience and understanding in her tone, but she wanted to get in and out of this town as fast as she could.

She never should've signed up for this assignment in the first place.

She was too close to the case. Too many emotions had been attacking her since it landed in her lap.

Callie glanced between both of them again, this time landing her gaze on her. "No, I haven't." Then she turned to Seth. "What's going on?"

"It's nothing that—"

"Barry's dead. We can't find Evan, and I thought Stacy might know," Seth said, cutting her off.

Oh, maybe she'd reevaluate her opinion of him. That wasn't very nice. She was the deputy here.

Although, she wasn't being very nice to Callie either. But she had no choice. She was here to do her job, not make friends.

Before she could give him a few choice words for interrupting her, Callie staggered back, covering her mouth with her hands as a gasp escaped.

Without thinking, she leaned closer to him and whispered, "Subtle. You didn't sugarcoat that at all."

He twisted his head and their eyes met as he inched even closer to her. "Well, you're not much better than me, Pepper."

The way he said her name, so disgusted, made her stomach twist with unease. Boy, she was a real people person.

"You okay, Callie? I'm sorry that came out so..." He shrugged as if he didn't have the right word. "Right now, it looks like an accident, but Logan wants to talk to Evan."

Wiping a few tears away, Callie nodded, appearing to have gathered her composure. "Barry always came in for his morning coffee. He was in a good mood this morning, like most days. I can't believe...I can't believe he's dead." Callie stepped closer to the counter. "You don't think Evan had something to do with it, do you? I know...I know you two aren't friends anymore, but...I don't understand, Seth."

Seth frowned, his shoulders drooping. "I don't think he hurt anybody either, Callie. But Logan needs to talk to him. Thanks for your help. I'm sorry for upsetting you. I didn't mean to."

A tiny smile appeared on Callie's face before vanishing as if it never existed. "I know you didn't. I wish I could tell you who called Stacy and where she went, but I can't."

"If you hear anything, let the sheriff's department know." With that, she turned around and walked away. No other pleasantries to be had. She couldn't even find an ounce of sympathy in her heart at her callous behavior.

She slid in the car and immediately cranked the engine, blasting the heat on high. Less than a minute later, Seth joined her in the car.

"We'll try her house. What's the address?" she asked, shifting the car in reverse, her foot waiting to transfer from the brake to the gas pedal. She might know the town itself, businesses and whatnot, but she didn't know where every single resident lived.

"I thought you were just having a bad morning, me running into you." Seth slowly looked in her direction. "Turns out, you're just not very friendly."

"And you were nice in there? Just tossing out Barry's dead?"

He turned his gaze to peer out the front window. "I don't know why I said that the way I did, but I didn't mean to. You, on the other hand, it seems to come naturally."

She had no response because he was wrong. So very, very wrong. Nothing about her behavior this morning was natural or right.

But she couldn't tell him that. She couldn't explain anything.

Well, okay, she could be standoffish, but that's because she didn't always know how to connect with people. People always took her expressions and attitude the wrong way, even when she was trying to be nice.

But right now, she couldn't focus on how she was acting.

"What's the address?"

He glanced at her. "Do you even care what I said?"

Averting her gaze, she pulled out her phone. "Hi, Charlotte, Pepper here. I need the address to Stacy Cotton's house."

She ignored Seth as she wrote down the address as Charlotte rattled it off.

Did she care what he said? Of course, she did.

It was breaking her heart and ripping it to shreds that the man next to her hated her. That the icy tone of voice coming from Charlotte said she hated her. That soon everyone in this town would hate her.

But it didn't matter. None of it did.

The only thing that mattered was finding out the truth and doing what she had to do.

3

WITH THE DOUGHNUT halfway to his mouth, he paused in midair when his phone went off. Setting the glazed doughnut back on the napkin sitting on top of the file of his latest case, he grabbed his phone.

"Hey, sweetheart, what's up?" Danny said, amused that Kat was calling him already—and slightly dreading what she had to say.

They had a delightful morning getting ready for work. Him to the FBI field office in the Cities, and her to Dr. Matthews' practice where she worked as a nurse. He always had to get up earlier than her because of the commute. A little over an hour drive. It sucked, but it was worth it to be with her. He'd do anything for her. Sometimes, she woke up with him, very horny and very eager to please in bed...and the shower. Like this morning.

Right before she kissed him goodbye and he walked out the door, she brought up the subject of kids. What did he think about kids?

It threw him so off-balance. One, because it was such odd timing to bring it up. He was leaving for work. Two, because they had kind of grazed the topic already. Yeah, they'd eventually have kids.

Just not right now.

Which was what he said and then kissed her again and rushed out the door.

Hell, he still needed to put a ring on her finger. Of course, he knew he wanted to spend the rest of his life with her, but he still had this irrational fear she wouldn't say yes. That he would lose her somehow. Losing Kat was the last thing he ever wanted.

"We have a situation."

Her broken tone of voice put him on high alert. His Kat never sounded broken and lost.

"What's going on? What happened?" If he had to leave and come back home, he wouldn't hesitate. Deke, his partner and best friend, would understand. Deke was still in the break room probably grabbing more than one doughnut for himself.

"Barry's dead. Logan can't find Evan to ask him what happened, and Seth's out there looking for him." Kat scoffed. "Apparently, he's with the new deputy, who, according to Charlotte, isn't nice. Why wouldn't Logan hire someone nice? After the way Derek up and left town—"

"Kat, take a deep breath," he said sharply—maybe too sharply—cutting her off. But damn, she was hopping from one thing to another in one long breath. He rarely heard her lose control. Although, with Derek recently leaving, he wasn't too surprised.

Shit. He didn't want to think about any of that right now.

"Let's start with one thing at a time. How did Barry die?"

He heard Kat huff, then sigh loudly. "He was crushed by a vehicle he was working on."

"The equipment malfunction?" That would be Danny's

first thought, but only because Lucky was a small town. He'd gotten to know everyone in the short span of two months. Barry was a wiz when it came to cars. Getting crushed by one didn't sound like something that would happen to a man like him unless it was an accident.

"Logan doesn't know yet. Evan should've been at work, but he wasn't. He's not at home, and he's not answering his phone." Kat paused. "It's suspicious."

Oh, yeah, Danny would agree. And after Evan held back information pertaining to his sister's abduction, he didn't trust the guy. But he also kind of understood why he didn't say anything. He was willing to let the past go and move on from it all. He had even encouraged Seth to make amends with him, but he hadn't done it yet.

"So, I'm guessing Logan called Seth to try to find Evan. How did he take it?" Because Danny imagined Seth didn't take it all too well.

"Fine, I guess. He's out searching with the new deputy. I already said that. Aren't you listening to me?"

Right. The not-so-nice deputy, according to Charlotte. He wasn't even touching that conversation because it would lead to talk about Derek, and he didn't want to talk about him either.

"Do you need me to come home? Does Logan need me?"

Another sigh echoed through the phone. "No. No, I don't need you to come home, and as far as I know, Logan doesn't need you either."

Her words hit his chest and punctured his heart like a knife had twisted slowly until it made a full three-hundred-and-sixty-degree turn. *No, I don't need you.* Those were the only words that penetrated.

He should've stayed longer to have the kids talk. Hell, he

didn't understand why she brought it up when he was leaving for work in the first place.

The sadness and distress he heard from the first word she spoke suddenly disappeared. Cheery, happy Kat rambled through the phone.

"I wanted you to know. That's all."

Right now wasn't the time to get into an argument. At times, when they tried to have a conversation, it easily turned into some heated arguments. So, instead of addressing all the concerns he had, he simply said, "I'll call you on my way home. I love you."

There was a moment of silence.

Then the words he always loved to hear. "I love you, too."

He hung up with Kat. Deke sauntered into his office with two doughnuts on his napkin, then twisted his lips into a wry smile as he took a seat across from Danny. "I thought I'd give you a sense of privacy, but I was totally eavesdropping from outside the office. What's our next move?"

Danny smiled, so happy nobody but Deke was his partner. That Deke moved from Florida and joined him in Minnesota when he didn't have to. He even moved to Lucky and did the commute with him. It made the drive easier for them because they had each other for a distraction on the long drive. Most of the time they talked about their latest case and what they planned to do that day.

"I'm going to call Logan to find out more details and what he needs from us, if anything."

Deke crossed his leg over his knee as he took a bite of one of his doughnuts. "Works for me."

And although he didn't get along with Logan in the beginning, they were pretty much friends now. If Logan needed him, he'd drop everything he was doing and help him out.

They were going to be family soon, after all.

Logan had surprised Aubrey at Christmas and proposed. Everyone knew they'd get married eventually, but it surprised Danny when Logan popped the question to his sister so soon. They hadn't been dating that long. It felt rushed. Of course, Aubrey had been all smiles and delight shone in her eyes. She couldn't have been happier, which made him happy. That's all he ever wanted was for his sister to be happy. He kept his concerns and worry to himself, but in the end, he knew Logan was the right man for his sister.

Nobody ever said it, but it lingered in the air like smoke from a fresh fire. Was he going to propose to Kat soon?

He had no idea. Maybe if he found the nerve.

SETH BLEW out a frustrated breath when Stacy didn't answer her door. He didn't even look at Pepper as they walked back to her patrol vehicle. The aggravating—beautiful—woman wouldn't have anything nice to say anyway.

Damn, how could such a gorgeous woman on the outside be so vicious and cruel on the inside? It wasn't right.

Pepper closed her door a lot softer than he shut his.

"Do you think Evan is the one who called her?"

Without making eye contact, he shrugged. He had no clue. Probably, but he wasn't sure he wanted to admit it.

These were his—well, former best friend and ex-girl-friend, but still. He couldn't imagine them involved in a murder. Although he had broken up with Stacy—and she had started to date Evan—he was cordial with her. They were still friendly. Evan, he was another story. He hadn't been too nice to him.

"Drugs are getting more popular in this area. Your friend..." She cleared her throat. "...former friend has two brothers who were involved with drugs. That could be why his boss was murdered."

Seth finally turned his head in her direction. "Logan told you all that in the space of two minutes when you talked?"

She stiffened in her seat, her hands clenching, then her body relaxed as if he imagined her odd reaction. "I can't do my job if I don't know the people in the town."

Well, that didn't answer his question. What did she even mean by that?

"What do you know about me?"

She twitched in her seat but didn't remove her gaze from his. "It's not pertinent to the case. What's our next stop to find your former friend?"

Again, she didn't answer his question, which made him wonder what she knew about him. Hell, what she thought about him.

Strangely enough, her opinion of him mattered. It shouldn't because he wasn't even sure he liked her.

He averted his gaze, staring out the window. "He has a cabin a few miles out of town. He might've gone there."

"Address."

He shook his head at her brusque tone. She didn't even ask for it. More like demanded it.

But, not having the energy to argue, he gave her the address and leaned back in his seat as she drove away from Stacy's house.

Where did Stacy go?

What the hell was going on?

He woke up today expecting to grind out another hard

day's labor. Instead, he was searching for his ex-best friend and ex-girlfriend.

"Why did you break up with your girlfriend? How did she end up with your best friend?"

He shifted his head her way, his brow arching. "Is this information pertinent to the case?"

She sat ramrod straight in her seat as she drove the vehicle. "No."

A slow grin emerged, unable to hide it. "Then, why do you want to know?"

He hated gossip and talking about his shit and what all went down two months ago with anybody, even Logan and Kat. Anybody else, he would've told them to mind their damn business.

But he was curious why she wanted to know.

"Well...Pep. Per?" He deliberately said her name slowly and punctuating each syllable.

The way her hands clenched on the steering wheel said it aggravated her. Good. He was going out of his mind with aggravation—the annoying kind...and the sexual kind.

She was gorgeous, and it was impossible to wipe that from his brain, even if she didn't have a great bedside manner.

Something in his gut told him she was acting this way for a reason. She was hiding something. He couldn't exactly say why he thought that, but his instinct had never steered him wrong before.

"Forget I asked."

A low snicker floated out of his mouth. Highly unlikely he'd forget anything about her.

They made it to Evan's cabin with no more words spoken between them. When he didn't see any vehicles parked or even tread marks to indicate Evan stopped here, he knew this was a dead end.

But Pepper was nothing, if not efficient. She got out of the vehicle, knocked on the door, and even walked around the property. He stayed in the nice warm car while she did her thing.

When she got back into the car, rubbing her gloved hands together, he couldn't help but joke around with her.

"Need help warming up?"

"I'd die for a hot chocolate right now with extra marshmallows. If you can provide that, then yes, warm me up," she replied with a tender smile attached to each word.

Wow. He didn't expect that. But, hey, he could work with it. He'd love to warm her up...in any way possible.

"I can make the instant kind of hot chocolate. Anything fancier than that and you're out of luck. I'm not the greatest cook or chocolatier or whatever you want to call it," he said with a chuckle.

Like a bolt of lightning striking too close and sending a shock down his spine, her back stiffened and her smile disappeared.

"Where to next? He didn't show up here."

How odd.

It was like night and day,

Jekyll and Hyde.

Erasing the weird conversation out of his mind, he replied, "Let's try my family's cabin next."

She finally looked at him, her brows pleated in confusion. "But you're not friends anymore. Why would he go there?"

"Just because we aren't friends doesn't mean he wouldn't go somewhere familiar if he's in trouble. He might not call me, but he might think it's the last place we'd look for him."

His eyes narrowed. "He was my best friend for nineteen years. I know him like a brother. It's worth looking."

Nodding, she averted her gaze and put the car in reverse. Soon, they were on the road again and hopefully to Evan. He didn't know how much longer he could stand to be in her presence.

The constant back and forth confusion was too much for him right now.

BERATING herself for forgetting who she was, she tried to ignore the man sitting next to her. How could she be so stupid? Joking around with him. She couldn't afford to get attached to anyone here, least of all this guy.

Except he made it so easy with his infectious smile.

She parked in front of a small, quaint log cabin with two rocking chairs covered with snow on the porch. She hoped they found Evan inside. One, so she could get far, far away from Seth. Two, so she could start finding the answers to complete her goal.

By the tire tracks embedded in the snow, there was a possibility. Or, at least, evidence he was here.

"Someone was here recently," she said matter-of-factly, pointing toward the tire tracks.

"It wasn't any of us. Aubrey likes coming here, but it's been a crazy few weeks, and I don't think Aubrey and Logan have been up here. The same goes for Danny and Kat."

How did she respond to that? Make it seem like she didn't know who those people were? Because she did. She tried to be as prepared as possible before coming to this small town. She researched the few people she had to. Logan, as the sheriff of the town, had been close to the top of her list. Because she dug for information on him, she knew Aubrey was his fiancé.

And, of course, she knew all about the Bartens. Each and every one. She screwed up earlier mentioning Evan and his brothers being involved with drugs. Because she didn't learn any of that from the sheriff. Hopefully, Seth never realized it because then he'd start to suspect something was up with her.

By researching and dissecting their lives, she knew who Agent Danny O'Rourke was and that he was dating Katrina Caldwell, or Kat, as everyone called her, and that Aubrey was his sister.

Yet, Seth...

Not much had popped up in her research about him other than he had been good friends with Evan. Nor had much information popped up on Evan either. But his brothers...Wayne and Joshua—too much information had surfaced.

"So, what I'm saying is, it could've been Evan or Stacy."

Her head swiveled in his direction when his disgruntled words echoed between them. Perhaps she should've responded with something, anything. Hearing his sad, wounded tone of voice tore her up inside. She hated that feeling.

Because making attachments was bad. Bad. Bad. Bad.

"Do you have a key to the cabin? I'll check it out."

He pulled out a set of keys and jangled it between them. "I'll come with you."

Tilting her head, she held his intense gaze that said he was prepared to argue with her. How much did she want to argue with him?

"Fine, but stay behind me. I have a gun; you don't."

Arguing with him would be futile, she decided. Best to keep him close.

"I can take care of myself," he muttered.

"Are you sure? Your testy attitude tells me you need a lot more coddling than is necessary." She cracked a grin before opening her door and stepping outside.

Then she mentally berated herself for speaking without thinking again. She had to stop doing that.

She couldn't afford to speak so freely. Getting into arguments with men—especially handsome, sexy men, who make you want to disrobe and let them do sensual things, would bring her nothing but trouble. The last thing she needed was the sheriff looking deeper into her background and realizing she wasn't who she said she was.

Not until she knew for a fact she could trust him.

Groaning and fisting her hands, she shoved her illustrious thoughts away and stalked through the snow to the front door. After waiting a few seconds when Seth didn't appear right by her side, she turned around.

Seth took his time getting out of the car and shutting his door. The walk from the car to the front door was also very tentative, as if he looked ready to bolt back to the car at any second.

She took a deep breath to hold in her comment that wanted to escape. That she understood his hesitancy. He might not be friends with Evan any longer, but that didn't mean anything. He still cared about his friend deep down inside.

"You can wait in the car." She said it firmly, trying to make it sound like an order. She didn't say it to be a bitch, although he'd probably take it that way, but to give him a way out, an excuse not to come inside.

His eyes narrowed, his jaw clenching.

Yep. He thought she was a bitch.

Then he stepped closer, which made her step to the side to avoid making physical contact and opened the door without unlocking it.

"We don't lock our cabin. We've never had an issue."

Hating herself for the retreat, which she thought spoke volumes, she ignored what it meant and shoved past him, walking inside first. Plus, she had no response to his comment. She couldn't believe they wouldn't lock their doors around here. It wasn't safe. And why had he dangled the keys in front of her if he knew it wouldn't be locked?

The cabin was small. One large room that connected the living room and kitchen, one bedroom that was vacant of any person hiding, and a small bathroom that was also empty.

She did her job, though, inspecting every room for any clues. She walked out of the bathroom with the garbage can, set it down on the kitchen table, and pulled out her phone to take a picture.

"What's inside?" Seth asked, walking away from the door closer to her.

She had to force herself to remain aloof and hide her surprise. He hadn't moved once from his spot as she searched the cabin. Odd, considering he insisted on coming inside with her.

She pointed at the garbage can. "Bloody rags. Evan must be injured. The blood looks fresh."

Her stomach churned with disgust, especially with the way she said it so toneless and like she was reading off a bland report about the weather. Sometimes, the only way she could function was to pretend nothing mattered.

By the way Seth's face paled and he jerked away from the table, the news hit him hard.

"How much...how much blood do you think he lost?" Seth finally asked as his eyes darted toward the couch.

She didn't miss the way his hands trembled, although he had them fisted tightly together.

Detached and aloof. That's how she had to be. She wouldn't be able to do her job otherwise.

"Not so much that I think he's losing it at a fast pace, but enough where it's probably a semi-serious injury. Do you want to have a look?"

His gaze seemed to glaze over as he stared at the couch. Then he whipped his head in her direction. "No."

"I'll bag this as evidence. You can wait in the car." Again, she said it as an order, hoping that he'd follow it even if he took it as her being a dictating bitch. She couldn't stand the sadness in his eyes and the hollow of pain that radiated around him.

"Fine."

Without another word, he stalked out of the cabin.

After taking a few pictures and grabbing an evidence kit from the trunk of her patrol vehicle, she bagged everything. Then she called the sheriff with an update. He'd want to know Evan used his cabin as a pit stop.

Based on her research, she knew this cabin had also been where Agent O'Rourke and Deputy Bolten shot and killed Joshua Barten. Kat had been injured as well.

Her mind trailed to Seth. Maybe that's why he hadn't walked too far from the front door. Because his sister had been hurt here. The memories too much to bear?

She knew the feeling. How memories could tear you apart inside, weigh you down, make you feel like you were on your last legs of life. Some days she wished the memories would disappear. Other days, she wanted to relive them until the answer popped out and said, "Boo!"

She forced herself back into work mode and gave the sheriff a brief rundown of everything.

The sheriff sighed. She even pictured him running his hand down his face, something he had done quite frequently in the few brief minutes they talked this morning.

"How's my brother doing? He hasn't been back to the cabin since...well, since our sister Kat was injured. I've left him alone, knowing he doesn't want anyone helping him with how he's feeling, but I'm thinking that might've been the wrong thing to do. My brother is hurting, and I don't know what to do."

Oh, boy.

That was some heavy stuff to be throwing at a new deputy. The sheriff barely knew her. What was she supposed to say to any of that? Was this how small towns operated?

At least her assessment had been right. Seth hadn't been comfortable walking inside because it conjured memories of his sister, injured and hurt.

And she was the last person to give advice. She sucked at the whole let's-be-a-happy-family thing.

"He's fine."

Wow. That was harsh and abrupt. But she wasn't here to make friends, and she didn't know if she could trust the sheriff. Although, before she even arrived in the small town, her research—and her gut—had said she could trust him. It still said she could trust him.

But trust was an elusive thing. She rarely trusted anyone.

Hell, she couldn't even trust anyone in her own family. So, could she really trust her gut?

"Right. Well, good. I'm glad to hear that. I'll call Kat and let her know Evan's injured. I'll start having Charlotte call the local hospitals and urgent care facilities in the area. By the sounds of it, he'll be needing to see a doctor soon."

"What would you like me to do next?"

Sheriff Caldwell sighed again. "I need you to find Evan, so keep working with Seth and hopefully you two find him soon."

She disconnected with the sheriff, dreading having to continue working with Seth. Because she lied to the sheriff —about so many things—but especially about how his brother was doing.

Seth was not fine.

And it wasn't her job to make him feel better.

Even though she kind of wanted to.

4

HE SLAMMED the door harder than he intended, then winced when he saw Aubrey's expression from the kitchen as she pulled something out of the oven.

"Is everything okay?"

Nodding, Seth walked toward her as she set the pan on a potholder sitting on the counter. "I'm fine. What's that? Smells delicious."

Aubrey's eyes narrowed. "You always say fine, but it never sounds like it." She looked at the pan, her eyes staring hard at it. "And I attempted my hand at lasagna. It probably tastes horrible. It looks funny."

Seth stepped closer, inhaling another dose of the delicious aroma. He had no doubt it tasted great. Aubrey was often hard on herself, especially when she had a bad night the night before. So, her comment was a good indicator that was the case.

"The way it smells, I know I'm going to love it." But Aubrey didn't always like to talk about her bad nights, so Seth was going to ignore it. Because he understood not wanting to talk about pain.

Her brows puckered, then she smoothed her features as she met his gaze. "Honestly, how are you? It had to be a rough day for you."

That was no lie.

Trying to find Evan...

Stuck in a car all day with Pepper...

Not finding Evan...

Rough day didn't even describe it.

"I'm fine."

A hard slap to his back jarred his teeth, making him wince once again, but this time from pain. He looked at his brother Logan who appeared out of nowhere. Logan didn't do anything but grin as he headed for the fridge and pulled out two beers, handing one out in his direction.

"We all know you're not fine. When will you stop pretending it's fine?"

Seth sighed. "Are you wanting to fight? Is that why you slapped my shoulder so hard?"

Logan took a swig of his beer. "I didn't slap you that hard." Then his eyes softened when he looked at Aubrey. "But you had a tone with Aubrey." His eyes met his. "So, watch it."

Aubrey stepped closer to Logan and playfully tapped his cheek. "Leave him alone. He didn't have a tone. Let's all calm down. If Seth said he's fine, he's fine."

He shared a look with his brother, wondering why he was on his case. This morning he wasn't that bad with his attitude when Logan laid it all on him what he thought Evan had done. If anything, he took it rather well. So why was Logan acting like he was about to have another toddler moment and storm out of the house?

Then it hit him.

"Did Pepper call you?"

Logan's brow rose. "For updates, yes. Why?"

Hmm. Well, okay, maybe she didn't say anything to Logan. Not that she had much to complain about him. He should complain about her and whether she was a good fit for this town.

She was rude, brazen, outspoken...and so damn beautiful. It was her beauty that gave him a hard time trying to forget why he shouldn't like her even a little bit. And she had a few brief nice moments that he couldn't forget. Although she wore her hair in a tight ponytail, not a strand of hair out of place, it was sexy. He imagined a few times yanking her hair out of its place and messing it up. Get a rise out of her, watch as her face bloomed with anger. She was cute angry...annoying, but cute.

And he still thought she was acting, putting on a front for some reason. She was hiding something. Seth just couldn't pinpoint what that might be.

Logan waved a hand in front of his face. "I lost you there. Is there something I need to know?"

Seth shrugged. "She's...different. Why did you have to hire her?"

A ragged hand ran down his brother's face. Seth knew it was a sensitive subject, but hell, if he had to deal with his issues with Evan, then Logan had to deal with his.

"I'm down a deputy. With Derek up and quitting, I didn't have many options. She comes with a reference from an old coworker of mine in the Cities and a great background in law enforcement. Is there something I should know?"

Seth shrugged again. "She's fine, I guess. She doesn't have much tact when dealing with people."

This time, Logan shrugged. "As long as she does her job well, I can't afford to fire her. Not to mention, I need more of a reason other than not 'much tact dealing with people.'"

Before he could respond, the front door opened and in walked his sister Kat and Danny. Aubrey smiled wide at their arrival and shooed them all toward the table to have a seat. Hellos went around, but it all soon died down as they situated themselves. Aubrey cut the lasagna and they all dug in.

"So, any progress since the last time we spoke?" Danny asked, then scooped a forkful of lasagna into his mouth.

"Nope. Seth and Deputy Wilson searched everywhere today. Nothing panned out. He's injured, though." Logan looked away toward his plate. "He used our cabin to clean up a wound."

Seth saw Aubrey lay a hand over Logan's in a comforting way. Those two used the cabin the most. It was probably hitting Logan hard that another tainted memory hit their special place.

"No leads at all, Seth?" Danny asked.

Seth pushed his lasagna around his plate. "I checked every place I could think of. He wasn't anywhere. Stacy still hasn't returned home, so I can only assume that they disappeared together."

"How helpful was the deputy? I didn't hear nice things about her," Kat grumbled as she slammed her fork down toward her plate to grab another bite.

"What are you talking about?" Logan asked before Seth could respond.

"Charlotte. She said there was something weird about her and that she's not very nice. I don't know why Derek left." Kat glanced at her food.

Tension filled the room. More tension, anyway, because Seth felt it as soon as he walked in the house and Aubrey asked him how he was.

"I don't know what to say, Kat," Logan said with a weary sigh.

"He's your best friend," she shot back.

Logan dropped his fork. It clanged against his plate. "I think you know why he left. He didn't say it, but I think we all know."

Danny shifted in his seat. Aubrey kind of cleared her throat. Logan and Kat stared each other down. And he sat there wondering why he wasn't the one causing the scene. Normally, he screwed up, pissed everyone off, and stormed out the house. The way Kat looked right now, she was two seconds away from doing just that.

"Kat, sweetheart, I think—"

"No!" Kat shot up from her chair, interrupting Danny. "You don't get it." She dropped her fork and shook her head. "I'm not hungry. I'll see you at home."

Then she walked away from the table, grabbed her jacket, and walked out of the house.

Danny stood up, smiled at his sister Aubrey, then nodded at Logan. "I better go with her, especially since we drove together. Let me know if you need Deke and me for any help. My offer still stands from this morning."

Danny was gone and out the door a few seconds later.

Seth finally grabbed his first bite of lasagna and shoved it in his mouth. Pure deliciousness swirled around as he chewed. The spices, the flavor, the cheese. Aubrey made a mean lasagna.

"This is good stuff, Aubrey. Thank you."

Aubrey faintly smiled but said nothing.

Logan looked at him funny.

"Must be PMS. Kat usually doesn't act like that," Seth said with a chuckle. "At least it wasn't me this time."

Logan rolled his eyes, then joined him in laughter. Even Aubrey laughed.

Although laughter filled the air, the tension remained.

He knew his sister was hurting that Derek left. They had dated briefly a few months ago. But Kat could never see him more than friends, even though she tried. Before they had dated, they were the best of friends. Not as close as he and Logan had been, but good friends. And the reason he left—probably because he didn't win Kat's heart. They all knew it. They just couldn't say it out loud.

But he had his own problems to deal with.

Like locate his best friend—*former* best friend—and find out what the hell happened.

Because Evan might be a lot of things, but he wasn't a killer.

SHE THREW AWAY the empty container for the bland TV dinner she bought and then pulled open the fridge. Besides stocking her refrigerator with the easiest meals possible, meals she could nuke in the microwave, she also bought wine. Lots of wine. There were some things in life she couldn't change. If she had to pretend to be someone she wasn't, then she needed some way to find relief at the end of the day.

Of course, she had to stay levelheaded and in control. No more than one glass of wine a night—maybe two.

While she hoped not to be in this small town for long, she was starting to see it could be a lot longer than she anticipated.

Evan Barten was supposed to be her first lead in her

quest. What were the odds the first day she arrives in town his boss is murdered, and he goes missing?

Highly unlikely. Which meant someone knew she was coming and decided to lock down any chance of her finding answers. Maybe. She could be creating a theory that wasn't true. It could be a coincidence.

Slamming the fridge shut without grabbing any wine, she stalked to her bedroom. She had to stay sober at all times. Time to get back to work. All the information she needed to do her job was spread across her bed.

She was grateful she managed to find a tiny house to rent. It wasn't large by any means. One-bedroom house, one bath. A garage that wasn't attached, but she was able to lock it, so she considered it a win. No bathtub, just a shower. That made her slightly sad because she enjoyed soaking in the tub now and again, but did it matter? She wasn't here for a leisure vacation. She was here to find a killer and do what was necessary.

She always got her perp.

This time would be no different.

Besides the background on every Barten, a few other essential people to her case, she had information on the one murder she couldn't erase from her mind.

No matter how many times she looked over the file, burned her eyes staring at the crime scene photos for hours on end, combing through every word, she never saw a reason why this young woman had been murdered.

But, of course, the reason didn't matter at the moment. The person who killed her was hiding in this small town. She only had to find out where he was located. And who was helping him to keep out of sight.

Anyone in this town could be helping him. Even people in the sheriff's department. She didn't know yet, and that was a problem. Of course, she didn't suspect anyone in the sheriff's office was a criminal in disguise.

Her gut had been churning all day, but not with suspicion.

Hopefully, tomorrow, she wouldn't have to be cooped up all day with Seth Caldwell.

First, he wasn't a cop. He didn't have the expertise.

Second, he was so annoying. His attitude and arrogance were too much.

Third, he was too handsome for his own good. He was a distraction she couldn't afford to have.

When she spoke to the sheriff before signing off for the day, it wasn't clear whether she'd have to work with Seth again in the morning.

Going through her normal routine, she went through the case file piece by piece until her eyes couldn't stay open any longer. By two-thirty in the morning, her eyelids were drooping so badly, they shut without resistance.

She woke up with a stiff neck and a sore back from falling asleep in a sitting position, a gruesome crime scene photo still in her hand at five in the morning.

Gathering the papers scattered around her bed, she shoved everything back into the large manila folder and hid it in the vent across from her bed.

Maybe a little over-the-top, but she couldn't be sure if anyone knew the real reason she was here. Better to be safe than sorry.

She showered, dressed in her uniform, and grabbed a quick bite to eat. By six o'clock, she was out the door and heading for her car. Just as she was about to start the vehicle and head to the sheriff's station, she paused.

She wasn't due until seven-thirty. She had already annoyed Charlotte on her first day. She couldn't afford to keep antagonizing people in the town, especially the people she worked for. The more suspicious people became, the more likely they'd start researching her background with a fine-tooth comb, and she couldn't have that.

Begrudgingly, she got out of her car and sat in her living room in the dark on the old worn couch until the clock finally struck seven-fifteen. Then she jumped up off the couch like a firecracker and headed for her vehicle once again. She made it to the sheriff's department a few minutes later, still walking into the building early.

The look on Charlotte's face said she wasn't amused, which amused her. Normally people would be happy she was on time, even a little early. But hey, she didn't exactly go out of her way to make friends yesterday on her first day on the job.

She could try a little harder today. Of course, even before she came to this small town she had never heard of, she never made friends very well. No matter how hard she tried —or didn't try—she just wasn't a people person.

"The sheriff would like to speak to you."

That's all Charlotte said before returning her attention to whatever she was working on at her desk.

She nodded, pretending not to care that Charlotte was very brusque and rude.

If anything, her nerves ramped up some.

The sheriff wanted to speak to her. About what?

Did Seth say something about her?

Oh, damn it. She shouldn't have been so rude.

Knocking once on the doorframe, she waited no more than two seconds before the sheriff looked up from his desk, offered a smile, and waved her inside. "Have a seat, Deputy Wilson."

She cringed at the title, then blanked all expression from

her face. If he fired her on her second day, then so be it. It wouldn't stop her from her mission, only make it a lot harder.

He must've seen her wince because an apologetic tilt of his lips appeared as he said, "Sorry. You want to be called Pepper. Which is great. We're like a family here. I want you to fit in and feel like family."

She smiled, appreciating how sincere he sounded. What a change of pace from where she normally worked where everyone was out for themselves.

"Thank you, Sheriff. I appreciate you giving me the opportunity to work here."

So very appreciative. It had been pure luck when she saw the advertisement for a new deputy. It made her job so much easier. Although it wouldn't have deterred her from her goal, it was making things run a lot smoother.

"Thank you for working with Seth yesterday. You two did well."

Her brows knitted together. "We didn't find Evan or Stacy." Something she found unacceptable. But when she put her mind to something, she got the job done.

His hand circled his hot steamy mug of coffee in front of him. "No, but you know he's injured and that Stacy is most likely with him. That's something." With his free hand, he grabbed a small stack of papers and handed it to her. "Unfortunately, Barry's body needs to be transported to a larger city that can perform the autopsy. But, based on Dr. Matthews' quick examination, it looks like he was murdered."

She took the papers from his hand, glancing at the report. "Although crushed by the car, Dr. Matthews appeared to find a large gash to the back of his head. So, someone knocked him out, then dropped the car on top of him."

"That's my guess. The question is, why?"

Oh, yes, she was looking for a lot of whys lately. Just one more to add to the list.

"And we think Evan did it?" she asked as she looked up from the report.

Sheriff Caldwell appeared perplexed before smoothing out his features. "I don't want to think he did. It's not the guy I know. But I can't say for sure."

"He's not a killer."

She snapped around in her seat when she heard the harsh tone come from behind her. Seth stood in the doorway, his expression displaying his displeasure. He looked ready to fight his brother.

Interesting. Especially since she didn't know whose side she'd take if a fight suddenly broke out. On one hand, it should be her professional duty to stand up for the sheriff and protect him. On the other hand, she liked Seth—against her better judgment—and she understood the pain behind his tempting green eyes.

Sheriff Caldwell stood up and ran a hand down his face, then he smiled as if there wasn't any tension zapping between the two. "Morning, Seth."

Seth met her eyes briefly, then they flashed back to his brother. "I stopped by to see if you had any news on Evan, but obviously, you don't."

"Did you talk to Kat at all this morning?"

Seth shook his head. "You?"

Sheriff Caldwell shook his head as well. "Aubrey called her and spoke to her. She said she's fine. Sounds like someone else I know."

Rolling his eyes, Seth crossed his arms. "Do you need my help today or not? Otherwise, I have to get to work."

She finally stood up, directing her full attention at Seth. "I thought we exhausted all avenues yesterday to locate him. I don't think you're needed today."

She didn't need him in her space—cramming his way inside her heart.

Not many men could ever reach inside her heart with ease. Sure, she dated, when she found the time, but she had never met a man who hit her emotionally like Seth. He made her feel so many things, it was hard to sort them out.

Cocking his head to the side with a sly smile twisting his lips, Seth replied, "Well, I wasn't asking you, Pepper."

Sheriff Caldwell blew out a breath. "There's one place you didn't look, and one place I haven't visited yet."

Seth's eyes narrowed into tiny little slits. "He wouldn't go there, even if he was dying."

"Maybe not, but we have to cross it off the list," Sheriff Caldwell said as he headed for his jacket hanging on a coat rack in the corner. "We'll all three go. He hates me. I have no idea how he'll respond to a new face, especially a woman. And he never seemed to have a huge problem with you, Seth."

"Yeah, but I wouldn't say I was his favorite either. Evan and I got into a lot of trouble together as kids."

She couldn't stand that she didn't know who they were talking about. So, she decided to ask. "Where are we going?"

Sheriff Caldwell met her gaze. "Mr. Barten's house. Evan's father. Evan hates the man, and there's no love lost between them, but he could've gone there if very desperate."

"This is such a dumb idea, but whatever, I'm in. I need some coffee." Then Seth walked out of the room.

Based on all the reports she read about Mr. Barten, she

wasn't sure what to expect other than a very disgruntled, angry man—who also happened to hate women. Yay her.

"I'm ready when you are, Sheriff."

He nodded and donned his jacket.

"What was the reason you called me to your office?" Her heart started hammering in her chest as she finally asked the question she'd been dreading an answer to.

Sheriff Caldwell looked puzzled for a moment, then grinned. "To show you Dr. Matthews' preliminary report. We won't have an official autopsy report for a few weeks. And to talk about a plan of attack. Looks like we have one. Shall we?"

He gestured for her to lead the way.

She didn't hesitate to follow orders. Because she couldn't afford to get fired so soon.

Which meant she had to try hard to play nice today.

But sometimes she had a hard time playing nice.

That was the problem.

5

Seth didn't know what to do and decided letting his brother take the lead was the best option. Especially since he didn't know if Mr. Barten had a gun waiting and ready by the front door. The old man owned a lot of weapons.

The door was partially open, Mr. Barten's head peeking out, his right hand dangling by his side, while his left hand was hidden behind the wall. He wouldn't put it past him to have his shotgun leaning against the wall, waiting and ready for anything. Hell, the last time Logan showed up at his house, he pulled a shotgun out and aimed it at him. They arrested him, and the charges were still pending. He had a court appearance soon. It didn't mean Mr. Barten wouldn't try it again. It was very plausible he had a gun ready.

"We won't take much of your time, Mr. Barten. We're looking for Evan. Do you happen to know where he is?" Logan asked as if they were talking about the weather and if it was going to rain later.

Mr. Barten stared hard at him before spitting in their direction. "That sorry piece of shit. Nope. Now git off my property. Don't make me tell Marybeth."

He heard Pepper inhale sharply. She was standing on the other side of his brother but otherwise said nothing. He wasn't at all surprised by Mr. Barten's words. The man had no love for Evan, and vice versa. There was no way Evan came here, which was what he tried to tell Logan. Although, the part about Marybeth, his wife, was odd. She had passed away quite a few years ago. Seth had heard rumors he still talked about her as if she were still alive. He almost felt sorry for the old man...almost. He was cruel and evil, even to his late wife.

After a few more words back and forth with Mr. Barten, they finally retreated to his brother's vehicle. Thankfully, Mr. Barten had been wise enough not to pull a weapon on them. As soon as they were tucked inside with all the doors closed, he shook his head as he laughed. "I told you so."

A short chuckle escaped Logan's lips before he sighed. "I had to try. None of this makes sense."

Seth turned away from Logan and stared outside as Logan started to back out of the driveway. His brother was right. None of this made any sense. Evan wasn't a murderer. Sure, he was a liar. But hurting someone he looked up to as a father figure, especially when his real father didn't give two shits about him, didn't make a lick of sense.

"Are you sure there's nowhere else he would go that you can think of?" Logan asked, the hope in his tone like he'd miraculously think of something.

Oh, how he wished he could answer his brother's silent prayer. "No, sorry."

He had thought of every place, all the old haunts they used to frequent together, and nada. Evan hadn't shown up anywhere he could think of.

Then Seth twisted toward the back seat. "You're quiet. Nothing to add, chatterbox?"

He couldn't hold in the smile as he called her that, especially when he knew she was not a chatterbox at all. By the look of disgust on her face, she didn't like it. It didn't stop him from laughing a little.

"Perhaps what we need to be asking is where would Stacy go?" Her eyes glared at him heavily, as if she were preparing to strike him dead with a harsh blow.

"That's a good idea. We've already exhausted every avenue with Evan. It only makes sense Stacy might take the lead, especially if he's injured," Logan replied.

Here we go.

He knew it was coming.

"You knew her best, Seth." Logan didn't say anything else.

"I talked to her parents last night. They haven't heard from her."

After having dinner with Logan and Aubrey, he couldn't help himself. He swung by Stacy's parents' house and asked a few questions. They needed to find them. Not just because Barry was dead but because Evan was hurt, too. They might not be best friends anymore, but he didn't want him to die.

Of course, her parents didn't know anything, nor did they say much. He wasn't on the top of their fan list. Hell, they never did like him much even when he and Stacy dated.

"I didn't know you talked to them," Logan said with a hint of surprise. "Did they have anything useful to say? Because when I stopped by yesterday afternoon, they didn't have much to say to me."

"Nope. You know they don't like me." Seth shoved his hand in the direction toward the back seat. "Maybe little miss sunshine will have better luck."

Nothing.

No response.

He called her two names, neither very appealing, especially in the tone of voice he used, and she didn't react in any way.

Talk about being an ice queen.

Although, he didn't understand why he was being a dick either. She didn't do anything to him. Sure, she could be standoffish at times, but she also searched every nook and cranny he could think of yesterday to find Evan. She didn't complain or groan or whine at all the driving they had done yesterday. And they had ventured to quite a few locations around Lucky and the surrounding area. It had been a long day cooped up in the car with her.

He was frustrated.

Frustrated they didn't find Evan.

Frustrated they didn't find Stacy.

Frustrated his friend might be dead.

Hell, sexually frustrated as well.

It didn't mean he should take his frustrations out on her.

She might've not reacted to his brisk tone, but his brother was another story. He cleared his throat and threw him a dirty look. Seth shrugged but didn't offer a word of apology, even though he should've.

"That's a fine idea." Logan cleared his throat, then tilted his lips into a devious grin. "Why don't you and Pepper work together once more? This time looking in places Stacy might go."

He clenched his jaw, but held back spewing hurtful words at his brother. Only because he knew Logan was waiting for it. He wanted to hear Pepper refuse to have him hanging around her again, especially after his harsh attitude.

Except she said nothing. Still silent.

"Pepper, does that sound like a plan?" Logan asked, although with his eye on Seth as he said it.

"Yes, sir. We'll find them today."

Turning his attention back outside, he sure hoped they did. He'd work next to temptation one more day if it brought him to Evan's doorstep.

His best friend—*former* best friend—couldn't die.

Logan drove back to the sheriff's department where he and Pepper moved to her vehicle.

Before he could give her a good place to start, she was off driving.

"Where are you going? You don't know where Stacy would run off to."

"Her parents' house. You said I'd have better luck and you're right. They weren't home yesterday when we knocked on her door, but maybe they will be today."

He couldn't stop the laughter. "You're kidding, right?"

Glancing at him out of the corner of her eye, the death look she gave him sent chills down his spine. "Meaning?"

"You weren't exactly a people person yesterday. Nobody likes you here. What makes you think they'll talk to you?"

Dead silence answered him.

Tension filled the air—more so than what was already there.

Shame suddenly filled him. His words repeated in his mind.

Nobody likes you here.

Shit. That was kind of harsh. He just continued to insert his foot into his mouth. He might be frustrated with a lot of things—sexually frustrated with her—but Stacy's parents were no more likely to talk to her than they were to him or Logan.

An apology sat on the tip of his tongue, yet no words

emerged. He didn't even know how to start an apology. Saying sorry was not one of his better traits. It usually took him a while to conjure that emotion up.

Nothing more was said as they drove.

She put the vehicle in park, didn't even look in his direction and opened the door. "Stay in the car."

He had no problem with that. He was still trying to figure out the right words to apologize. Plus, Stacy's parents were less likely to say anything if he stood on the doorstep.

He wondered as she made her way up the short walkway whether they were even home. It was still early morning, but they had probably already left for work.

Or not.

The door opened rather quickly after Pepper knocked. The harried, nervous expression on Mrs. Cotton's face was obvious why they were still home. They were waiting for their daughter to return.

Ever since they broke up, Stacy had moved out of his house and back home with her parents until she found a place of her own.

Mr. Cotton joined his wife at the door, his expression morose, but also animated at times. He was curious to know what they were saying because it didn't appear they were telling Pepper to get the hell off their porch.

Hmm.

It looked like she *was* having better luck than him. He needed to apologize for his cruel words.

A few minutes later, she walked back to the car, immediately rubbing her gloved hands near the heater.

"Well?"

"They haven't heard from her since she left for work yesterday morning. They've called everyone they could think of: friends, family, old acquaintances. Nobody has heard from her."

She put the car in drive and started backing up.

"Where are you going now? I'm still the one with the knowledge of where she'd go."

Geez, Seth, why don't you just keep acting like a dick.

"Are you? Because all I see is an asshole with a chip on his shoulder."

Ding. Point one to her.

She hit that on the mark. He couldn't deny it. He was acting like an asshole.

Before he could respond—with a much-needed apology —she said, "Her dad just got done looking at his bank account. Stacy used one of his credit cards last night. About thirty minutes from here. He was ready to go racing there and digging on his own. I assured him I'd find his daughter for him. He gave me the address to the store."

Uh.

Well, okay.

Seth could admit that Pepper was much better equipped at her job than he realized.

"Nothing to say to that, Romeo?" she asked with a chuckle laced with sarcasm.

He couldn't hold back his own chuckle. "Drive faster."

Pepper only responded with a short laugh and a shake of her head—and a heavier foot.

UGH! She needed to stop engaging with Seth Caldwell. No laughing. No teasing. No putting him in his place, even if he needed it.

Nobody likes you here.

That hurt. It hurt more than she cared to admit.

It wasn't the first time she moved somewhere and nobody liked her. Hell, it wouldn't be the last time either. That didn't mean she liked to have it thrown in her face so brutally. As a child, they moved around too much. Getting evicted here and there. Moving because her dad had found trouble he needed to escape. That's what gambling did to a person. Moving had been a very common occurrence, and each new school always brought on the hope that people would like her this time. She'd make friends a little easier.

Nope.

It never got easier. Only harder.

Seth should be grateful he had someone he could call a best friend. She'd never had a best friend in her life.

It was nice to shove the wonderful information she got in his face. Ha! Take that! She found a lead before anyone else. With a little hope and luck, they'd find Stacy and Evan soon. Whether she'd be able to interrogate Evan without anyone knowing was a different story—if he even had the answers she needed.

They made it to the town of Neptune twenty minutes later because she had been a little heavy on the gas. The address led her straight to main street in the quaint, small town.

"A drug store? That can't be a good sign," Seth muttered as he exited the car.

No, she had to agree on that account. Evan and Stacy probably left Lucky, drove straight to this drug store and hunkered down somewhere. The question was, where?

She walked briskly and with an extra pep in her step to reach the door before Seth. It took all her strength not to smirk at him.

"Hello. I'm Deputy Wilson." She pointed to the sheriff's emblem on her jacket. "I need to ask you some questions."

"Hey, Seth." The clerk ignored her, besides the glance at her chest, and directed his attention to the aggravating man standing next to her. Oh, and he had no problem holding his smirk in.

"Hey, Roy. I didn't know you worked in Neptune. When did you start here?" Seth asked as if they had all the time in the world. They absolutely did not. She had a case to solve and a town to ditch. She couldn't do any of that if she didn't find Evan.

"About three months ago. It's a part-time gig two days a week. You know I work with my dad the other days at his shop in Lucky."

"Wonderful. Were you working last night?" she interjected. She didn't have time for their reminiscing.

"Maybe," Roy said as he leaned against the counter with a shit-eating grin like he knew all the answers to her questions. His eyes grazed her chest again. "What's a pretty lady like you going to give me if I say yes?"

She could honestly say these were the times she enjoyed exerting her authority.

Yanking on the front of Roy's shirt, pulling him closer, she leveled a hard glare. "How about I give you one second to answer my question like a gentleman or I slap some cuffs on you for impeding an investigation."

"Okay, geez. Can't take a joke, I see." Roy laughed nervously as he backed away, but only after she let him go. She had all the control in the situation and Roy knew it.

"Well, Roy?"

"Yeah, I was working last night. Why?"

"Did Stacy Cotton come in here and purchase anything?

Was Evan Barten with her?" she asked briskly and to the point.

Roy glanced at Seth, who wisely hadn't stepped into the conversation. Then Roy looked back at her, his eyes straying to her chest one more time. "Yeah, Stacy popped in. She was in a real hurry. She wasn't much for conversation, just like you. She wasn't with anyone."

"What did she buy and did she mention where she was headed?"

"I don't know. I didn't pay attention. I rang the shit up. Chips, snacks, band-aids, maybe. She asked if the Snake Toad Trail was clear. That nasty storm we had in the summer brought down quite a few trees, blocking the path to some of the cabins. I told her I had no idea. Because I don't."

"Try to pay more attention next time to the customer's purchase instead of their breasts, Roy. It would help." On those parting words, she turned around and walked outside.

What a pig.

A shiver rushed down her spine as she slid in the car. And Seth was friends with that creep. She was very thankful it was winter and her jacket had been zipped up tight. Poor Roy couldn't even get a peek at her breasts.

She started the car as Seth slid into his seat. Rubbing her hands near the vent, she inhaled deeply to find the strength to stay calm and in her groove.

"I know where the cabins are he's talking about. I know which one Stacy would head to."

She put the car in drive. "Good. What's the address?"

"Nice job with Roy. Not many people put him in his place when he's acting—"

"The address, Seth," she said, cutting him off, turning

her head to meet his gaze. "I'm done with pleasantries with you. Give me the address and then zip your lips."

Seth's eyes narrowed, yet a hint of confusion lingered in his gaze. "Pleasantries? I'm not sure we've ever exchanged anything close to that. I was trying to say—"

"I don't care what you have to say."

Well, she did. But she certainly couldn't tell him that. She couldn't say how she appreciated him letting her control the situation. So many times in life other people loved to step in and take control. Make her do this and make her do that. Especially men. Like they were the boss of her. She never had any say. She never had any control of her life.

But back in the store, Seth stood to the side and let her lead. It had felt nice, but very foreign. And she couldn't afford to like him. To let him get under her shield and into her heart. Nothing good would come from it.

Seth nodded and looked away. He rattled off the address and then silence descended.

Silence was good.

It was for the best.

She pulled behind what she assumed was Stacy's or Evan's car in front of a golden-colored cabin nestled in the woods. Glistening white snow surrounded it.

The silence was about to end.

Because Seth didn't listen to her protests to let her go first. He dashed out of the car and straight to the cabin door. He didn't even knock.

6

His legs were frozen, immobile. His eyes zeroed in on the body sprawled across the floor near the couch. A pool of blood was stationed near the side of her body and ran through her beautiful chestnut brown hair.

Stacy was...

Oh, God, she was...

His stomach started to churn, bile coating his throat. Two cold hands suddenly grasped his cheeks and shielded his view from the horrifying scene.

"Don't look. Go back to the car where I told you to wait," Pepper cocked a brow, "and stay there."

The coldness blowing into his back from outside didn't bother him, but the chilliness from her hands sent a shiver down his spine. Surprisingly, not in a frightening way. Her touch might've been bone-chilling cold, but her hands on him kept him anchored to reality. Because seeing Stacy lying dead on the floor was enough to send him to the pits of hell.

They broke up. She moved on to his ex-best friend, but that didn't mean he'd ever wanted to see her hurt.

"Seth, I need you to listen to me." She leaned closer, her hot breath fanning his lips.

It made him ache to close the distance, to get his mind on something other than what his eyes just saw.

Then, before he could do something truly crazy like kiss her, her hands dropped and shoved at his chest. Her stern look that insisted he follow her directions wasn't the least bit frightening as she likely intended. Instead, he thought it was adorable.

Deciding to listen, he swiftly turned around and headed back for the car, dreading each step he took. He shouldn't be retreating, acting like a coward.

But that's exactly what he was. A coward.

He couldn't look at Stacy's lifeless body for another moment. And if Stacy was dead, then that meant Evan was dead as well. Walking around the cabin, searching for his body wouldn't be the best thing for him. He couldn't say how he'd react.

Break things. Smash everything into smithereens. Which would inadvertently compromise any evidence.

Or he could do something unmanly in front of a woman and break down and cry.

Cry for the loss of a childhood friend. A friend he never took the chance to reconcile with.

He should've met Evan for drinks. He should've cleared the air between them.

He forced himself to look out the window, but he couldn't see anything of importance. Pepper had closed the door.

She was such an enigma. Downright cruel and closed-off, emotionless. And other times, compassionate and caring.

The way she took hold of the situation and grounded him back to reality—he didn't understand.

More than likely, she did it because it was her job, not because she cared. He needed to get any lustful thoughts about her out of his head right this second. Starting any sort of relationship with her, even just a sexual one, wasn't a smart idea.

Plus, he still needed to apologize for his behavior earlier and the things he said.

His hand reached inside his coat pocket and clutched his phone.

He should call his brother, too. Give him an update.

His hand unfurled from around the phone.

No, he'd leave that task to Pepper. It was her job, after all.

Again—nothing but a coward.

He perked up in his seat when the cabin door flew open and Pepper came heading straight for his side of the vehicle. He managed to open his door and step half out by the time she reached him.

"What's going—"

"She's alive. Slow pulse, but alive. We don't have time to wait for an ambulance. Help me carry her to the car, but be gentle. I don't know what kind of injuries she has. She has an obvious head wound, but she was also shot in the stomach."

Seth didn't stop to ask more questions. He followed her inside the cabin, this time not freezing at the sight of Stacy lying unconscious on the floor.

Please don't let her die.

He said a silent prayer that Stacy would make it as he gently scooped her into his arms. Wordless, he followed Pepper outside, then carefully laid Stacy in the back seat after Pepper opened the door. Trying his best not to jostle

Stacy too much, he joined her in the back seat with her head resting on his lap.

Pepper suddenly thrust her jacket toward him. "Press this to her stomach as hard as you can. We don't know how long she's been lying there bleeding, but she can't afford to lose any more blood."

He did as he was told, shoving the jacket hard onto Stacy's bloodied wound. A soft moan erupted from her lips, but she didn't open her eyes or say anything.

"Hang on, Stacy. You're going to be fine," he whispered, as he pressed harder, eliciting another quiet moan.

Pepper started to back up and turn the vehicle around in the small driveway and nearly got stuck in the snow when he heard the back tires spinning.

"Be careful. Don't get stuck."

"No shit, Sherlock," Pepper snapped as she gently twisted the wheel another direction and put her foot on the gas again.

Thankfully, they moved forward and headed for the road without further worry.

"This is bad. Who..." he cut off the rest of his question, afraid to voice it out loud.

Did Evan do this? Why would he shoot Stacy? Pepper never mentioned a word about Evan. Was he dead? Did she find him in there? Or was he...

Gone.

First, Barry. Now, Stacy. It didn't make sense, but it all seemed to point to Evan. Unless...

"Did you find Evan in another room? Is he...is he dead?"

Pepper hadn't immediately rushed out of the cabin, indicating she must've searched the cabin.

"He wasn't there, but I saw evidence he was. More bloody rags in the trash."

They both went silent after that.

What could he say? They both had to be thinking the same thing. Evan did this.

Or someone else did it and took Evan with them.

Yeah, that sounded like a more plausible reason. He liked that scenario better than the first one. Because no matter the issues between him and his friend, he couldn't imagine Evan physically hurting anyone.

He listened with a strained ear as Pepper called his brother, relaying everything. She kept one firm hand on the wheel, driving like a bat out of hell, holding the phone in her other hand, talking with a brisk, in-control tone.

How could she be so calm and collected right now? His hands were shaking, yet he made sure to keep the jacket tight against Stacy's wound. His heart was pumping double-time. His nerves were so wired with tension, he was ready to shout out a bloodcurdling scream filled with anguish and despair.

Before long they were jerking to a stop in front of the emergency room doors, although he swore it took forever to reach the hospital.

Within seconds, Stacy was whisked out of his arms and out of his view. Blood covered his hands, his heart pounded like a raging animal hyped on meth and his eyes were on the verge of unleashing the floodgates.

Pepper appeared by his side, standing with that same stern look she loved to wear with the sun shining brightly behind her. It was weird the way the sun penetrated his gaze. Maybe he was finally losing his mind to reality. Because the way the sun reflected around Pepper, it haloed her like an angel.

A bright, defining angel sent from heaven to make everything in his shitty life better and brighter. More alive and happy than he'd been for the past four months since the first day Aubrey came into their lives and he found out his best friend was lying to him.

"Let's go. Get out of the car."

An angel?

What the hell was he thinking?

Pepper was more like a deranged demon from hell. Her forceful, direct words said enough.

Yet, he followed her instructions like a lost little puppy looking for a new home. He couldn't help himself.

As he stepped out of the car with shaky legs, the sun still surrounded her, like a beacon of light directing him to his forever home.

Except he wasn't a damn puppy, and Pepper was the last woman who would ever want him.

———

SHE HATED THE SAD, forlorn look on his face. Utter devastation and for a woman who had moved on to his best friend. She never had a man care about her that much. Hell, she never would. Her entire life was filled with bad memories and baggage that would not be easy to sift through. No man ever stuck around long enough to see the real her.

Seth wouldn't either, especially because she wasn't even showing him the real her.

They stared at each other while the cold, brutal wind whipped around them. There wasn't snow in the forecast, but with the way the wind wailed and tunneled around them, it felt like some sort of storm was brewing.

She honestly didn't know what to say. So far, she'd only said what was necessary to get Stacy some help. And the way Seth stood frozen like a statue, she knew she had needed to step in before he completely lost it.

Thankfully, Stacy wasn't dead—yet. With the amount of blood she lost, she could still perish. With a quick search of the house, she didn't find Evan hiding.

She didn't know what to think. Was he behind this? Murdering his boss and then trying to kill his girlfriend?

Or was someone else behind it—the same person she was looking for—and they now had Evan? If that were the case, she had to be extra careful. This man wasn't someone to trifle with. He could hurt her as much as he hurt...

She had to stay focused and in control. Especially for Seth.

Seth continued to stare at her, his eyes glazed over with fear and confusion. Obviously, it was up to her to take control of the situation once more and keep him centered.

"Come on. Let's clean you up." Then she lightly pushed on his back to walk forward instead of grabbing his hand like she had the strong urge to do.

It was so strange how much she wanted to comfort him. To let him know he wasn't alone in this.

And yet, he was alone. Because no matter how much she wanted to be his friend and offer a shoulder to cry on, she had to maintain her cover. At all costs.

She spoke quietly to a nurse about what she needed, then followed the nurse with Seth in tow to an empty exam room. She gestured for Seth to sit down on the bed. He did nothing but stand in the middle of the room. She waited impatiently, tapping her foot, while the nurse fetched clean clothes for him.

"Take off your clothes."

A low, masculine chuckle floated seductively to her ears.

"I didn't know you liked me like that, Pepper. You don't have to tell me twice."

Her face burned as her eyes rounded when Seth started removing his jacket, a sly grin on his face.

Sure, she told him to take off his clothes, but she forgot to add a few words along with that sentence.

His shirt came off next.

Pure, handsome glory stood before her. A strong, chiseled chest, defined in all the right places. Seth Caldwell worked out. Smooth chest, yet with a hint of hair leading below his belt line. Almost like it was playing a bit of peek-a-boo. Come see more, if you dare.

She really needed to find her words. The man was undressing right before her eyes. Have mercy on her soul, she didn't want him to stop.

But he had to.

His hands reached for the button on his jeans and unsnapped it.

"Stop!"

His eyes twinkled with mischief. "But you told me to take off my clothes."

Remember who you are. Remember why you're in this town.

"You didn't let me finish my sentence."

"Oh, you sounded like you were done speaking."

"This isn't the time or place for such things, Seth."

His grin inched up a notch, all sexy and inviting, just like his naked chest begged her to come closer and touch. One little touch. "I'd be more than happy to remove my clothes for you somewhere else, Pepper."

"I didn't ask you to remove your clothes for that reason. You have blood all over you." Her eyes glided to his jacket he had tossed onto the bed. Although it had been zipped up, the bottom of his shirt had also gotten stained with blood, as had the top part of his jeans.

Just like that, the reminder of what happened, why they were even at the hospital, flooded back into his features. His eyes lost the merriment, his smile disappeared. A shiver wracked his body, and she knew it wasn't from a chill in the air.

"The nurse is bringing you a set of scrubs. I'll leave you alone to change without an audience. You should wash your hands first."

He looked down at his hands, raising them. The horror that filled every facet in his expression made her heart ache. She wanted so badly to step closer and offer any sort of comfort. A touch to the shoulder. A friendly smile. Encouraging words.

But she did none of that.

She stood firmly in her spot, waiting for him to say something, anything. When he didn't respond but walked over to the sink, she took that as her cue he didn't need anything from her.

She left the room and headed for the waiting room.

Not even a minute went by when Sheriff Caldwell stormed into the area, a harried expression on his face.

"Where's Seth? Is he okay? Any word on Stacy yet?"

She cleared her throat and tried to keep all emotions out of her features. "He's changing. He had quite a bit of blood on him. I haven't heard anything about Stacy yet. I imagine it'll be quite some time before we do. I'm sorry, Sheriff. She lost a lot of blood. We did the best we could."

Sheriff Caldwell's expression softened. "Of course, you did. I know that. And I am so glad you were on the case and found her when you did. I know Seth is grateful as well."

Well, what did he mean by that? Did Seth still harbor

feelings for his ex-girlfriend? Part of her wouldn't be surprised. He did give that impression on a few occasions. It wasn't her place to ask. None of these people mattered to her.

Oh, the lies she loved to tell herself.

They mattered. They mattered in her quest for justice. They mattered because deep down, she wasn't an unfeeling bitch, even though she portrayed it so well.

"The question is, where is Evan? Like I told you on the phone, I saw evidence he was there, but no sign of him. I didn't have a chance to search the premises outside, though."

The sheriff nodded as if he understood why she hadn't. "I sent Bolt there to check everything out and collect any evidence."

"I'll join him."

Because the last thing she wanted to do was stick around Seth. The man was digging under her barrier she erected a little too easily for her tastes. And she could not—absolutely not—let anyone close to her.

Sheriff Caldwell hesitated, then nodded. "You're right, he could use the help."

"Seth's in room two. I'll report in later, Sheriff."

Then she left the hospital before she changed her mind and checked on Seth one more time.

She had a job to do.

Getting to know Seth Caldwell better was not it.

———

SETH DIDN'T LOOK at his brother when he stepped into the exam room. The nurse had given him a blue-colored set of scrubs and he had just put the shirt on when Logan entered.

He'd have to take a shower when he got home because although he scrubbed his hands with a huge amount of soap, he still felt dirty.

"You okay?" Logan asked quietly.

He wanted to retort with, "Hell, no. How can I be okay?" Instead, he shrugged and then turned to the garbage can to throw away his clothes. He never wanted to see the items again in his life. Hell, if he could start a fire and burn them to ashes inside the hospital, he would.

"Don't do that," Logan said with a sharpness in his tone.

Seth paused, the clothes dangling in the air, and finally looked at Logan. "What?"

Logan breathed deeply then ran a hand down his face. "Your clothes have blood on them. Stacy's blood. It's evidence, Seth."

A shiver wracked Seth's body as he jerked and threw the clothes back onto the bed as quickly as he could.

"Did you find Evan yet?" He didn't want to ask—or even know the answer, especially if he was dead—but the question slipped out anyway.

"Not yet. Bolt's out at the cabin looking for any useful evidence, and Pepper is on her way to help."

His heart dipped at the news—and an odd moment of terror filled his veins. He couldn't explain why he suddenly feared for her safety. She was quite capable of taking care of herself. She had walked into that cabin with no fear and taken charge of the situation. He had no doubt she could defend herself.

He couldn't explain his sudden bout of fear. Maybe it was because Stacy was fighting for her life, someone he used to care about.

Damn. Was he saying he cared about Pepper? Already? So soon?

He couldn't answer that. His emotions and feelings were all jumbled in confusion, but he knew he didn't want anything terrible to happen to her.

Despite her frosty attitude on occasion, he liked her. He couldn't help it. Her beauty alone reeled him in.

"I'm sorry you had to see Stacy like that." Logan paused. "I'm also glad you found her, though. You two saved her life."

"She's going to make it?" Hope filled him up. He might not be dating her any longer, nor wanted to in the future, but he didn't want her to die.

Logan frowned. "Well, I don't know her prognosis, but if you hadn't found her, she would be dead."

"I'll stay and wait. I want to know. And you'll let me know when you find Evan?"

Logan nodded. "Of course, I will. But, Seth, you should go home. I'll keep you updated about Stacy."

Being home, all alone, for his thoughts to play mad tricks on his mind was the last thing he wanted.

"I'll stay."

Then he walked around Logan and exited the room. Logan didn't immediately follow, which made him assume Logan was bagging up his clothes. For evidence. He still couldn't believe it.

When he walked into the waiting room, he saw Stacy's parents running toward the automatic doors. His entire body stiffened when he made eye contact with her mother. The woman never did think he was good enough for her daughter. And maybe he wasn't. He tended to screw up and make things worse in every area of his life, even with his own family.

"You! This is your fault!" Stacy's mother screamed at him. "Get out. What are you even doing here?"

Seth didn't know how to respond. Although he didn't know how this was any of his fault. Maybe it was. Maybe if he had never broken up with her, she would've never gotten closer to Evan, and she would've never gone off with him like she had.

But the feelings between them had fizzled out and he couldn't keep doing the same song and dance with her. He ended things with her and refused to go back and try again. He didn't love her anymore. They weren't right for each other.

Stacy's mother's eyes grew wide when he still didn't respond. She stepped closer and was about to put her hands on him when Logan appeared out of nowhere and stepped in front of him.

"Mrs. Cotton, none of this is Seth's fault. If anything, you should thank him and Deputy Wilson for finding Stacy when they did. She lost a lot of blood, but she's in good hands now. What I don't want to do is arrest you for assaulting anyone." Logan's tone of voice was firm, yet consoling. Even though Seth couldn't see his face, he knew Logan had a tender expression to soften the blow of his words. Seth always had envied his brother being able to take charge and control any kind of situation.

"Marcy, let's go find someone to give us information. Ignore the boy." He grabbed his wife around the shoulders to comfort her and most likely hold her back in case she decided to try something again.

Seth lightly ground his teeth at the words *boy* but said nothing. They were hurting, worried about their daughter, and it wasn't anything new. They never did like him.

"You find who did this, Sheriff. You make them pay," Marcy said with a shaky voice, yet filled with steel.

"You have my word."

Then her parents walked away to the nurses' station.

Logan turned around and met his gaze with a concerned look. "Are you ready to leave now?"

Well, after the outburst by her parents, it would be wise if he left.

"Yeah, I guess. I have no choice, it looks like."

"Come on. I'll drop you off at home."

Seth didn't argue and followed Logan outside to his vehicle. It didn't take long for Logan to drive him home. Not much was said. He barely mumbled goodbye before exiting and rushing to his front door.

Not because it was brutally cold out, but because he needed to be alone. He needed to break down without his brother witnessing anything.

All his emotions going haywire in the hospital were reaching their breaking point. He didn't think he could hold back any longer.

As soon as he closed the door, he slumped against it and slid down to the floor. Silent, hot tears streaked across his face.

His thoughts rolled around like rough waves crashing in the sea.

Stacy could die.

Evan was missing.

His life was a mess.

Something seemed to be bothering Kat.

And Pepper...

His thoughts were so confused about her, they couldn't settle on one particular thing.

Yet, tears rained done. He released all the pent-up emotions that had been building for a long time.

7

PEPPER ROTATED her neck and let out a slow breath to release all the tension from her body. It kind of worked.

Opening her car door, she stepped outside and tried not to think about Seth and how he was doing at the hospital.

She should've stayed with him a little longer.

Or not.

What would be the purpose? She wasn't here to make attachments—least of all with him.

She had a job to do, and right now that was to find Evan Barten.

She had stopped at home first to grab another jacket and then came straight to the cabin.

Steeling her features, she stepped inside the last place she wanted to be—because she had to be honest with herself, she wanted to be with Seth. She hadn't liked leaving him like that, so lost and alone, hurting. But she had no choice.

Deputy Bolten stood up where he had been crouched down near the small pool of blood from Stacy's wound. He smiled and nodded as he capped what looked like a swab from the blood. "Deputy Wilson."

She returned a nod. "Deputy Bolten."

She had met him briefly yesterday. That was about the extent of their pleasantries yesterday as well. He smiled at her, so she had to assume she hadn't offended or pissed him off yet like she had with so many other people.

She had only been in town for two days and she already knew so much about him as well. People liked to talk, and maybe because they didn't know her well, they liked to chat her up. Mrs. Dunburry, who ran the boutique in Lucky, had stopped her yesterday to have a conversation. More like, dig up information on her. And no matter how hard Mrs. Dunburry tried to dig, she wasn't able to pry any information out of her. She knew her abrupt attitude had rubbed Mrs. Dunburry the wrong way. Oh, well.

She could already tell the woman was a huge gossiper. Mrs. Dunburry had freely shared that Deputy Bolten had been shot four months ago. It had taken two full months for him to return to work. Since being shot, he was more serious and subdued, rather than his normal chipper, fun-loving self. Guess getting shot and almost dying could do that to a person.

Not that she was going to ask Deputy Bolten about any of it. It wasn't any of her business, nor did it matter concerning her mission. Her gut told her from the first hello she could trust him.

It didn't mean she was ready to tell them the truth.

"Find anything useful yet?" she asked as she walked around the cabin, keeping her eye trained for any nuances. "And you can me Pepper."

He nodded with a gentle smile. "Call me Bolt." He placed the swab he had collected into his evidence kit. "I only got here a few minutes ago. I walked around a little bit but didn't see anything catch my eye. It looks like they spent the night as the bed wasn't made, but I thought I'd start here and then work my way around the cabin."

"There's also bloody rags in the trash can in the bathroom. I'm assuming they're from Evan's wound. Do you want to bag that up and I'll look around outside?" She decided to phrase it as a question instead of barking orders. She could try a little harder at being nice. She couldn't help she tended to take charge and get things done no matter how it made people feel. Ruffling peoples' feathers was a forte of hers. Of course, she had coworkers, but she had yet to call any of them friends. Not many people she worked with actually liked her. It was never something that bothered her because the job itself was the most important factor, not whether people liked her.

Oddly, she found herself wanting Bolt to like her. Wanting Sheriff Caldwell to like her. She figured with how she started with Charlotte that would be an uphill battle getting the woman to like her. Only after two days, her gut said she could trust these people and she was going to follow her gut like she always did.

"That's fine." His tone of voice didn't suggest malice or derision, which made her heart soar for a brief moment. At least one person didn't completely hate her.

Did Seth hate her?

She wasn't tender on his feelings at the hospital. She could've been a bit more sympathetic.

Whatever. It didn't matter.

Of course, repeating that didn't seem to be registering, because it did matter to her. She didn't want Seth to hate her.

In two short days, the man had weaseled his way under

her defenses. Defenses that were normally impenetrable by anyone. Even her own family.

Clearing those dangerous thoughts from her mind, she walked back outside. It was hard to tell glancing at the driveway how many vehicles had been here. She had already been here once, now back again, added in with Bolt's tire tracks and the other car sitting there, it was difficult to pinpoint whose tracks were whose. Who had shown up? Or maybe nobody showed up at all and Evan hurt Stacy. So why didn't he take the vehicle sitting in the driveway?

Heading back to her patrol car, she ran the license plate of the car. Evan's registration information pulled up.

Okay, so it was Evan's car.

If he fled, why didn't he take it?

And where was Stacy's car?

When she left the diner yesterday morning, she drove away in her vehicle, according to Callie, and she didn't appear to have been lying about that.

Had both Evan and Stacy driven to this cabin? Did Evan flee in Stacy's car?

Unsure of what was more likely—and it didn't matter, they needed to find her car—she put a BOLO out on her vehicle, then stepped back outside.

Approaching the car, she tried each door, finding them all locked. Peering inside, she didn't see anything out of the ordinary besides some blood on the seat, most likely from Evan's wound.

Mentally noting to ask Bolt if he found a set of car keys in the cabin, she started walking around the outside, taking her time so she didn't miss anything vital.

When she got around to the back side of the cabin, she saw a set of footprints emerge from the other side of the house. As she got closer, she noticed the distance between each print.

Someone had been running.

There looked to be two sets of prints. Following the prints back toward the front door, she could only assume one thing. Evan ran and someone followed.

Deciding to follow the footprints, she tried to keep her mind focused on the task and not how Seth was doing. But no matter how hard she tried, her mind kept conjuring up images of him. His sad eyes. His morose expression. The pain enveloping every facet of his body.

She couldn't even fix her own pain; it was pointless to try to fix his.

The cold wind slapped her in the face as she walked farther and farther away from the cabin. The steps didn't appear to go in a straight line, but they were rather zigzagged and erratic.

Evan tried to keep them on their toes...or the person had been shooting at him. She was inclined to believe the latter.

After following the footprints for about twenty minutes or so, she finally came across a road. The same road that led to the cabin itself. Unfortunately, the footprints stopped there.

The question was, had Evan gotten away?

Or did they grab him?

She wished she had an answer, especially for Seth. Which was wrong to even want.

As she made her way back to the cabin, she thought of Seth once more and how she could attempt to put a smile on his face. He had a devilish-charming smile she just adored.

What was the point in denying it?

She liked Seth Caldwell.

And it was only setting herself up for heartache.

———

SETH KNOCKED his head against the door, mentally berating himself for acting like a crybaby. How long had he been sitting on the floor crying? He had felt his phone buzz and ring in his pocket, but he didn't answer it. It was probably Logan checking on him. His brother never could let things lie. Or maybe it had been Kat calling him to check on him. Either way, one of his siblings had called.

He didn't want anyone to bother him right now. To see the evidence of his weakness.

Inhaling and exhaling a few times, hoping the tears were done, he finally stood up. He was a bit wobbly, but he didn't fall on his ass, so that was a good sign.

He headed straight for the shower. He had to clean every inch of his body. Although none of the blood appeared to have touched his skin besides his hands, he felt dirty and disgusting.

He made sure to turn the water as hot as it could go. Maybe it would burn some of the guilt from him as well.

Why didn't he meet Evan over drinks and talk about their issues? Why didn't he try to make amends?

He might not ever get the chance. In all likelihood, he was dead. Just like Stacy would die. She had lost so much blood, half of it had spilled on him, even as he had held that jacket to her like a vice grip.

But whenever he thought about Evan and seeing him again, he never could find the right words. He didn't know what to say. He wasn't even sure an apology from him would be enough.

Evan lied—for over two months he kept to himself that

his brother Wayne had approached him. Okay, sure, it had nothing to do Aubrey's abduction, but he had seen Wayne. Why Evan thought he had to lie about it blew his mind. He couldn't understand why he would lie. So what, that his brother saw him.

Which made him think he was still lying about something.

With the occurrence of the latest events, it didn't seem too farfetched anymore. Of course, he had never voiced his concerns to Logan—or Danny—that he still had a small inkling Evan was lying about something. Why bother? They all wanted him to let it go and move on.

Well, he did. Without even attempting to find out answers from Evan, and now, he might not get another chance.

By the time he stepped out of the shower, his skin was raw and red, and he still didn't feel clean. He felt hollow and empty and filled with so much desolation he thought about getting back in the shower and trying to scrub himself once again.

He grabbed an old pair of jeans that fit perfectly around the waist, with worn patches on the knees. He needed comfort and stability. A damn pair of jeans he'd had for the past five years that still fit with perfection was going to do the trick. How laughable. Swiping a black shirt from the closet, he threw it on, then ran a hand through his wet hair, smoothing the strands back.

More tears wanted to flow.

His bottom lip wobbled as his eyes filled up with water.

Shit.

Not again.

He would not cry again.

A loud knock on his door had him jumping.

Well, he should've figured one of his siblings would come knocking on his door, demanding to know how he was doing. Just great. Not what he wanted to deal with. He wanted to be by himself and wallow in his self-pity...and cry some more.

He'd ignore them. They would go away.

Another knock sounded.

Or not. When did his siblings ever walk away? They didn't.

Swiping another hand through his wet hair, he headed for the front door. He rubbed his eyes, trying to erase any evidence that he'd been crying. He couldn't believe he cried, to begin with. How pathetic.

Okay, so his brother—or sister—was about to see how pathetic he truly was. That he couldn't even hold it together. Whatever.

Because if he didn't open the door, they would open it themselves. Neither one of them would leave just because he refused to answer the door.

Steeling his spine, attempting to display an indifferent expression, he wiped his face one more time, then swung it open.

Double shit.

Not his brother.

Or his sister.

"Can I come in or are you just going to stand there gawking at me?"

He couldn't understand why Pepper stood on his doorstep—or how she knew where he lived. He imagined she would be just as persistent as Kat and Logan would be.

He stepped to the side and let her enter.

Great. As if he hadn't already made a complete fool of

himself with her, now she knew how pathetic and weak he truly was.

He knew his face had the marks of his tears still lingering, even after taking a shower.

Closing the door slowly, not that it would delay her reason for stopping by, but it gave him two extra seconds to find his composure.

Then he turned toward her.

Before he could say anything, she reached up and brushed his cheek. Her hand stilled in position.

"You must really love her. I'm sorry."

Her soft touch, the concern in her eyes filled up a part of his heart that had been empty for so long.

Love Stacy? Not anymore. Not for a long time. He had just gone through the motions because it was safe and comfortable. Same for Stacy. They never wanted to branch out and see what else was out there.

But "I'm sorry?" What did that mean? Was Stacy...dead? Did she not make it?

He couldn't find the words to voice his concerns because her hand was still pressed to his cheek, her eyes gazing at him with such affection. Like she...cared.

Before he could think about the consequences, he placed a hand on her hip and drew her closer. Then his lips met hers.

A soft, languid kiss that scorched his soul and made him suddenly believe in happily ever afters.

HIS LIPS WERE like molten lava, hot and raw, yet soft like a feather. Her hand stayed pressed against his cheek as her other hand grabbed the front of his shirt, making a fist.

His hands strengthened around her waist as the kiss deepened.

Oh, the magical things she was feeling. The desire flowing through her veins. The want and need coursing through her body.

She wanted more.

More of him.

Damn it!

No!

This was all wrong. She couldn't give in to her wants and needs. Nothing mattered but her mission in this small town.

As painful as it was, she pushed away from him and let go, taking a few steps back. They both stood a few feet apart, chests heaving, shallow breaths filling the small foyer as if they had run a marathon.

His eyes looked red as if he had been crying. The desire she felt in his lips morphed into the sadness she first witnessed when he opened the door.

Why did he kiss her if he still loved his ex-girlfriend so much? He had to by the evidence marked on his face.

"By the look on your face, I feel like I should apologize for kissing you." His eyes roamed around her entire body, landing back onto her eyes. Yet, no words of apology left his lips.

She tried to smooth out her features and display nothing of what she was truly feeling. Like how much she wanted to kiss him again. How much she wanted to be locked in his arms. She had felt so safe and protected. Warm and cared for. She couldn't remember the last time she felt remotely close to that.

"That will not happen again." Her tone was sharp and lethal.

He shifted on his feet. "What are you doing here,

Pepper? My brother told me you were on your way back to the cabin. What did you find?"

"I was there."

She didn't add anything else because there wasn't anything else to add. They didn't find much of anything. Stacy and Evan had spent the night, appeared to have cleaned and dressed Evan's wound, and that it's. Besides the footprints she found that led to a dead end, she had no answers for him.

"And?"

"And we found nothing of importance. I'm sorry." She was sorry. She wished she could help take away his pain by giving him some answers, and she couldn't.

"So, what are you doing here?" Seth asked with a disgusted tone as if he didn't just kiss her and take her breath away.

Which was fine with her. She needed to forget how wonderful the kiss was.

"I thought you might want to join me again. To search for your friend."

That was the honest-to-God's truth. They made a good team. She liked working with him, even though she could be a world-class bitch on occasion.

It had nothing to do with the fact she liked being around him.

Absolutely not.

"My brother asked you to come here?"

How did she answer that? Because, no, the sheriff did not. He called her when she left the cabin and mentioned he dropped off Seth at home, but he didn't tell her to pick him up and continue the search for Evan.

She felt compelled to see him. It sounded like a good excuse for her reason for coming by.

Maybe this was a bad idea.

By the looks of his wet hair, he had just gotten out of the shower. His hair was swept back in its usual perfection, although one tiny strand looked like it wanted to break free from the rest. For one brief moment when she eyed that tiny piece, she had been tempted to smooth it back for him. Touch him in a way she had no right to touch him.

What was she doing here?

This was a bad idea.

"You either want to come or you don't. It doesn't matter to me."

They stared at one another for what felt like ages before Seth finally nodded. "I need to find a new jacket. Give me a minute?"

"Be quick." Then she pulled out her phone like she had something pressing to look at when in reality, she didn't know what else to say.

He walked back to the foyer a minute later.

"I'm ready if you are."

She nodded and then headed for the front door and stepped outside. She didn't have a good response. She was far from ready for anything. Seth followed without a word.

It was tense and silent as they both got in the car. She couldn't quite define the tension, either. It didn't feel like the original tension before the kiss.

Now it felt like sexual tension.

Lots of it.

Just great.

More worries to add to her plate. Like how she was going to resist Seth Caldwell. He was a very tempting man. His smile, his humor, his kisses. She wanted to get to know him so much better, and she couldn't.

And if—when—he learned the truth about her, he'd hate her.

Ignoring her tumbling feelings, she turned in his direction.

He looked back.

They did nothing but stare at each other until Seth finally cocked a tiny grin. "Where are we going?"

She couldn't hold back her own tiny grin. "I thought you might have an idea."

His grin dimmed as he glanced outside. "I wish I knew. These days, I feel like I barely even knew my best friend."

"I kind of lied inside your house." She had no idea why she blurted it out like that, but it was out in the open now.

Seth trained his eyes back on her, wariness and a bit of distrust coating his gaze. It was the last thing she wanted to see.

"What do you mean?"

"I said we didn't find anything, which we didn't." She inhaled softly. "But I found some footprints leading away from the house. If I had to make a guess—and it's merely a guess— someone else showed up at the cabin and shot Stacy and Evan ran. They chased him. The footprints ended at the road and the trail went dead. I don't know what happened from there. So, I guess, the question is, where, if Evan got away and is still on foot, would he go?"

"In that area?" Seth shrugged, indicating he had no clue, which disappointed her. "We used to go to that cabin all the time, the three of us. Drink, party, have fun. Lots of memories there. I even went there with just Stacy. We would grab beer and snacks from town and head straight to the cabin. When we left, it was back to Lucky. We didn't frequent anything else in that area."

She nodded, even more disappointed. Hearing stories

about him and Stacy was not what she wanted. Why did he still love that woman? She moved on with his best friend. He should hate her on that principle alone.

But who was she to talk? She was an arrogant, impolite bitch. At least, based on her actions the past two days, that's how she figured everyone classified her.

In reality, she was lonely. She worked, slept, worked, slept, and so on. She didn't have a social life. She didn't have friends. She didn't have a boyfriend.

She didn't have anything but herself.

How sad and lonely.

Her phone buzzed in her pocket. Pulling it out, her brows knitted together.

"Bolt."

"Pepper."

She wanted to giggle at how they greeted each other, but she held in the laughter that would show a side of her she rarely let out.

Why was that?

Maybe because anytime she laughed growing up, nobody joined in. Laughing alone wasn't any fun.

"You put a BOLO out for Stacy's car."

He said it as a statement rather than a question, and she wasn't sure how to respond. Yes, in a sarcastic tone seemed like the most appropriate answer she'd give to someone else, yet with Bolt, she hesitated. She had also failed to inform Sheriff Caldwell she'd done that.

Had she done something wrong? Was she supposed to get permission before she put a BOLO out because she was the new deputy?

When she didn't respond, he continued. "A park ranger found it and called us. Do you want to meet me here?"

Hmm. Well, maybe she didn't do anything wrong.

"What's the address?"

He rattled off the address as she wrote it down in a tiny notepad she carried. Then she disconnected without saying goodbye.

"What did he want? What did he find?" Seth asked with a slight panic in his tone.

Her hand itched to reach out and comfort him, but she stopped herself before the impulse took over. "Stacy's car. Let's go."

She put the car in reverse and headed to the address Bolt had given her with directions from Seth. It led to an overlook on the side of the road leading to one of the many hiking trails in the area. It was also in the opposite direction from the cabin in Neptune, so there wasn't a chance Evan would come for Stacy's vehicle if he was on foot. She pulled next to Bolt's vehicle and met him by Stacy's car.

The doors were locked and the windows were all intact. Nothing appeared to be amiss inside the vehicle.

"I didn't realize you'd be with, Seth," Bolt said as he glanced between the two of them with a puzzled expression, yet didn't add anything more.

Seth shrugged. "I've been helping search for Evan from the beginning. I want to find him as much as you guys."

"Well, there's not much to see here. I don't see anything odd inside and we can't open it without a warrant," Bolt said. "I figured I'd have Sam, Barry's son, come tow it." Then he winced. "That's a bad idea. Forget I said that. I just thought the vehicle should be back in Lucky, not here in Mulhene."

"I know a guy here in Mulhene who can tow it," Seth offered.

"Give him a call," she said briskly, deciding she had to maintain her original personality, especially with Seth.

There could be no more kissing.

He eyed her funny, then nodded and stepped away to make a phone call. She walked around the area while he talked on the phone. Bolt waited patiently by the car. She didn't see anything stick out, although she wasn't sure exactly what she was looking for. When she neared the railing, the view stopped her. So breathtaking. The trees dotted to and fro with snow covering the limbs, sparkling like diamonds in the spotlight. The tiny sounds of nature that echoed her way sent a very brief moment of peace inside her soul. A tweet of a bird. The rustle of leaves.

She could get used to living here, and it had only been two days.

Too bad she couldn't.

"He'll be here soon." Seth's voice broke her moment of serenity.

She met him by Bolt and nodded she heard.

"So why do we think her car is here?" Bolt asked.

"My guess is they ditched it after he called her for help. They only needed one vehicle. Whoever is after him, I suspect they were trying to create a different trail." Her brows pleated, despair slipping in. "It sadly didn't work."

"I know a few people in Mulhene. We can ask around if they saw them in town," Seth suggested.

"Let's do it." She met Bolt's gaze. "Bolt."

"Pepper."

So tempted to smile again, but she refrained and headed to her car. Seth followed.

"You know, if I didn't know any better, I would say you like Bolt."

This time a small bout of laughter escaped. "Excuse me?"

"You weren't once mean or rude to him."

That hurt.

But it was the truth. That's how she acted with people more often than not. It wasn't usually her intention, but a lot of the times her personality came off as rude and closed-off.

Seth must've realized what he said because his eyes flashed with regret. "I didn't mean—"

"Don't hold back just because we shared one tiny kiss. It didn't mean anything, and I won't break."

If only that were true.

She could feel herself slowly withering and breaking inside.

But he didn't need to know that.

Nobody in this town needed to know that.

Get in and get out. That's what she needed to do.

She was here to arrest a murderer.

Or kill him.

She still hadn't decided which option she liked better. She had never killed a person before, but there was a first time for everything.

8

LOGAN PLACED a warm hand over Aubrey's arm as she slid her arms around his neck from behind.

"Are you okay?" she whispered before placing a soft kiss upon his neck.

That felt like something he'd been asking her for the longest time, ever since he found her alone and injured in his cabin with no memory. That wasn't something she should be asking him.

And he didn't know how to answer. Was he okay? Yeah, he was, for the most part. Except he worried constantly about his brother and sister. Were they okay? Kat was upset about Derek leaving, and she wouldn't talk about it until she was ready. And the things with Evan and Stacy—he knew for a fact his brother wasn't okay.

"Logan? Talk to me, please."

He squeezed her hand. "I'm worried about Kat and Seth. That's all. I'm fine."

He kept ahold of her hand as she walked around him and slid onto his lap. "How is Seth holding up? Any news on Stacy and Evan?"

"Stacy's out of surgery and it looks like she's going to make it." He breathed a sigh of relief. "And Evan...we still don't have a clue where he is. Pepper and Bolt searched all day for him. Seth was in the mix, too. I'm not sure it's the best thing for him to keep working on the case, and yet I'm the one who started it. I don't want tension between us again, but I want him to back off."

"I thought you dropped him off at home after the hospital."

He did. Then, after getting an update from Bolt, he found out Seth arrived with Pepper when they found Stacy's car. He didn't like it, but what could he do? Get into another fight with his brother? He should've never asked for Seth's help in the beginning. That's where he made his first mistake.

"I did, but he was back with Pepper helping to find Evan."

Aubrey laid her head on his chest. "He'll be fine, Logan. He's concerned about his friend."

"You're probably right. Hopefully he lets it go tomorrow and goes back to work. I should call Kat. See how she's doing."

"Or you can let Danny make sure she's all right. You know what's bugging her."

He knew partly what was bugging her. Derek quitting and moving out of town had shocked everyone, especially him. He had thought Derek let his feelings for Kat go and made amends with her. He thought they were friends again. Then one day, he left, leaving everyone reeling from shock.

But something else was bugging Kat and he didn't know what it was.

"Then maybe I should call Derek."

Aubrey brushed a hand across his cheek in a comforting gesture. Her soft touch always soothed him.

"Or maybe," she said sitting up, her hand still cupping his cheek, "you should kiss me and relax. You're always trying to take care of everyone. Let me take care of you. Derek made his choice to leave; Kat will open up when she's ready, and Seth needs time to deal with what's going on. It can all wait until tomorrow. Let me make you feel good."

Aubrey pushed him back on the bed, a beautiful smile lighting up her face.

Well, it wouldn't hurt to let everything else slide to the back of his mind, especially when he had the most gorgeous woman in the world in his arms.

"I love you, Logan," Aubrey said as her hands slid down his chest in an erotic gesture.

God, he loved this woman so much.

Then his mind only conjured blissful thoughts as Aubrey continued her beautiful torture upon his body.

———

DANNY REMOVED the last dish from the table and put it in the sink. He could do the dishes now—or he could find out what was bothering Kat.

He had another busy day at work, but his mind had been on Logan and Seth and everything going on in Lucky recently.

And Kat.

His mind was never far from Kat.

Wiping the table with a wet rag, he threw it in the sink and decided he'd come back and finish the dishes later. Time to find Kat and make her tell him what was going on.

She'd been acting weird ever since she asked him about kids yesterday.

He found Kat in the bathtub almost filled to the brim with warm, bubbly water.

She looked at him, smiled, then rested her head against the tub. "You don't mind if I take a bath, do you?"

"Of course not." Then he started to unbutton his shirt.

"What are you doing?" Her eyes glossed over his naked chest and appreciation lit up.

"I thought I'd join you. You don't mind, do you?"

For a moment, his heart hammered in his chest that she'd deny him.

Then a wicked smile spread across her face as she sat up to make room for him.

He shed his clothes and joined her in the tub, sighing in contentment when she rested against his chest. Wrapping his arms around her, he held her close and pressed a kiss to the side of her head.

"I love you, Kat."

She played with some of the bubbles sitting in front of her. "I love you, too, Danny."

"Do you think it's time you tell me what's wrong?"

She stiffened, yet didn't respond.

His lips found her neck, pressing soft, butterfly kisses. "You've been tense since yesterday morning when you asked about having kids. I didn't mean to brush you off. If that's what's bugging you, let's talk about it. But I don't like how you seem to be pulling away from me." He inhaled and slowly released his breath, then pressed another kiss to her long, slender neck. "I feel like you've been pulling away from me since Derek left."

"I can't believe he left."

"But he did." Then his body stiffened as a realization hit

him. "You love me, but if you love him more, then I—" Shit. He wanted to say he understood, but he didn't. He loved Kat with every breath in his body. He'd do anything for her.

Hell, he moved across the country to be with her.

He'd even let her go if he wasn't what she really wanted.

Kat grabbed his hands that were tight against her stomach and squeezed hard, the water flowing in gentle waves as she moved.

"He's a friend, Danny. I love you more. I swear I do. It just hurts that he left so abruptly. That he thought he had to leave. I never meant to hurt him."

"Maybe he'll come back one day. He might just need time to himself." His hands strengthened their grip with hers. "I don't like how you seem to be pulling away from me. Tell me what else is wrong."

"I...I don't know what's wrong with me. So much has happened in the last few months and it's catching up to me. Getting shot...Seth hurting because of Evan...Aubrey and her nightmares...Derek leaving..." Her voice hitched as if she were trying to hold back tears. "Life is so short, Danny. I feel like mine is flashing before my eyes. I feel like everything is spinning out of control, and I don't know how to stop it."

Danny felt her body shake within his arms and he knew the tears were coming down, although she didn't make a noise. He held her close, pressing kisses to her neck, soothing her as best as he could. He wasn't good with words. He didn't know what to say, afraid he'd say the wrong thing.

But he had to say something. He couldn't stand her crying, the pain wracking her body.

"You don't have to stop anything. You just have to be you. My beautiful, strong, loving Kat. You love to be there for everyone, but you forget that we're here for you, too. I'm always here for you."

"I know you are."

"The talk about kids..." He exhaled, wondering if he should even bring that conversation to the forefront. "I'm ready to start whenever you are. I'm ready for everything. This is a terrible place to ask, but will you marry me?"

A low giggle escaped from her sweet lips. "Naked in the bathtub, asking me to marry you, how is that terrible?"

"Well, I don't have a ring for you yet, and I'm not down on one knee." He leaned closer, cocooning his head near her neck. "And you're crying. I hate when you cry. But I need you to know how much I love you. How much I want you in my life forever. Marry me, Kat. Let's make a baby and just forget about everything that's plaguing us. None of that matters right now. You and me, that's what I want to focus on."

Kat sat up and twisted around in his lap, nestling herself in the perfect spot, water splashing over the rim of the tub. Then she cupped his cheeks and leaned in for a kiss.

"Yes, Danny, I'll marry you."

His hands slid up and down her waist as his heart slowed down to a steady rhythm because it had been beating like crazy since he walked into the bathroom.

"That's what I like to hear." He grabbed another kiss as her hands wove through his hair. "And the baby making?"

"Oh, let's start that right now."

And they proceeded to do just that.

———

SETH SLOUCHED INTO THE COUCH, staring at his TV but not really seeing what was on the screen.

He had called the hospital an hour ago asking for an update on Stacy. She hadn't woken up yet, but she was in the clear. She would be okay.

Evan, on the other hand, was another story.

He had no idea how bad his injuries were, and until Stacy woke up and could tell them, they wouldn't know how bad it was. Evan could be in the hands of someone dangerous. If he had his guess, it all had to do with drugs and his lowlife brothers—Wayne and Joshua—somehow. Which was crazy because one was locked up and the other was dead.

They didn't find any helpful clues in or around the cabin today. Nor did they know where to search for Evan anymore. Right now, they were in a waiting game for Stacy to wake up and shed some light on the situation.

He fiddled with his phone, willing it to ring.

He had called Logan a little bit ago, but he didn't answer. Maybe Aubrey was having a bad night. She sometimes regressed and had moments where the dark truly frightened her. Most nights were pretty good, though. Or maybe Logan was busy with work.

He even tried calling Kat, and she didn't answer either. She was probably ignoring him. The shit with Derek was bugging her, and until she was ready to talk, she'd keep it to herself.

But he wanted to talk to someone. He wanted to not feel so alone because right now he felt like the world was ending and he was the last man standing.

He couldn't shake the bad feeling that Evan was dead. That whoever took him—if someone had—had killed him.

Pepper had worked hard this afternoon trying to dig out any clue they could to find him. After searching the area around Stacy's car, they had headed back to the station and starting pulling out old case files dealing with any drug arrest. He had mentioned his concern about Evan's brothers, and Pepper had agreed it was something they should look into. Bolt had shown up a bit later and joined them. Talk about drugs had ensued.

The uptick in drug arrests in the area had increased lately. Logan had started to worry the Cheetahs, the gang Wayne had worked for in Florida, were starting to infiltrate their small town. So, digging into any case that might pop up a small lead was worth it. He didn't think they'd find a link to Evan that way because Evan wasn't involved in the drug scene, but he didn't argue.

He obviously didn't know his best friend. He hadn't talked to him in over two months. What did he know about Evan anymore?

There had been too many cases to comb through. They didn't get very far, and of course, Evan had never been picked up for drugs, so again, he figured this was a fruitless endeavor. But Pepper—even Bolt—thought it was necessary to find the leader of the drug gang in the area. If they could figure out who was running the operations in the area, then they could question him and hopefully find Evan. Assuming Evan's disappearance even had to do with drugs.

He had left the station before Pepper. He had even insisted she go home. They all needed a break. But she had looked determined to spend the night, if necessary, to find the answers they needed.

It was odd. The fierce determination in her eyes. It felt like...more than just finding Evan was important to her. He couldn't quite put his finger on it, but it felt like Pepper was hiding something.

God, he was starting to become suspicious of everyone. What was wrong with him?

He abruptly stood up.

No one was answering the phone. He didn't think—if he had Pepper's number—she'd answer either.

But she couldn't turn him away if he knocked on her door.

He knew Charlotte kicked her out of the station for the night. She ran a tight ship.

It was a small town; it wouldn't take much investigation to find out where she lived. After making a quick stop to the gas station, feigning the need for an energy drink, he got the information he needed. Patricia, working behind the counter, gave him Pepper's address with barely any need to nudge it out of her. Living in a small town had its advantages at times with the gossip flowing freely, and Patricia was one of the more gossipy gossipers in town.

Pepper had rented a small house near the edge of town from old Doc Roberts. He had moved away three years ago to live down south with his daughter and grandkids. His son still lived in town, who told Mrs. Dunburry that Pepper was renting his dad's place, who then spread the word viciously to everyone else. Not much was kept a secret around here. And she wasn't particularly liked, so he figured everyone wanted their eyes on her just in case...

He pulled into her driveway, glad to see the lights blazing through the windows. Not that it was that late at night, but after the day they had, he wouldn't have been surprised if she went to bed early.

Knocking on the door before he changed his mind, he shifted on the porch, filled with anxious energy.

Maybe this wasn't the best idea.

The door swung open.

Oh, yeah. This was a terrible idea.

Pepper had on a loose tank top with no bra on and an

old pair of sweatpants. Her hair hung down around her shoulders, looking soft and sexy and ready for his hands to mess it up.

The woman was downright gorgeous.

And he wanted nothing more than to kiss her breathless until she moaned his name and begged for more.

Yep.

He made the wrong choice.

Because he didn't think he could keep his hands to himself.

Before he could stop himself, or she could utter one word, he stepped inside, shut the door, and pulled her into his arms.

9

SHE DIDN'T KNOW what to do—and his lips on hers were so tempting, she didn't do what she should do. Push him away.

Instead, she found herself grabbing the front of his jacket and pulling him closer. The movement made a small needy groan escape from his lips as the kiss deepened.

This was wrong.

But it felt so right.

No! This was definitely wrong.

A bruised moan left her lips right before she pushed on his chest and stepped away from him.

As much as she enjoyed that kiss, and oh, boy, she enjoyed it, they couldn't kiss. They couldn't be friends. They couldn't do anything that would bring them closer because when he found out the truth, he would hate her.

"I should apologize for that."

She cocked a brow, waiting for Seth to do just that. Not that she wanted him to be sorry. She certainly wasn't sorry because it had been a delicious kiss. Men weren't foreign to her. She had her fair share. But that kiss...

One of a kind.

Her heart dipped at the realization. That thing. That something she had searched and hoped for all her life suddenly stood in front of her.

Someone worthy of her affections.

And in a few days, or whenever she completed her goal, he would despise her.

They continued to stare at one another. Her waiting for an apology she didn't want and him wrestling with a decision on his face, yet no words left his mouth.

She couldn't take the silence anymore.

"What are you doing here?"

He shrugged. "I'm not really sure, to be honest. I didn't feel like being alone."

This time she might've shown her shock because she tried very, very hard to hold her emotions in check. But his admission was mind-boggling.

"So, you came here? To my house? So you wouldn't be alone?"

She couldn't understand it. Why, after the way she treated him most of the time, would he want her company? What about his brother or sister? Anyone but her?

"Well, you keep things interesting. I like that." Then he grinned and headed into the living room, taking off his coat as he walked.

Her jaw dropped a fraction when she watched him sit down on her couch and grab the remote control. She followed him but didn't sit down.

"What are you doing?"

The TV clicked on.

"Channel surfing. Unless you had something specific you wanted to watch."

She frowned, glancing from him to the TV and back to him. What game was he playing? First, a kiss? Now, this?

His eyes twinkled with delight as he patted the empty spot next to him. "Damn, you're adorable when you frown like that, all confused and out of sorts."

"I am not out of sorts," she said with a clipped tone. There. Much better. That was the tone of voice she needed to be using with him. She needed to let him know she was, without a doubt, not out of sorts. At all.

Well, she was. But she would never let him see it.

He patted the spot again. "Then have a seat."

Propping a hand to her hip, she arched a brow with deadly intent. "You can't just walk into my house, kiss me, then make yourself at home like I gave you permission to do so. Because I did not. Now, get out."

Then she pointed her finger toward the door to prove she meant business.

The humor in his eyes fizzled, then he looked away from her, his shoulders drooping. "Okay, maybe I didn't make you out of sorts with that kiss," he flickered a glance at her, then looked away again, "but it sort of threw me off. I was already feeling..." He shrugged, running a hand through his hair, messing it up. "I feel...jittery. I don't know how to explain it. It sounds like Stacy is going to make it, but Evan is still missing. He could be dead. I have all these thoughts and scenarios running through my head, and I didn't want to be alone. My brother and sister weren't answering the phone and I...I thought of you as my last resort."

He finally looked at her, his eyes blazing with pain and heartache. "Does that make you feel better? To know you weren't the first person I thought of."

No, that didn't make her feel better. It hurt. It confused her. She'd liked the thought he wanted to be with her out of everyone else. Silly her. He only sought her out after he exhausted all other efforts.

Well, she asked for it. He could've left all of that to himself, but she just had to go and act like her usual bitchy self.

He stood up. She flinched and took a step back, unable to hide her reaction.

"I don't want to apologize for that kiss. I enjoyed it. It felt like you did too before you pushed me away. But I'm sorry I did it. I won't bother you again. I'm sorry you hate me for some reason."

Then he grabbed his coat from the couch and started to walk past her. Before she could stop herself, she reached out and snatched his hand. He jerked and stopped, turning slightly.

The confusion she probably wore a few minutes ago when he tried to make himself at home on her couch now masked his face.

"Seth…"

What was she doing?

This was wrong.

She was supposed to keep her distance. Not make any attachments. Do what she came here to do and leave town.

Grasping her bottom lip with her teeth, a war raged inside her mind as he waited for her to finish speaking. His hand felt so warm and soft—and strong. Like he could take all her problems and fix them.

"I don't hate you," she finally said in a whisper.

He took a step closer. "Can I kiss you again?"

Her lips curled up into a tiny smile because she couldn't resist. He looked so earnest for one more kiss.

"I said I don't hate you. That doesn't mean I wish to kiss you."

His eyes glided to her lips. "That's not what your eyes

were telling me...or your actions." He squeezed her hand. "Otherwise you would've let me leave."

She pulled on his hand, indicating she wanted him to take a seat once more. Then she let go of his hand and pushed lightly on his chest. "Have a seat. I'll make some popcorn."

"That's it. The conversation's over?" he asked with a chuckle, but took a seat.

"Nothing can happen between us. No more kisses. You should've never done that, to begin with."

Because now all she would dream about and wish for was more kisses. More of him. And she couldn't have anything.

A sly grin touched his lips. "Maybe not, but I enjoyed it. Admit it. You did, too."

"It doesn't matter. What I want doesn't matter. I'm only here to do one thing."

Her lips snapped shut, berating herself for almost confessing what that *thing* was.

Seth's brows puckered low. "Your wants matter. Why deny yourself of what you want? What are you here to do, Pepper?"

Pain sliced through her, tearing her to shreds. Oh, how she wanted to confess. Break down and tell him everything.

But she couldn't.

"I'm here to do my job. I can't do that if you're distracting me. I don't like distractions, Seth. That's when things go wrong."

His jaw tightened as if her words hurt him. She didn't mean to hurt his feelings. It was honestly the last thing she wanted to do, but he had to understand she wasn't here to play nice and be friendly. She was here to do her job and that was it.

"Then maybe I should go. I'm sorry I even came."

She was sorry, too. But then again, she wasn't.

"Stay." A slow breath released, as she wondered what the hell she was doing messing with both of their hearts. "You're not the only one who doesn't want to be alone."

———

OH, her words gutted him. They made him ache to stand up and wrap her in his arms. Why was she denying them the passion so clearly evident between them?

But he wouldn't force himself on her. When—not if—she was ready to kiss him again, she would. He could see it in her eyes that she wanted to do it again.

"If you're picking the snack, I get to pick the show," he finally said. He decided to ignore her confession. For both their sakes, it was better they kept their friendship, if one could call it that, at a distant level. Which meant he had to stop thinking about kissing her.

She gave him a tight nod and then walked out of the room.

Seth still wasn't sure why he came over here. After that tense moment, he was thinking it wasn't the brightest idea he ever had. When she walked into the living room with a bowl of popcorn that made his mouth water, he knew he made the right decision.

They may not always get along. He may want to kiss her like she would provide his last dying breath. But her presence calmed him. His jittery nerves worrying about Stacy and Evan settled down. His mind emptied of everything else, solely focused on her.

Maybe that wasn't a good thing, either. But right now, he

didn't care. Anything to get his mind off his best friend and whether he was dead or alive.

"The sports channel, really?" she said dryly as she sat down next to him on the couch. Not close enough so they were touching, but near enough where he could reach the popcorn bowl.

He shrugged. "You don't like sports?"

He didn't look too hard for something to watch. It didn't matter what was on TV because all his senses were tuned to her. The way she shifted on the couch as if she were trying to find a comfortable position. The light scent of roses, although the popcorn smell was overpowering everything else. But for that brief moment when she had been in his arms, she smelled like a beautiful red rose. He couldn't be sure if it was her shampoo or perfume she wore. Whatever it was, he wanted to get closer and inhale another deep breath.

"I never have time for them," she replied as she scooped a handful of popcorn.

He took a small handful and popped a few into his mouth. "Is your job the only thing that matters to you? What about your family?"

She tensed.

He hadn't meant to make her uncomfortable, but he had clearly touched a sore spot. His family was everything to him. Even though they argued and got mad at each other on occasion, they always forgave each other and moved on. He'd be lost without his family.

Pepper fascinated him. He wanted to know every little thing about her, starting with her family. Because if her job mattered so much, even to the point of ignoring her family, where did that leave him?

Because as crazy as it seemed, he wanted her. He wanted

to pursue a relationship with her, even if it was only sex. She got his blood pumping, his heart hammering, and his desire skyrocketing more than any other woman ever had— including Stacy. He couldn't ignore those feelings.

"I take my job seriously."

He chuckled, aching to utter, "No shit." But he kept the quip to himself. He wasn't sure what to say because she ignored the family part altogether, which didn't bode well for his chances.

"Do you ever take anything seriously?" Her intense look as she asked the question was like she was staring straight into his soul, grappling for the answer.

He'd be the first to admit he could act like a petulant child way too often. Of course, he'd only admit that to himself, not anyone else. Maybe because he was the youngest. He always got his way, teetered on the edge of breaking the rules. He rarely got into trouble for things his sister and brother got nabbed for all the time growing up.

But he knew he had to start acting like an adult. Like someone people could rely on and trust. Because there were times when Logan looked at him like he was a failure and he couldn't trust him for anything.

"I wish I could give you some sort of sob story about why I act the way I do sometimes. But I can't. It's just who I am." Seth grinned. "Do you ever act irresponsibly?"

A tiny grin appeared, although Seth could tell she was trying to suppress it. "I like your honesty. For not trying to bullshit me."

He popped a few pieces of popcorn into his mouth, chewing and swallowing before responding. "You'll always get honesty from me. It might not be eloquent and delicate to your feelings, but I don't lie."

Her gaze turned away. Her entire body tensed once again.

Odd.

He hit another nerve.

"Can you say the same thing, Pepper? Will you always be honest with me?"

His heart pounded as he waited for her answer.

For some reason, he feared what it would be, and he couldn't explain why.

10

PEPPER SHOOK HER BODY, trying to get the nerves out of her system before the elevator door opened.

It had been a long evening sitting next to a man she was starting to like a little too much. Seth made it so easy with his infectious demeanor and humorous character. He let his guard down a lot last night as they sat channel surfing, not staying tuned to one particular show.

She, on the other hand, didn't let her guard down an inch. That didn't stop him from trying to pry her open, dig into her background and get her to spill the beans—on anything.

When he asked that disastrous question—will you always be honest with me—she almost threw up right then and there.

Because, no, she wouldn't. She was lying to his face left and right.

Of course, she continued to lie when she answered, "Yes."

That one simple word gutted her. It twisted her insides,

ripping and pulling until she ached as if someone beat her to the last inch of her life.

But she had no choice. She had to lie for her safety—and to achieve her goal.

The elevator door swished open, and she stepped into the brightly lit corridor and made her way until she found the nurses station.

"Sheriff Caldwell is expecting me. Which room is he in?"

She didn't bother with pleasantries. The hospital might not be located in Lucky, but by the look on the nurse's face, she already knew that Pepper was not a people person.

Right. She could try a little harder at pleasantries.

"Please."

"Room 234. Down the hall, last door on your left."

"Thank you." The simple polite response didn't make up for her initial abrupt greeting, but it made her feel better. Stopping outside the door, drawing in a breath, she mentally prepared herself. She could soon be within reach of all the answers she needed.

Then she opened the door and stepped inside the dimly lit hospital room where Stacy lay on a bed, her eyes closed.

Odd. Sheriff Caldwell called her this morning telling her to report to the hospital instead of the station saying Stacy had woken up. Her surgery went well yesterday, and she would be out of the hospital within a week or two.

Sheriff Caldwell smiled at her as he greeted her in a friendly demeanor. Out of everyone, besides Seth and Bolt, the sheriff always treated her with respect and a jovial attitude. No matter how abrupt and standoffish she acted, he never deviated. She liked that about him. If she had any intentions of sticking around town, he would be perfect to work for. It was too bad she couldn't stay. Especially when he learned the truth.

"You got here fast. She's been in and out since about five o'clock this morning. I thought I'd wait for you and let her rest before I started asking questions."

Considering she was up at four o'clock this morning, unable to sleep for so many reasons, she could've been at the hospital the first moment Stacy woke up.

"Has she said anything?"

Sheriff Caldwell shook his head. "Not much at all. With surgery and all the medication she's on, we might not get much out of her right now. She needs rest."

Well, she didn't have time to let this woman rest. She needed answers. Of course, she could only push her luck so much before the sheriff might start taking a deeper look at her. That could never happen.

"Good morning, Sheriff Caldwell," a nurse with long blonde hair and a peppy smile said as she walked into the room. The nurse nodded at her in greeting, then approached the bed.

"Good morning, Beth. How are you today?"

"It's a slow shift, so it's always a good day when that happens." Beth started doing vital checks on Stacy, which prompted her to open her eyes.

Pepper internally groaned at the way Stacy could barely keep her eyes open. It didn't look good for her. She'd have to wait for the answers she desperately needed.

"How are you feeling this morning, Ms. Cotton?" Beth asked Stacy as she placed the blood pressure cuff back onto the vitals monitor.

"Tired. Sore. It hurts," Stacy whispered, blinking slowly as if trying to wake herself up.

"Where does it hurt?" Beth asked softly.

"Everywhere." Then Stacy closed her eyes, her hands grabbing the blanket into a tight ball.

"I'll get you some more medication for the pain. Sheriff Caldwell is here. Are you up for answering some questions?" Beth asked as she smiled at the sheriff, although her gaze said she was prepared to kick them out if she had to.

Stacy nodded, then opened her eyes, fixing them on the sheriff.

"I'll be right back," Beth said, then shifted her attention to the sheriff. "Make it quick. She needs her rest right now. You can always come back later."

"Thank you, Beth. We won't be long." The sheriff waited until Beth stepped out of the room, then walked closer to the bed.

She moved closer as well, hoping to get in some questions, but she remained quiet and waited for the sheriff to speak first.

"Stacy, it's Logan. You up for a few questions?"

The grogginess in Stacy's eyes made Pepper feel almost sorry for her. She looked like she was in pain. But should she feel sorry for her? She chose to answer Evan's call and go with him. She put herself in this situation.

"Where's Evan?" Stacy asked with a shaky voice instead of answering the sheriff's question.

"We were hoping you could tell us. Deputy Wilson," Logan pointed at her, "only found you at that cabin. There was no sign of Evan. What happened?"

Stacy turned in her direction. "Thank you."

She nodded. Perhaps she should step in because the sheriff's calm, soothing demeanor wasn't getting them anywhere.

"Who shot you?" Her voice held no sympathy. Not like the sheriff's or the nurse.

Stacy's eyes glazed over in fear. "I don't know."

"Why did Evan call you?"

"He was hurt. Someone shot him in the shoulder. He wouldn't tell me why." Stacy looked away.

"I don't believe you." She felt Sheriff Caldwell shift next to her as if he didn't like what she said, but he didn't comment.

Stacy's eyes snapped back to her. Her hands clutched the blanket. "Who are you?"

"The sheriff already told you. You're stalling. You're lying. Which almost makes me believe you do know where Evan is. Did he shoot you?"

Stacy's bottom lip started to tremble. The action made her sick to her stomach. This woman was recovering from a gunshot wound and she was acting like she only received a scrape. But that's who she was. Straight and to the point. No bullshit. No remorse. She should never forget that. That's how she got the job done. Her boss loved that about her. Everyone else, not so much.

"Two men showed up to the cabin. It all happened so fast. One of them shot me, and the other went for Evan. But Evan didn't shoot me. He ran. I heard him run."

Tilting her head, she eyed Stacy with a razor-sharp gaze. She didn't think Stacy was lying about that. It all sounded like the truth.

The question was, did Evan manage to escape, or did they take him?

"Why did Evan call you?"

Stacy frowned. "I told you. He was shot."

"Yet, you don't take him to the hospital. You don't call the police. You run with him and try to help him all by yourself. You do all of that, yet you say he wouldn't tell you why he was shot."

Stacy glanced down at her blanket. "No, he wouldn't."

"Look at me," she said as if she were a parent about to deliver the most severe punishment on the planet.

Stacy's eyes shot to hers.

"You're lying. Nobody does that unless they know what's going on."

"I love him. I'd do anything for him." Stacy inhaled slowly, exhaling just as slowly.

"Four months ago, you loved Seth Caldwell. Forgive me if I don't believe your bullshit. We can charge you with obstruction, if you'd like." Pepper heard Sheriff Caldwell suck in a sharp breath, but he still said nothing.

Stacy's bottom lip quivered again. "Seth and I had a complicated relationship. I did love him. That doesn't mean I can't love Evan now."

Rage started to bubble up in her veins. For Seth. She couldn't explain why she even cared. But the fact this woman went from Seth to a loser like Evan pissed her off.

"Skirting around the issue doesn't ignore the fact you're lying and refusing to tell us who shot Evan and why they did."

Stacy averted her gaze once more. "I don't know why."

"Deputy Wilson, please go wait out in the hallway," Sheriff Caldwell said with a brusque tone.

She jerked in surprise, cringing inside that she allowed him to see her shock. Without a word, she turned around and walked out of the room.

Now her rage was simmering from Stacy *and* the sheriff. She was on the verge of getting the truth out of Stacy. She could feel it—and he stopped her.

Beth smiled at her, although she looked confused why she was standing outside the room, and entered, shutting the door behind her.

The sheriff walked out a few minutes later.

He sighed, running a hand down his face. "That was a bit harsh, Deputy Wilson."

"She's lying, sir. I was doing my job." She was trying to complete her mission.

"Unfortunately," he started, and she dreaded hearing the rest. He was going to fire her, which would make her job a hundred times more difficult. "I believe you. She's lying. I never thought she'd lie like this. And why? I don't understand. I told Stacy she has until this afternoon to tell us the truth, or we'll be charging her with obstruction of justice."

She tried to keep her composure and not display her excitement that the sheriff was on her side. She couldn't believe it. "Yes, sir."

"For the time being, let's try to work this case at every angle. We need to find Evan."

Forcing a smile down, she nodded. "I'm on it, sir."

Oh, she was so on it.

She'd find Evan if it was the last thing she ever did.

"CHARLOTTE, SO GOOD TO SEE YOU," Danny said as he walked inside the sheriff's department.

Her smile widened until she landed on Deke, who stood behind him. "How can I help you, Danny?"

Danny chuckled at the weird byplay between the two, then sidled up to the counter and rested his arm. "Is Logan in?"

"He is. He returned from the hospital about an hour ago. You can go on back." She smiled again at him, but glared at Deke.

He thanked her and headed for Logan's office.

"What did you do to upset her? She always has a smile

on her face," Danny asked in a low voice as they walked down the long hallway to Logan's office.

"I didn't do anything," Deke grumbled in a sulky voice.

"Maybe that's the problem." Danny laughed as he knocked on the doorframe of Logan's office.

Logan's head popped up from reading something on his desk and then he waved his hand for them to come in.

"What are you two doing here? Is everything all right?" Logan asked as they took a seat in front of his desk.

"We want to help find Evan." Danny leaned forward. "Kat's been on edge lately. Ever since Derek left. Last night she was worried about Seth and...I want to help. I need to do something."

Deke threw a hand in Danny's direction. "I'm here because he's here. What do you need from us?"

Logan sat back in his chair and ran a hand down his face, the exhaustion evident. "I'm sorry Derek leaving has put a strain between you two. And Seth...I think he's okay. She shouldn't worry."

"I wouldn't say there's tension between us, but I do feel like she's a million miles away sometimes."

Danny wasn't sure right now was the best time to confess he proposed. It wasn't like they were going to keep it a secret, but he'd wait until Kat was with him to share the news with her family. And he still needed to buy her a ring. Her tension had reduced somewhat last night, but this morning, it was back full force. That's when he decided he needed to stick around town and help out Logan. He needed to be near Kat in case she needed him. Danny was lucky his boss understood and was lenient enough to let him stay.

Logan grabbed the folder sitting in front of him and laid it closer to them. "A few possible suspects. I have no clue where Evan might be and Stacy is awake and recovering from surgery, but she's not talking. She's claiming she knows nothing. We think she's lying."

"We?" Danny asked as he and Deke scanned the contents in the folder.

"My new deputy. Pepper Wilson. We interviewed Stacy together earlier this morning." Logan paused. "I know a few people have said she's a bit...harsh. I saw it firsthand. But she's been doing a good job."

"Yeah, Kat hasn't officially met her, but she hasn't heard nice things." Danny chuckled. "I can't fault Deputy Wilson taking charge and getting the job done."

"Neither can I," Logan replied with a laugh of his own.

Deke tapped the folder. "So, you think this shit going on with Evan has to do with the Cheetahs. They're still heavy in this area dealing drugs?"

"I can't prove it, and I can't get a search warrant based on my gut, but I think their main operation is on Mr. Barten's property. Makes sense since his two sons were a part of the Cheetahs. I don't know how Evan fits into it all, but yes, I think they have something to do with his disappearance and the death of Barry and hurting Stacy," Logan replied.

"So, we have three heavy hitters to look at," Danny said as he continued to read the contents in the folder. "Don Lacey, Brett Nelson, and Juan Hernandez. All high up in the Cheetahs. Have they been spotted in the area? They mostly run the business in Florida, by the looks of this."

"We haven't been able to stop the flow of drugs in the area completely, but we've arrested some of their people. I'm not sure if they're here or not." Logan sighed as he ran another hand down his face. "If whatever happened to Evan has to deal with the Cheetahs, then one of them is responsible, if not all three of them. They have to be giving the orders, at least."

"I'm assuming you spoke to Mr. Barten?" Deke asked.

Logan nodded and chuckled. "He had no information for me."

"Do we think Evan is dead?" Danny asked, sitting back in his chair.

"He's wounded. Gunshot to the shoulder, according to Stacy. I can't say whether he's alive. Whether he managed to get away when they shot Stacy or if they have him." Logan glanced at the clock on the wall. "I gave Stacy until this afternoon to tell me the truth or I'd be pressing obstruction charges."

"Think the threat will work?" Danny asked as a grin grew. "Because I can take a crack at getting her to talk."

"I hope it will. Maybe I'll let Pepper have another try. I could tell she made Stacy uncomfortable. I like Pepper. She might be a bit rough around the edges, but I like her."

By the few things he had heard, Danny had to agree with Logan. It sounded like he'd like her, too. He could be a bit rough around the edges as well, especially when it came to his job.

"So, you want our help or not?" he asked.

Logan grinned. "I would never pass up on the FBI offering help. I appreciate it."

Deke stood up. "We should start a deep background on these three men. Find out if they're in the area. I'll go see if Charlotte has a computer I can use."

Danny watched as Deke walked out, his steps quick and eager. A low chuckle escaped.

"Something I should know?" Logan asked as he chuckled along with him.

Danny turned his way and shrugged. "I have no clue. I have my own worries right now to be trying to figure out what's going on with Deke and Charlotte."

"Yeah, I don't think I want to figure that one out either. Do you and Kat want to come over tonight for supper? Maybe try again."

Before Danny could answer, a knock sounded near the door. They both looked over to see Seth.

"Come on in," Logan said, waving a hand. "What are you doing here?"

"Just curious how the case is going. Do you need my help?" Seth took a seat in the chair Deke had vacated.

"I don't think so. Danny and Deke are on the case now. I think we exhausted all the places you'd know to look for Evan. Plus..." Logan's voice trailed off as if he didn't want to finish his sentence.

"Plus, you think the person who shot Stacy has him, don't you?" Seth said as he exhaled deeply.

"It's a high probability. We'll find him," Logan reassured his brother.

Danny didn't add that it might not be alive. Even though he knew Seth hadn't reconnected with his friend, he knew Seth would take it hard if it turned out Evan was killed.

"Let me know if you need me. If you need me to tag along with Pepper. I don't mind."

Danny grinned at the eagerness in Seth's tone of voice. Interesting. Most people in town didn't like her. But if Danny had to guess, Seth wasn't one of those people.

"I will. Thanks, Seth. We saw Stacy this morning. She's recovering well."

Seth nodded but didn't ask Logan for any further information.

Logan nodded back, then asked, "So, dinner tonight? Will you two join us?"

"Not tonight. I need to catch up on...stuff." Seth didn't elaborate and Logan didn't ask for clarification.

He should go over to Logan's house just to see his sister. But he wanted to buy Kat a ring and talk with her on how they should share their great news.

"We'll pass, too."

"Well, if either of you changes your mind, Aubrey's making pot roast tonight."

Danny couldn't deny that sounded good.

They worked all day long, digging into the background of all three men in the Cheetahs. All three had a long list of arrests, most of them from Florida, which was where the head of the Cheetahs gang operated. They had only started to branch out in this area due to Wayne and Joshua Barten.

Like Logan had said, they could never get any charges to stick. They were smart and cunning, knowing how to work the system and keep their hands clean.

Through all the digging, with the help from Pepper and Bolt, they were able to find everything they could about them, but not where they were located. The men had been spotted in the area on occasion, corroborated by a nearby agency, but they had no physical address for them. That posed a problem. If they wanted to ask them some questions, they'd have to find them first.

And that's where Danny agreed, once again, with Logan. Mr. Barten had to be giving them access to his land. Without a warrant and probable cause to search his land, they couldn't step foot on his property.

Danny and Deke packed up and left the sheriff's department around six o'clock, nowhere closer to their prize, but that didn't mean anything. They were like two bulldogs. They didn't stop until they caught their bad guy.

Strangely, Danny had sensed the same mentality from Pepper. He saw the hard edge in her. He also saw a bit of wariness whenever they connected eyes. He wasn't sure what to make about that, but he liked her.

When he got home, he found Kat already in the kitchen making supper. Sliding his hands around her waist, he kissed her cheek as he inhaled the wonderful scent of spaghetti cooking on the stove.

"How was your day?" he asked as he peppered a few kisses along her neck. She didn't try to stop him. Last night, although they had a fun time in the bath, he felt her pull away again this morning, which had punctured a hole in his heart. He had no idea what he had done wrong.

"Long."

Although she was allowing him to hold her, she was still in her own little world, barely responding to him.

He had asked her to marry him. She said yes. Why did it still feel like a huge distance was splitting them apart?

"I need you to talk to me, Kat. You're scaring me. Did I do something wrong this morning?"

She stiffened in his arms and stopped stirring the sauce as his quiet words resonated around them.

Then she relaxed and rested against his chest, dropping the handle of the wooden spoon. "You're amazing. You didn't do anything wrong."

He squeezed her tighter. "Then why do I feel like you're pulling away from me again?"

Twisting around in his arms, she stared at his chest for the longest time before lifting her gaze to his. "I keep thinking about Derek."

His heart plummeted.

She brushed his cheek, something he adored every time she touched him like that. "It's not what you think. I swear I love you. I just thought Derek and I made amends. I thought we were friends again. Then he suddenly leaves town and I feel like it's my fault. I feel weird about being happy when he's unhappy. And I'm so, so happy with you."

"He made his choice to leave. That's on him, not you. What can I do to make you happy again? I proposed last night. I'm not sure what could top that. And shit, I still need to buy you an actual ring. I swear I will. Do you want me to track him down and drag his ass back here?"

A beautiful, tender smile emerged. Then she kissed him deeply and thoroughly. "You would, too."

"Damn straight, I would. Anything for you."

Her hands grabbed the back of his shirt tightly, yet she wore a sweet smile. He wasn't fooled. She was pretending to be happy.

"I didn't mean to bring up the subject of kids at such a bad time."

"I'm not opposed to kids. I thought we had this settled last night." He didn't know what else to say.

He honestly wanted kids someday. They even had sex without protection in the bathtub. What more could he do or say to let her know he was all in for everything?

Her hands on his shirt strengthened in their grip. "Well, when do you think we'll be ready for kids? I know what happened last night, but are you truly ready?"

His brows puckered low, confused. "I wouldn't say it if I wasn't."

"I know, but...I'm just...making sure."

He was so confused. None of this was making sense. Her hesitation. Her nervousness. The constant talk about kids. Then his mind starting spiraling, going back and forth through the past few weeks, searching and looking for clues as he would on one of his cases.

"You haven't had your period in a while."

She bit her lip and shook her head.

"You keep bringing up the subject of kids."

She nodded, her eyes filled with worry.

"Holy shit. You're already pregnant."

Her bottom lip started to tremble. "And you don't seem happy about it. You don't seem like you want kids yet."

A crazy laugh let loose. Then he grasped her cheeks as he planted a light kiss to her lips. "This is why you've been worrying like crazy about Derek. Your hormones are out of whack. You're having a baby. Our baby." He kissed her again. "Of course, I'm happy. I'm ecstatic. A little frightened, but ecstatic. Don't worry like this next time. You have to talk to me about these things right away, Kat. I love you. So damn much."

"I love you, too, Danny."

He pulled her into a hug, holding her gently. A baby. Holy. Shit. He couldn't believe it. Was he ready? Would he be a good father? He felt like he failed his sister, having had to raise her himself when she was a teenager.

"Do you still want me to track down Derek? I don't want anything upsetting you. Not when you're pregnant."

Her arms tightened around him. "No, you're right. That's on him for leaving. I'm still a little stressed, though."

"Why? How can I help?"

"I'm worried about Seth and all this business about Evan and Stacy. He has to be taking it hard. Yet, I don't know how he's taking it because I've been in my own little world so worried about telling you everything."

He pressed her closer, kissing the top of her head. "He's doing okay. I saw him today. Hell, I think he has the hots for Deputy Wilson. That's a good distraction for him right now."

Kat pulled away from him, cocking a brow. "Don't say that. I don't like her."

"You haven't even met her yet," he said with a chuckle. "She seemed decent to me. A little uptight, but good at her job."

"Well, Charlotte doesn't like her, and that's all I need to know."

"Enough about everyone else. Let's celebrate. We're having a baby and we're getting married." Then he turned off the stove and lifted Kat into his arms and proceeded directly to their bedroom.

SETH EXHALED, shivering from the low temperature outside, then knocked firmly on the door.

What was he doing?

This was crazy. Ludicrous. She'd probably slam the door in his face. He should've taken his brother up on the offer of supper tonight. Aubrey made a really good pot roast. Except, he found himself making his way here instead.

The door opened.

Pepper looked indifferent, not annoyed, nor happy to see him. Just—indifferent. She was wearing black sweatpants with a light purple T-shirt with a unicorn on it. Her hair was in its ponytail this time, but she had removed her makeup. He wanted nothing more than to take her hair out of the ponytail and mess it up. Drive his fingers through her long tresses and kiss her senseless.

"Hi."

He decided he'd settle with a simple hello before he attempted to kiss her. She didn't look too receptive to a kiss at the moment.

"What are you doing here, Seth?"

He lifted the grocery bag he had in his hand and smiled, hoping she wouldn't close the door on his face.

"I brought better popcorn and a six-pack of beer. I thought we could channel surf again together."

"Better popcorn?" Her eyes gazed at him like two laser beams bent on destroying the Earth.

"The popcorn you had last night...well, I'm not a fan of kettle corn. Not cool, Deputy. Not cool."

Her lips pressed together in a thin line, yet slightly twisted as if she were trying hard not to laugh. "Does it have extra butter? I either like super sweet or super buttery."

He wiggled the bag. "If you let me in, I'll tell you."

She opened the door wider and waved him in. "If it's not extra butter, I'm booting you out."

He set the bag on the floor as she shut the door. Taking off his jacket and hanging it up on the small coat rack in the corner, he smiled. His boots came off next.

"No extra butter, but I have a box of Milk Duds, too."

She rolled her eyes and then grabbed the bag from the floor. "You're lucky I love chocolate. I'll make the popcorn."

He thought about following her into the kitchen but decided not to press his luck. He was already pushing the limit by showing up to her house again for the second night in a row.

The day had been long, worrying about Evan, wondering how Stacy was holding up. Although, Logan had called him asking if he was sure he didn't want to join them for supper. After he declined, Logan told him they had pressed charges against Stacy. She was mending from a gunshot wound, but now she was facing charges because she refused to cooperate. He couldn't understand why she'd lie, especially with the threat of being arrested.

Not his problem. At least, that's what he had to keep reminding himself.

Yeah, what a long day.

Besides all the worrying and wondering, he had missed Pepper.

Two days working alongside her and he missed her. He didn't understand it. But when his brother asked if he wanted to join him and Aubrey for supper, he knew right away he wanted to see Pepper instead. He declined without even knowing whether she'd want to see him.

Taking a seat on her couch, grabbing the soft cotton blanket she had been using, he placed it over his lap with a smile. If she wanted to use it, she'd have to share it with him.

She walked into the living room a few minutes later with a bowl of popcorn, two beers, and the box of Milk Duds. He grabbed one of the beers, lifted the blanket for her to cuddle under, and couldn't hide his silly grin when she didn't argue or complain. She took a seat close to him, her thigh brushing his as she snuggled under the blanket. She settled the bowl of popcorn between them.

"So why are you here, Seth? Honestly?"

He took a sip of beer, debating how to respond. "I don't know. Would it be crazy to say I missed you?"

Her eyes flashed in surprise. "We barely know each other."

"Maybe I want to get to know you more."

She looked away, her knuckles turning white as if she were squeezing her beer bottle hard. "I already told you I can't afford to get distracted."

Yeah, he remembered that, all right. He didn't understand then, and he didn't understand now. But, Pepper was a complicated woman. An enigma. A puzzle.

And he really, really wanted to get to know her more.

"We all need a little distraction in our lives."

Her head whipped back toward him. "Is that what I am? A distraction for you? Because you don't have Stacy anymore."

He pressed his lips together to stop himself from blurting out something he might regret. He was already on shaky ground with her. And he did tend to blurt out things before thinking about it.

"Stacy and I are done. We have been for the past few months."

"But you still love her." Her eyes held a sadness as those words slipped free.

"I don't. I miss having someone in my life, but I don't love Stacy. We were like oil and water. We just didn't mix, even though we tried and tried and tried."

"So, I'm the rebound." She scoffed before taking a long swallow of her beer.

"You're someone who challenges me, who makes me feel more centered and calm when a lot of the times I feel like I'm floating in chaos. You're beautiful and confident, and sexy as hell. I'm here right now because I want to be, not because you're my only choice."

She slowly met his gaze, her eyes shimmering with unshed tears. "Nothing can happen between us, Seth. Don't say things like that to me."

He wanted to shout out, "Why?!" So much pain lingered in the depths of her eyes. Pain he figured she was trying to hide from him—from the world.

Instead of challenging her, he reached for the controller on the coffee table. Flipping through the channels, he stopped when he came across a documentary on lions.

She grabbed a handful of popcorn and started to eat,

chomping quietly next to him. He grabbed a handful as well, focusing on the show.

All of his senses were trained on her—the way she would shift now and again, her thigh brushing his. The light chewing sounds she made as she ate the popcorn. The sweet rose scent that drifted his way every time she leaned toward the popcorn bowl. The sultry sound of her voice as she made comments here and there about the show.

He liked Pepper, and he knew he had a huge uphill battle trying to win any tiny little affection from her.

He was all in.

Better to do that than worry about his best friend, who was more than likely dead.

11

SHE GRABBED her jacket from the coat rack and inhaled, mentally preparing herself for another day on the job.

Four days had gone by since they found Stacy. Four days of trying to extract any and all information from her. And nothing. The woman was still lying, maintaining she knew nothing about why Evan called her after he got shot.

The sheriff had pressed charges against her. Stacy was still in the hospital, but it didn't stop him. Of course, he didn't want to arrest her, but the charges would stay until she came clean.

It wasn't looking good for her.

Why would she lie?

That was the million-dollar question.

Pepper slammed her front door shut and locked it before heading to her vehicle. Wondering and worrying about it wouldn't solve anything. She'd just have to find her target another way. And soon.

She couldn't stay here much longer. Because the longer she stayed, the harder it would be to leave Seth.

Oh, Seth.

That man had somehow wiggled his way inside her heart.

Four days.

That's all it had taken for him to get past her defenses. Make her weak. Make her wish for things that could never be possible. Once he knew the truth, he'd hate her.

She should tell him to stop and stay away from her. But each night when he stood on her doorstep with a gentle smile and a delicious treat, she found herself inviting him in instead of demanding he leave.

Tonight, she'd be stronger. She wouldn't let him inside.

If only she believed it.

She checked in at the sheriff's department, receiving an icy glare from Charlotte and headed back outside to her patrol vehicle. She tried to stay out of that woman's way as much as possible. The less contact she had with people was better anyway. She couldn't afford to build any more relationships like she was unfortunately doing with Seth.

Although, Sheriff Caldwell didn't seem to have a problem with her. Nor did Agent O'Rourke, Agent Sumnter, or Deputy Bolten. She liked all three of them, especially the FBI agents. Although, part of her told her she should keep her distance, especially them. If anyone would be able to detect what she was really doing in town, it would be those two. But they were helping on the case, and she had no choice but to be in their vicinity. So far, no such luck on making any progress. They'd been trying to find a reason—any reason—to get access to Mr. Barten's property. They had also been knocking on doors and ruffling feathers with people associated with the Cheetahs. She had to admit, every time they met a new person in the gang, she got a tad nervous. Because as soon as she found her target, she'd have to leave. And she wasn't ready to leave Seth.

But nobody was talking.

They couldn't find Evan.

Stacy wouldn't talk.

And she had no idea where to find her target.

Lunchtime came fast. The morning had been slow patrolling the area. If Agent O'Rourke or Agent Sumnter had found something, they would've told her. Unfortunately, the entire morning rolled by without a peep.

Evan seemed to be a dead end—perhaps even literally speaking. She hated to think that, but four days had passed and nada. It didn't look good that he was still alive. Even if they did find him, she wasn't too positive he'd know where to find the man she was looking for, or if she'd even get a chance to speak with him alone.

Her best bet right now was finding out where the Cheetahs head operations were, which they all figured was on Mr. Barten's property. Which meant, she might have to trespass and do some digging on her own.

She didn't relish the idea at all. Because she did everything by the book. But this case...her reason for being here...she just didn't care about the damn *book* and doing things right. She only wanted a murderer off the streets and justice.

To find peace and solace, something she had yet to feel in her life.

Pulling into a parking spot in front of the diner, her stomach grumbled. When she opened the door and stepped inside, the few patrons in attendance glanced her way, yet nobody waved in greeting.

Yeah, she didn't make many friends in this small town. No surprise there. She didn't make friends in any town she ventured to.

She took a seat in one of the booths near the back away

from everyone. Callie was at her table within ten seconds of her settling in.

"Your usual?" Callie asked with a sweet smile.

Although she wasn't always pleasant—more like brusque and to the point—Callie always treated her with kindness and respect. Honestly, she wished the woman wouldn't. She didn't deserve it.

"Yes." Even though she was trying to maintain her distance from everyone, she added, "Thank you."

Callie nodded and walked away to put in her order. The same thing she had ordered every day when she stopped by for lunch. A glass of water with a ham sandwich on rye bread. She was a creature of habit. She rarely tried new things because she was what people called a picky eater. She could take one look at something and know right away she wouldn't like it without even trying it. It always drove her sister...

Nope. She couldn't let her mind drift there.

She didn't say anything when Callie dropped off her water. Pulling out her phone, she started to enter the passcode to unlock it when a person entered her space. Figuring it was Callie, she lifted her head with a smile because she could try to be nicer to one of the few people who was actually nice to her. Then her lips dipped into a frown when she came face-to-face with Kat Caldwell.

She had yet to officially meet the woman, but she had seen her around town a few times. The look on Kat's face said this wouldn't be a pleasant meeting.

Kat slid into the booth on the other side of the table, no happy expression littered anywhere.

"Can I help you?" This was odd, but she preferred to get whatever Kat wanted over with and then enjoy her lunch in peace.

"Stay away from my brother."

Laughter escaped before she could stop herself. "That's kind of hard when I work for him."

Kat leaned closer, her eyes shining like the devil possessed her. "I mean my brother Seth."

Oh.

This was...unexpected.

Did Kat know he came over to her house every night? It's not as if they advertised it. She lived on the outskirts of town, with no neighbors directly next to her. Although, there were a few houses on the way to her house. Perhaps those people told Kat he'd been visiting.

But why did she care?

They stared at each other for the longest time. She had no response to her demand. Because, even though she should stop seeing him, she didn't know if she'd have the strength.

"I don't like you," Kat finally said.

"You don't even know me."

Nobody did. Not even Seth.

She was living one big lie.

"I know enough to know I don't like you. You're rude and disrespectful. You're selfish."

Yeah, that sounded like her, especially when it came to her job. And her job was her livelihood. Kat wasn't wrong.

But nobody told her what to do.

"And you're messing with the wrong person. I'll do whatever I want to do."

Kat smiled wickedly. "This is a small town. It could start to get real uncomfortable living here. I don't do things like this, but I won't have someone like you hurting my brother. He's already going through enough with everything that's happened with Evan and Stacy."

Someone like you.

Those words hurt.

Those words she had heard too many times.

Someone like you doesn't deserve this. Someone like you will never amount to anything. Someone like you will always fail.

Boy, that was the truth.

She was failing her mission so far.

"There's just one thing wrong in your little threat." She shifted in her seat as if she were settling in to get comfortable.

She might be failing big time, but she wasn't ready to leave until she exhausted all efforts.

"What's that?"

"That you think I care."

Kat flinched as if surprised by her words.

She grinned. "I'm not here to make friends. I don't care who likes me and who doesn't. Do your worst, Kat. I love challenges."

"I don't know what my brother sees in you." Kat looked honestly baffled.

Hell, she didn't know what he saw in her either. Why did he keep coming by her house every single night? Nothing could happen.

A throat cleared and then a plate appeared before her as Callie set her sandwich down. "Enjoy, Pepper."

She nodded but didn't look away from Kat's penetrating stare.

"Are we done here? I'd like to eat my lunch." She picked up her sandwich, pretending she wasn't hurt. But she was. As much as she wanted to be good enough for Seth, she never would be. Kat knew it. She knew it. The whole town probably knew it.

Then without another word, Kat slid out of the booth and walked away.

She wished she could do the same.

Walk away from this town and never look back.

Except she couldn't walk away without her heart—Seth had it.

SETH SUPPRESSED a groan when he saw his sister Kat heading straight for him. Thanks to living in a small town, he had heard she and Pepper had some words today at the diner. If he had Pepper's phone number—something he planned to remedy tonight—he would've called her to make sure she was okay. Kat could be brutal when she wanted to be.

With him being the baby of the family, sometimes she did things that she thought was best for him.

He didn't need to be warned away from liking Pepper. Each night, he saw little glimpses here and there of the real woman inside. That hard exterior, so emotionless that she portrayed to the world was all an act. He knew it was.

And if he just waited patiently, he knew the real her would emerge soon.

But not if problems with his sister disrupted the small progress he'd been making.

Shivering from the cold, he tried to smile even though he wasn't happy with her.

"To what do I owe this pleasure?"

"Cut the crap," Kat said sharply. "I'm worried about you."

"Yes, I heard. Thanks for coming to me first before ambushing Pepper."

"Seth..." Kat reached out and touched his shoulder, but

he shook her off. He didn't want her comfort or whatever she was trying to offer. "What are you doing with her? She's not right for you."

"I'm doing what I always do, Kat. Making mistakes and screwing up," he said with the sarcasm lacing his tone.

"I don't like her."

"You don't even know her. Danny doesn't have a problem with her."

Kat hugged her arms around her body. Yeah, it was cold out and this conversation didn't need to be finished. There wasn't anything to talk about. He liked Pepper and it didn't matter what anyone tried to tell him.

"There's a lot going on right now. I don't want you to be shifting your pain into a problem you can't see."

"I'm not dumb, Kat. I know what I'm doing." Hell, he wasn't doing anything.

Sure, he stopped by her house every night, but nothing ever happened. They munched away on the goodies he brought over, had a beer or two, channel surfed, and then he left. Pretty boring, yet he enjoyed the time with her.

"What does Logan think?"

"Don't know and don't care. What I do and who I do it with isn't any of your business." Then he opened his truck door and climbed inside.

He hated to shut his sister out, especially with the way her face crumbled into agony, but he wasn't going to be told what to do. Kat didn't know Pepper. She didn't even bother to try to know her.

He flicked a small wave goodbye and then backed out of the parking spot. Instead of heading home to change like he normally did after work, he headed straight for Pepper's house. It was only five o'clock. He didn't even know if she'd be home yet, but he wanted to see her. He'd wanted to talk to her ever since he heard what happened at the diner. He had never wanted to push the boundaries of their friendship by asking for her number, but he was ready to do some light nudging into her personal space. He wanted—needed —her to know that he didn't care what anyone thought or said. He liked her.

When he pulled into her driveway, he smiled at the sight of her car. Grabbing the bag of nacho ingredients he had purchased before running into Kat, he headed for her front door with determined footsteps.

He knocked, his heart suddenly pounding.

The door swung open. She was still dressed in her uniform and the grim expression on her face didn't bode well.

"Hi." He wasn't sure how to proceed, feeling like he was on shaky ground, even though he wasn't the one who had emotionally attacked her today. "I brought nachos."

Her eyes glanced from him to the bag in his hand. "We can't keep doing this, Seth."

"Why, because my sister doesn't like it?"

Sadness dripped from her beautiful almond colored eyes. "You know why."

"I don't, actually."

She pressed her lips together tightly as if she were trying to hold back tears.

"Hey," he said as he shifted closer, putting a hand to her cheek, "what's wrong? Talk to me. Like, really talk to me. I don't know what's happening between us, but I do know I don't want it to stop. I like you. I like hanging out with you."

That was about as much as he would say. He didn't want to scare her away by telling her how much he thought about her throughout the day. How he missed her. How he plotted ways to get her to laugh and smile. Something she didn't do, so when a brief smile appeared, he had to conjure ways to see another one.

Slow and easy. As long as he kept things light and carefree, she didn't have a reason to push him away. But he couldn't keep being too gentle; he had to get past her barriers somehow.

Her eyes closed briefly. "Come in. You're letting in all the cold air." Then she stepped away.

He missed her immediately. The soft touch of her skin. The way she had leaned into his hand for a second as if she liked him touching her.

Setting the bag on the floor like he normally did, he took his coat off and hung it up and then slid off his shoes.

She stood far enough away that if he wanted to pull her into his arms, he'd have to move closer. In their routine, she always grabbed the bag he brought over and prepared the food while he waited in the living room. This time, she didn't move a muscle.

Her eyes glided to his coat on the rack and his shoes on the floor.

"Don't ask me to leave," he whispered, almost pleading.

He enjoyed these nights with her. It relaxed him. It got his mind off his best friend and whether or not he was dead.

She nodded. "Fine. I need to change out of my work clothes. You can get the food ready."

He blew out a thankful breath as she walked away without waiting for him to respond. Grabbing the bag from the floor, he headed for the kitchen. He didn't bring any beer today since they didn't drink everything he brought last night. Pulling two bottles from the fridge, he set them on the counter and then went in search of a bowl.

He poured some cheese dip into a bowl and put it in the microwave to warm up. Then he grabbed another bowl and poured half the bag of chips inside it. Carrying the beer and bowl of chips to the living room, he set it all on the coffee table and went back for the cheese dip. The microwave dinged as soon as he walked into the kitchen. Carefully, since the bowl was hot, he walked to the living room once again.

She still hadn't emerged from her bedroom. Not that it took him long to prepare everything. Five minutes, if that.

What was taking her so long?

He should just take a seat and wait for her.

Except he found himself wandering down the hallway in search of her bedroom. It didn't take long to find. It was a small house.

Her bedroom door was open. She stood in front of her closet with her back toward him in only a pair of pink sweatpants and a white bra.

He wasn't sure if she was aware he stood in her doorway, but as a gentleman, he should've turned around and waited for her in the living room.

But seeing her creamy, soft skin, the smooth curves of her body, the exquisite picture before him, he found his feet moving forward instead of backward.

The air crackled with intensity. Desire filled the room like heavy smoke.

He stopped inches from her, yet didn't touch her. He heard her inhale deeply, indicating she knew he was there. But she didn't turn around.

Raising his hand, he glided it as if he were caressing her from her shoulder down her arm, yet he didn't touch.

"God, you're so beautiful. I want to touch you so badly."

"You shouldn't be in here."

"I know. I didn't know what was taking you so long."

She stood rigid.

The last thing he wanted to do was make her uncomfortable, but damn, he was dying to touch her. To make her feel what he felt—charged with pleasure waiting to be unleashed.

"I'm sorry. I'll wait for you in the living room."

His hand hovered near her shoulder, then he snatched it away and turned around. He got three steps before she spoke.

"I said you shouldn't be in here, not that I wanted you to leave."

He turned around slowly.

She was facing him, her eyes dilated with the same intense pleasure he felt flowing through his veins.

His jaw clenched, his hands aching to pull her into his arms.

"What do you want?" He took a step in her direction. "Because I want you. I want to touch you until your body has memorized my touch."

He didn't know where those words came from, but they were true. He wanted to claim her until she begged him never to leave.

Less than a week, and he wanted this woman with so much passion it physically hurt to think he might never have her.

Her hands reached up and slid one strap down her arm. Then she reached for the other side and slid that one down, too. Her bra hung on, barely.

"I want you to touch me." She bit her lip before removing the bra completely.

He didn't hesitate. He didn't give her time to change her mind, although her eyes said she wasn't planning on it.

He pulled her into his arms and kissed her like it would be the last kiss they ever shared.

SHE KNEW THIS WAS WRONG, but it felt so, so right.

Being in Seth's arms was like finally finding a home. A place that she could fit in and be happy for once. Because her real home—if she could even consider having one—was pain and heartache and despair. Thinking about it always put her in a bad mood.

She should be honest with him first. Having lies between them didn't sit right with her, yet she didn't push him away.

The kiss turned hot, heating her skin and sending tiny tingles of anticipation running through her veins.

She pulled up on his shirt, tossing it away.

Their kiss turned fierce, yet choppy as they both fought to get the other person's pants off. As soon as they were both naked, they toppled to the bed eagerly.

"Condoms?" Seth whispered as he kissed his way across her chin and to her neck as one of his hands slid down her body in a smooth caress.

"I don't have any." The thought dampened her mood.

She didn't come to this small town to have sex. To meet a man and fall in love.

Oh, no.

Her entire body went stiff.

Seth stopped kissing her and lifted, his eyes boring into her with tenderness, yet a slight ache that tore her heart to pieces.

Neither said a word.

She couldn't open her mouth and confess she just realized she loved him.

In fact, what she needed to do was push him away and tell him this couldn't happen. She should tell him the truth.

"What's wrong?" A light kiss hit her lips. "And you didn't tense up because you don't have any condoms."

How could he read her so well? Nobody ever understood her like he could.

But she wasn't about to confess her love. Not when it wouldn't make a difference when he found out the truth about her. Her love for him would not keep her in his arms. He would hate her soon.

Which was why she couldn't tell him the truth about why she was in this small town. He would hate her, and she wanted a small piece of him before he turned her away.

Selfish? Yes.

Did she care? Yes, but not enough to confess.

This time she stole a kiss from him, then produced a smile she hoped he couldn't see through. "I'm hoping you have a condom because I want this to happen."

Did she ever.

Because this one moment in time would keep her memories through the end of her days. After tonight, she wouldn't have him in her arms again. She had made a decision earlier today while sitting alone in the diner after Kat left her reeling.

Once she put her plan in motion, there would be no turning back.

She couldn't even be sure her boss—her real boss— would like what she had planned.

His eyes narrowed as if he wanted to keep arguing with her and make her spill the real reason she stiffened in his arms. Then a sly grin punctured his lips.

"I always keep one in my wallet for emergencies."

A chuckle escaped. "Emergencies?"

He swallowed hard, his Adam's apple bobbing. "Maybe I was hoping something like this would happen."

"It probably shouldn't." Yet, she wanted it so badly so she could live off the beautiful memory.

"I'll leave if you want me to." His eyes said another story. That he wanted this moment to happen as much as she did.

"Grab the condom already, Seth."

He snatched a kiss, then got off the bed in search of his pants, digging out his wallet. Then a sweet, adorable grin touched his lips when two condom packages hit the bed.

"What can I say? A guy can hope, can't he?" he said, laughing, as he joined her on the bed again.

"Shut up and kiss me."

She slid her hands around his neck and pulled him closer, melting into his arms as his lips touched hers and his hands started lighting her body on fire.

They kissed, they touched, they roamed and learned each other's bodies as the heat and intensity grew. Before long, she was so inflamed with desire she couldn't wait anymore. She wanted him. All of him.

Grabbing a condom, she tore it open and slid it on him with ease. Seth was hard as a rock and just as ready for her.

Before he entered her, she tensed, her hands squeezing his biceps. "It's been a while. Be gentle."

It had been a very long while.

Two years, to be exact.

After her last boyfriend, who she didn't even want to think about, she had sworn off men—until Seth. He hadn't been physical with her. He had been attentive and attuned to her needs—when she let him be. It had been his words that cut her deep, that made her vow to never let a man get that close to her ever again.

You're so cold. So unresponsive. I can't keep doing this with you. All you ever do is work, and no matter how much I try to make this work between us, I can't be the only person putting forth the effort. And as much as I keep trying, the sex isn't what it should be. It's not worth it anymore.

His words hurt because they had been true. She worked too much to put forth a real effort in a relationship, and she couldn't deny it. She didn't say a word when he left.

After him, she vowed she'd keep all men at a distance, because what was the point? She wasn't worth it—he had said so himself. She'd fail at the relationship anyway, so why bother?

Why was she even bothering with Seth?

He kissed her, brushing his lips softly and slowly, telling her without words he understood how much he needed to be gentle with her.

Focusing on his hard, strong body on top of hers, she slid her hands up his arms and through his hair, adoring the way he sighed in contentment.

Then he entered inch by inch, taking his time. She relished in the way he was delicate about it as if granting her wish that he be gentle and cherishing her at the same time.

Her hands wove another path up his arms, through his hair, and settled at his neck, squeezing when he was fully inside her.

A kiss, as light as a butterfly, hit her neck. "Pepp—"

Her nails dug into his neck, cutting off his words. The way her name started to echo out of his mouth was too much. Too much emotion she didn't want to hear. How would she be able to leave him?

He winced, yet didn't say anything as he slightly lifted and met her gaze. Before he could say a word, she kissed him. From here on out, she wanted no words between them. Just sweat, moans, and bodies tangled as one.

The kiss, brutal and demanding, should've told him what she wanted. Seth wasn't an idiot. He took her cue and started thrusting deep and hard. His rough movements only spurred on the intensity of their kiss.

She matched his erotic pace, clinging to him as if she'd lose him if her grip loosened. The last thing she wanted was to lose him.

Too bad she was going to.

They moved as one, yet there was a ferocity in each thrust. In each sweep of her hand as she brushed his back with the command he push harder. In his stroke of hands as he gripped her hair and tugged in unison to her demands.

She never knew sex could be so feral and intense. She never could've foreseen them bracing and almost fighting in a way to get as much wanton desire out of each other as they could.

Then it hit her.

An orgasm so intense, she bit down on his bottom lip.

Seth moaned, perhaps in pain, perhaps in pleasure. Maybe a bit of both. She stilled in his arms and clung to him as he continued to thrust a few more times before tensing and groaning in bliss.

They stayed wrapped in each other's arms, only silence perforating the air.

She didn't know what to say. That—that was the most powerful, erotic thing she had ever experienced.

And it broke her heart she'd have to leave him. That he would hate her soon.

She should've never caved into this desire. He would really hate her when he learned the truth.

He finally lifted his weight off her and twisted to her side with a wily grin. "I am so damn glad I have two condoms."

Biting her lip, she tried to hide her smile. It was futile. She couldn't mask her happiness. Because she was so happy she felt like she was flying high, feeling the wind in her hair, the sun on her cheeks.

It wouldn't last between them.

But she could enjoy it while she had the chance.

"Let's have that snack and then make good use of that other condom."

His smile widened, as the desire ratcheted up a notch in his gaze.

"Sounds like a great plan."

He hopped out of bed and walked out of her room to the bathroom to dispose of the condom.

She crawled out of bed, her body deliciously sore in all the right places. Her mind zoomed to how he'd react when he learned she was lying. Since the beginning.

She didn't know if she'd survive losing him.

12

———

SETH BRUSHED a delicate hand down her side, not wanting to wake her up, but he couldn't stop the impulse to touch her.

When he came over last night, he never expected what happened. Making love twice, plus some extra delightful treats of exploring her body without the need of a condom. He certainly hadn't expected to spend the night, but he had.

A quick glance at her nightstand told him he'd have to get up and leave soon. He had to go home and grab a change of clothes before work. She had to get up and get ready for work as well.

Or they could play hooky. Spend all day in bed having fun and explore some more. Although he had touched about every inch of her body last night, he wasn't sure there was much left to explore. But it'd sure be fun.

Too bad it couldn't happen.

His mood dipped.

His best friend—ex-best friend—was still missing. As much as he wanted to write Evan out of his life, he couldn't. He just wanted Evan to be found safe and sound and to come home, explain the truth. Because no matter what he thought about his friend—a liar, for sure—he was no murderer.

When he brushed his hand back up her side, she shivered, then twisted his way. Her eyes were little slits as a smile brightened her gorgeous face.

"What time is it?" she asked in a sleepy voice.

"Too damn late in the morning and not enough time for what I really want to do." He then swiped a kiss before she could say anything that might bring his mood down even further. Because the slight flash of panic and irritation in her eyes said a storm could be brewing. He knew she was big on punctuality and would not want to be late for work. "It's not that late. But if we don't get moving, it'll make us late."

The flash of fire in her eyes died. "I can't be late for work." Then she started to stretch like a cat, arching, thrusting her breasts out as if tempting him to sin. "I guess something relaxed me way too much."

He pounced, unable to hold back any longer, smothering her with kisses. She giggled, submitted to his assault, wrapping her arms around him as the kiss to her lips turned tender.

"I can't be late," she whispered against his mouth.

"I know."

Reluctantly, because he didn't want to let her go, he released her and sighed as she slipped out of bed.

"I'm going to jump in the shower. Feel free to make some coffee and grab some breakfast if you'd like."

He nodded, appreciating the gesture. But he had to get to work, too. "Thanks. I can't be late to work either."

She paused in the doorway, still gloriously naked, with a troubled look on her face. Then it withered away in a blink of an eye as if he had imagined it.

"Have a good day at work." Then she walked out of the room.

No "I'll see you later." No "let's make plans." No "I can't wait to do this again."

Not that he expected it from her. On the contrary. She was terrible at displaying her emotions, but he was still disappointed she didn't give him a clue of what would happen later tonight.

Would anything happen again?

Could he be presumptuous he'd be invited back into her bed?

Well, he'd keep doing what he was doing. Dropping by at night with a snack and a little bit of hope she didn't slam the door in his face.

Of course, they had to have hit a turning point in their relationship. She slept with him. That had to mean something.

Blowing out an irritated breath at himself, he sat up. What the hell was he doing? He had no reason to worry. Whatever was happening between them was going somewhere. So, okay, she wasn't that great at expressing herself, but they had sex. He was able to get past her defenses and he wasn't about to back down. She meant too much to him to do anything but forge on and see where this relationship could go.

He swiveled his body, eager to get the day started so the night could come and he could resume right where he left off—with her in his arms.

Except, he twisted too much and his feet hit the bottom of her nightstand in the cubby hole and knocked some of the papers that were lying there to the floor.

Bending down, he started to gather them in a pile to put them back when one of the pictures punctured his gaze.

He slowly stood up as the brutality struck him in the gut. He dropped the papers onto the bed as if they had burned him straight to the core.

What the hell?

His body started to shake as he moved closer to the bed, a wobbly finger pushing the picture apart from the other papers.

He blinked a few times, thinking his mind was still groggy from sleep. But nope. The same picture glared at him.

A picture of a woman lying on a bed slashed from head to toe. Blood soaking the bedsheets. Her blonde hair tangled and stained.

He still couldn't understand what he was seeing.

Realizing he was stark naked, he got dressed and tried to erase the bloodied image from his mind. It didn't work.

She found him still standing by the bed staring at the picture trying to process the ramifications of what it could mean.

He met her gaze when he felt her presence. She stood near the door, horror etched across her features.

"How did—where did—Seth…" she finally uttered with a pained breath.

He glanced one more time at the horrific picture, then met her panicked eyes. "Why is there a picture of a brutally murdered woman here?" His voice lowered to a whisper. "Why does she look like you?"

His heart felt like it was ripping out of his chest. "Who's Lillian Chapman?"

HER ENTIRE BODY WENT RIGID, forcing down the urge to cry. She could feel the torrential emotion simmering, waiting to be unleashed.

She knew this day would come. She knew Seth would eventually find out who she was and hate her.

And oh, boy, he hated her. The dangerous glint in his eyes as he stared hard and unyielding at her, waiting for an answer, told her enough. He really hated her.

Because she had lied. She could see it in his eyes that he knew she had been lying from the start.

Just like his best friend. And he had yet to forgive his best friend of over 19 years for lying, there was no chance he'd forgive her.

She could only blame herself that he had found out so soon. Yesterday morning she had woken up surrounded by the papers she went over every single night, like usual, before falling asleep. She didn't have time to pick it up and hide it in the vent. So, she shoved it below the nightstand, telling herself she'd do it later. But then Seth showed up and she completely forgot about it...and here they were.

"I need some answers right now, Pepper."

She flinched at the way he said each word with such barely suppressed violence.

"Who is this woman? Talk to me, damn it," he demanded through gritted teeth, as if he had to control the urge to shout.

The jig was up. She had no choice but to confess. She honestly didn't think he or his brother or anyone else in the sheriff's department was a dirty criminal. So, it shouldn't matter; it was time to confess. Releasing a slow breath, she walked closer to the bed, but not close enough for Seth to be able to reach her. Not that she thought he'd hurt her, but she couldn't bear it if he touched her. She was ashamed of lying. But she'd had no choice.

She had been doing her job.

Her gaze glided to the photo she had looked at every day for the past month. Torturing herself. Berating herself. Blaming herself.

"Her name is Lillian Chapman. She was murdered a month ago." Her gaze slowly lifted toward his. "She's my twin sister."

Although they were twins, they were complete opposites. She was accomplished and smart, able to hold a job and be successful in her profession. Same as Lillian, who had worked as a dance instructor.

That's where the similarities stopped.

She was closed-off and struggled to connect with people. She liked things orderly and done in a certain way. She liked control, but she also didn't like being the center of attention. She tended to buck authority when she didn't agree with something but always did her job by the book. And her taste in men—ha, it wasn't even something she liked to think about.

And then there was Lillian. Beautiful and articulate. Gregarious and outgoing. Loved to be the center of attention. Loved men and flirting and showing off her assets way too much.

Which was probably what got her killed.

They looked almost exactly alike, except her sister had a small mole near the right side of her lips. She liked to wear her hair in a ponytail, straight and precise, not a strand out of place. It helped to keep it out of her face in her line of work. Her sister, on the other hand, loved to curl it with soft, beach-like waves, adding to the already slight wave she had naturally. She had tried to emulate her sister's look before. She could never get the waves down as eloquently as she could.

Seth glanced at the photo, then back at her several times before resting his gaze solely on her. "You have different last names. Are you married? What are you keeping from me?"

Well, here came the hard part. All her lies revealed. Because she couldn't let him think she was married.

She sighed, hating to spill the truth. "My name is Pepper Chapman. It's not Wilson. It doesn't matter what last name you attach to Pepper, it sounds dumb. My sister has such an elegant name—Lillian. And I'm named after a condiment."

She rolled her eyes at letting part of her insecurity show. Why had she added that last part? Even if it was true. Because, yeah, she'd heard the condiment joke about her name way too many times to count. Not once had her sister stuck up for her. Not once had she ever tried to get her friends to like her. Although, Pepper couldn't fault her. She didn't exactly make it easy for people to like her. She teased and picked on her sister right back.

Call it a defense mechanism.

They were polar opposites. They barely liked each other.

Yet, when she found out she was murdered, she couldn't find it in herself to leave it alone. She had felt like she failed her sister so many times in life, this was her chance at redeeming herself.

Seth's brows puckered, but he didn't comment about her name. Then his eyes swept across the contents on the bed once again. "What is all this? What are you doing here? Why did you change your last name?"

"You wouldn't understand."

Or, more like, she didn't want to confess yet.

His eyes pierced her with a deadly glare. "Try me. I'm so sick and tired of people lying to me. I want to hear some truth for once."

Damn it. She knew he'd clump her in with Evan, and that was the last thing she had wanted. But she fit right in. She was a liar.

"What can I say? My sister and I were never close. I'm pretty sure she hated me right out of the womb. We had our moments of peace, but mostly, we were always at odds with each other." Her eyes glided to the picture once more, pain ripping her apart inside at her sister's mangled body. "I tried a few times to get that sisterly connection with her, but she never accepted it. In her eyes, I was a bug annoying her. You know, she never told people she had a sister. Most people who knew her thought she was an only child."

How pathetic. She couldn't even get her sister to like her, so it never surprised her when other people didn't like her either.

She was just an unlikeable person.

"That doesn't explain what you're hiding from me." He paused, eyeing her intently. "I had a feeling you were holding something back. I should've trusted my instinct."

A strangled laugh escaped. She couldn't have agreed more. "I had no choice in the matter. I'm sorry, Seth."

He shook his head, his lips pressed tightly together as if he wanted to say something. "What are you sorry about? Tell me the truth."

Seth asked for the truth. For no lies.

Okay, then.

"I work for the FBI. I'm here undercover. And you're the only person who knows now, besides my boss."

A LOT HAD BEEN DROPPED at his feet this morning.

First, waking up, loving how well she fit into his arms. How much he didn't want to let her go. Such intense emotions he wasn't certain he could decipher—like, was he falling in love? Or just in lust?

Oh, then the part where she wasn't really the person he thought she was. That she'd been lying to him from the start. Lying to everyone.

Working undercover?

For what reason?

How could Logan not have known this?

He had no idea how to respond. To any of it.

"Why?"

Her eyes shifted away, gliding to the documents on the bed. He didn't want her shying away from him. He wanted answers, and he wanted them right now.

"Pepper, tell me now."

Her gaze snapped back to his, a mixture of awe and puzzlement lingering in her amber-tinted eyes.

What was that look for?

She bit her bottom lip, yet said nothing.

He took a step closer to her. She immediately retreated a step back.

Damn it. He didn't like how she kept withdrawing from him. Of course, why should he care? She lied. She had been lying since the first moment they met.

But a part of him understood why she had to lie. Hello, she worked for the FBI. Undercover work meant you couldn't tell people who you were. Even though she had ripped his heart out and stomped on it until there wasn't much left, he understood why she had to lie. But why here in his small town? What was she investigating?

Why didn't she tell him before they slept together? Had last night even meant anything to her? He swore he felt a connection last night. A raw and powerful connection. It couldn't have been fake.

Which was why his heart was bleeding uncontrollably right now. It had to have been all part of her cover. Maybe she was investigating his brother. Not that he believed Logan had done anything illegal.

They stared at each other for the longest time. Neither made the slightest movement.

"You're not going to tell me, are you?" he finally said in a deflated tone.

Just once he wanted the truth when asking for it from someone he cared about. Maybe even loved. Last night could not be forgotten even with the damning evidence before him.

She swiped a lock of hair behind her ear, her hair still freshly wet from her shower. A slight wave lingered in the strands. He remembered the way his hands glided through her silky strands, the way her eyes lit up with pleasure at the touch.

Damn it. He had to forget about last night. Clearly, whatever had been developing between them was over. Probably had never existed, to begin with.

"I can't, Seth." She shook her head. "I shouldn't have even told you that much. But believe me, I hated lying to you."

Hmm...was that her trying to tell him she cared about him? Because all the lies between them felt like she didn't. Yet, last night...

His mind couldn't erase any moment from last night or the desire lingering in her eyes.

"Does this have to do with my brother?"

"No."

Okay. Oddly enough, he believed her. Why wouldn't she tell him the truth, then?

"So, tell me what you're doing here? Why are you undercover?"

Her lips pressed into a tight line as if forcing herself to remain silent.

Oh, so she was going to test him, then.

"My brother is going to find this little tidbit about you intriguing. What do you think he's going to do with this information?"

The pain that scorched her eyes made him sick to his stomach. The last thing he wanted to do was cause her pain even though she had torn his heart out.

"You do what you have to do, Seth. My cover is blown, so..." She shrugged.

A mangled laugh escaped as he glanced at the documents lying on the bed one more time. Why was she acting like he didn't matter to her? "Does it have to do with your sister?" He looked at her. He obviously didn't matter to her. "Just tell me, Pepper."

Please.

She tore her gaze away, biting her bottom lip again. Oh, that gesture was enticing in too many ways. One in where he wanted to kiss her with an ache that told her how much he cared about her despite her lying. One in where he wanted to soothe her pain in any way he could. For losing her sister in such a brutal way.

He stepped closer but didn't reach out to touch her. "I'm so damn pissed that you lied, but maybe I can help you."

She didn't look at him. "You can't help me, Seth."

Because he couldn't resist any longer, he brushed his fingers lightly against her cheek. "You're not alone, Pepper. I can help you...if you'd just let me in."

Then he walked out of her room and left with his heart in her hands and his mind grappling with what he should do.

13

SHE HEARD THE DOOR CLOSE, but he hadn't slammed it. Surprisingly. He had walked out of the room angry enough. His words had been spoken soft, but she had felt the anger vibrating within him.

Of course, why wouldn't he be angry? She lied to him. Lied to everyone.

It didn't matter she was only doing her job. She had lied.

Her bottom lip trembled as her eyes glided to the papers strewn across the bed. Crime scene photos. The police report. Information galore about the Cheetahs gang.

Autopsy report.

Oh, she rarely looked at that document because she didn't want to imagine the last moments of her sister's life. The photos of her body said enough. But she had read it once.

Her sister had been stabbed multiple times. With her own kitchen knife. There was evidence she was raped.

Pepper honestly wasn't sure the last part was true. Yes, there were signs that a man had penetrated her before she died. But Pepper thought it had been consensual.

Because she knew who killed her sister. She'd heard him talking about it.

Shivering from the brutal memory that started her on the path she was on right now, she started scooping all the documents up. Every last paper was shoved back in the folder until she couldn't see anything.

Opening the vent, she hid the folder and plopped down on her bed.

How long would it take for the sheriff to show up?

What would she say?

She should call her boss. What would he say?

Instead of doing what she should do, she sat there and waited.

And waited.

When twenty minutes rolled by and not one knock sounded on the door, or even a phone call from the sheriff, she was unsure of how to proceed. She was going to be late to work today. That would be a first.

Seth had to have gone to his brother immediately.

So, what was taking the sheriff so long to arrive?

And why wasn't she calling her boss to inform him her cover was blown?

A lone tear slid down her cheek as heartache swept through, paralyzing her.

She knew why she couldn't call her boss. She'd never be able to confess she let her emotions get the best of her. Something she never let happen. It was one of the reasons he let her do this in the first place. He knew she was too close to the case—considering her sister was the victim—and hadn't thought it wise for her to go undercover.

But her sister deserved justice. She couldn't allow the Cheetahs to continue to always get away with their crimes. They were not above the law.

There were a few moments, rare moments, when she imagined killing the man who murdered her sister. That would be justice.

Of course, that was all in her dreams. She didn't think she'd have the courage to do it.

She believed in right and wrong. In the law. Killing a man—exacting revenge—wasn't something she believed in. It didn't stop her from picturing it from time to time in her mind.

That's right. She believed in right and wrong. And right now, it was completely wrong not to inform her boss of the latest development.

She grabbed her phone, her hands shaking as she dialed her boss's number.

"Find him yet?"

They always skipped pleasantries. They were more alike than she cared to admit. But it also made it easy to work under him and follow his directions.

She called him every day since arriving in Lucky. He always answered her phone call with "Find him yet?" She always answered with, "Not yet." That was the extent of their interaction. Straight and to the point.

"Pepper?"

Unfortunately, she had to deviate from their normal routine.

"My cover's been blown. Seth Caldwell, the sheriff's brother, knows I'm here undercover."

She heard him sigh heavily. "How?"

Ugh. She hated to lie. Where had lying got her here? Nowhere but to hurt a good man that didn't deserve more pain.

"He found my file on my sister...in my bedroom."

Her boss could infer what he wanted from that. Because that was the extent of all she could confess.

"I knew this was a bad idea."

She disagreed. They couldn't trust the Cheetahs. They had their hands in some of the pockets at the local precinct in Miami. They didn't know who was dirty and who was squeaky clean. When she'd gotten the phone call and talked to the lead detective about her sister's murder, she hadn't felt like he was even trying to find her killer. Because he had known who had done it.

The Cheetahs had a large territory in Florida. Their operation in Minnesota was nowhere near what they had in Florida. And when she learned her sister's killer had left the state, she knew she had to follow. Because her sister deserved justice. Not to be a cold case file sitting in a cabinet for years on end, especially when she knew who did it.

What would take the pain away from losing her sister? It wasn't that she missed her because she rarely saw Lillian when she was alive. She missed the fact she didn't have the option to call her up and attempt to make amends. To attempt to find some sort of sisterly bond with her.

To apologize for all the times she had made Lillian's life hell.

Sure, Lillian had said some pretty harsh and nasty things to her, but she had always dished right back.

The last time she saw her sister—about six months ago—she swore she had seen something in Lillian's eyes like she wanted to make amends.

Instead of reaching out and embracing the moment of sincerity, she acted like a colossal bitch.

Now she'd never know if they could've become friendly with each other. Maybe grab a coffee or something to eat and talk about life.

She didn't have that chance any longer because of one despicable man.

Burying her face in her hands, trying like hell to keep the tears at bay, she knew right then, even though her cover was blown, her mission was the same.

"Sir, I can still find him. I can still do this. I've gotten to know Sheriff Caldwell and Deputy Bolten, and they're solid men. You haven't told me that there have been reports he's been seen in Florida, which means he's still here. I can find him. Agents O'Rourke and Sumnter from the FBI field office in Minneapolis have also been helping on finding Evan Barten. They are also good men. I can trust these people. They can help me find my sister's killer."

"You're sure?"

Was she?

Her gut said so, and it hadn't steered her wrong yet.

"Yes."

"Bring them in the loop, then. And Agent Chapman," he said in a brisk tone, "the next phone call to me better be that that man is in custody."

Or else.

She heard that silent threat.

Or else she was done and had to come home.

Let a murderer walk away.

Leave Seth Caldwell and her heart behind.

GRAPPLING WITH A DECISION, it was a toss-up between being surprised and not surprised at all when he pulled into the hospital parking lot.

Seth knew he should've headed for the sheriff's office

and spoken to Logan about Pepper, but in the end, he couldn't do it. Not yet, anyway.

He had believed her when she said she wasn't here because of his brother. Which made him hesitate to blow her cover. What—*who*—was she investigating? He trusted his brother to help her, but...he just didn't know what to do.

He stared at the front doors to the hospital.

It had been five days since they found Stacy. She should be getting released in another day or two. Of course, that didn't mean life would be getting better for her.

She lost her job at the diner. She had charges pending for impeding the investigation. Not many folks were thinking too highly of her for withholding information either. She was bound to get some icy demeanor from a lot of people.

Seth wanted to feel sorry for her, but he didn't. Maybe a small part of him did, but mostly, he was pissed she wouldn't tell Logan what happened. Who hurt her? Where was Evan?

Which was why he had kept his distance and not visited her once. Not to mention, her parents had been by her side most of the time and he didn't want another run-in with them.

He was done holding back. It was his turn to take a crack at breaking her silence.

Since he had no clue whether to confess about Pepper to his brother, he had to shift his attention to something else. Maybe once he was done here, he'd have a better idea of how to proceed with Pepper's problem.

He waved hello at Tracy, the nurse sitting at the desk, producing a smile he had to force with all his might.

"Hey, Tracy. How's it going?"

"Slow, but good morning. And yourself?" she asked with

genuine sincerity as if she was having a great day...unlike himself.

"Just fine. I wanted to say hi to Stacy. Is she awake? I don't want to disturb her if she has any visitors right now either." In other words, he didn't want to go in there if her parents were here. He wouldn't be getting any information out of her if that was the case.

"She's alone right now. And yes, she's awake. Go on in." Tracy's eyes shimmered with sadness. "She could use a friend right now."

Ha! Seth wouldn't necessarily call himself her friend. Since they broke up for the last time, they didn't talk to each other. Sure, they were friendly in passing, but they didn't go out of their way to make nice and catch up.

"Thanks, Tracy. Have a great day."

She returned the sentiment with a brilliant smile and went back to the paperwork in front of her.

Seth let out a deep breath before knocking on the door and opening it. Stacy trembled in her spot as her eyes widened in surprise.

"Seth, uh, hi."

He produced a smile he didn't feel like offering, then took a seat next to her. "Hey."

She averted eye contact and fiddled with her blanket. "What...what are you doing here?"

"I don't know. I started driving and ended up here."

And boy, that was the truth. His mind had been a jumbled mess when he left Pepper's house.

Her head slowly lifted and met his gaze.

"I know it doesn't seem like it after the last few months of ignoring Evan, but I'm worried about him. The only thing I keep thinking is he's dead and I acted like an ass, not even giving him a chance to say his piece."

He wasn't sure why those words spilled out, but it felt cathartic in a way. Like a nasty infection, festering and growing, finally getting some medicine to calm the pain.

Her eyes glided away from him once more.

"I'm glad you're not dead. I know we're really not even friends anymore, but I would never want anything bad to happen to you."

Her bottom lip wobbled as her eyes glistened with tears. Her hands clutched the blanket. "Logan told me you and that deputy found me. That you saved my life." Her vibrant hazel eyes sparkled with agony and despair. "Thank you. I don't know what to say other than that."

He leaned closer, his expression intense, yet he made sure to keep his tone soft. "You can tell me what happened. Where is he?"

"I wish I knew," she whispered desperately. "I close my eyes at night wondering if I'll be opening them again in the morning. I can only assume I'm still alive because they know I won't say a word."

"Who, Stacy? Who is *they*?" He reached out and grabbed her hand, hating how she flinched and retreated from his touch, but thankfully, didn't make him let go. "Logan can keep you safe. The FBI is helping. They won't hurt you."

She squeezed his hand and held his gaze as the seconds ticked by. He didn't say anything, hoping against hope she'd trust him and finally tell the truth.

"Okay." She nodded, a few tears slipping down her cheek. "Okay, I'll tell you what I know. I'm just...so scared."

"Me, too. You have no idea." He wasn't just scared wondering whether Evan was alive or dead. He was also scared thinking about Pepper and what reason she could be here undercover.

"Evan called me in a panic. I met him at the lookout in

Mulhene. He didn't tell me much then because he was bleeding pretty badly. He said he stopped at your cabin first to try to stop the bleeding himself, but couldn't. So, we left my car and drove to Neptune where I bought supplies and headed to the cabin."

When Stacy stopped, he offered a dose of courage by squeezing her hand. She couldn't stop there, especially when he already knew all of that. He needed new information.

She inhaled and exhaled a few times before continuing. "Once I was able to stop the bleeding and get him patched up as best as I could, we argued. He didn't want to tell me anything. I didn't understand. Nothing made sense. He wouldn't let me take him to the hospital or call Logan or anyone."

Rubbing his thumb across her hand like he used to do when they dated, he smiled. "He can be stubborn. But so can you."

She returned a slight smile, although a few silent tears still trailed down. "I guess all three of us can be stubborn. What a trio we make."

"Yeah, I am stubborn, too."

Stacy pressed her lips together, a wave of anguish brushing across her features. "He said he was in the office when these two guys showed up at the garage. He said he recognized them and ducked down so they wouldn't see him. They asked Barry where he was and Barry wouldn't tell them. So, one of them knocked Barry in the head with his gun and then the other guy killed him. Evan made a noise, obviously shocked by everything, and they knew he was there. He said he ran for his car where they shot at him, which is how he got hit."

"Who were they? How does he know them?"

"I swear I have no idea, Seth. He wouldn't tell me. He just said they were bad guys that wouldn't leave him alone. I begged him to call the police, and he wouldn't." Her eyes implored him to believe her.

And he did. The torment in her voice didn't sound fake. That also sounded like Evan. Which made Seth believe this had to do with his dad and the Cheetahs gang. Maybe, even though Wayne and Joshua were out of the picture, the Cheetahs were still trying to recruit him into the gang.

Only speculation, of course, but he wouldn't be surprised. It always came back to Evan's deadbeat family making his life a living hell.

"What happened that morning you got shot?"

She inhaled and let out a breath slowly. "We had just taken a shower and gotten dressed. We were talking— arguing—about what to do again when the door busted open. These two guys came in. I'm assuming the same two that showed up at the garage by the expression on Evan's face. One of them grabbed me while the other went for Evan. Although, he's stubborn, remember? Evan started fighting with him. The guy who had me...laughed and...said, 'Bang. You're dead.' Then he shot me. I don't remember much after that. I don't know if Evan made it out of there or if they took him. It all happened so fast."

The tears were coming down so heavily, her words were choppy and broken. Seth wanted to pull her into his arms and comfort her, soothe her somehow. Instead, he settled with squeezing her hand. He couldn't take her pain away. He couldn't diminish the horror and terror she survived. Part of him was still pissed she didn't tell his brother any of this. It's not like any of it was that helpful. She hadn't given him much information—like the name of who shot her.

"I recognized them, Seth. I know at least the one guy's

name. He came into the diner sometimes. He was the one who shot me."

"Tell me a name, Stacy."

She closed her eyes as she laid back. "Brett. I only know his first name. He always scared me when he came into the diner. I'm pretty sure he's a drug dealer. And if he finds out I gave up his name, he'll kill me for good next time."

Finally, somewhere to go. A lead. A name. Hopefully, a trail to find Evan.

First, he'd call Danny to make sure someone was on guard to protect Stacy until this case was closed.

Then, he'd go find Pepper.

He got one woman he used to care about to talk.

Well, he had to get the woman he now *loved* to talk.

Damn. Yep, he loved her.

Yeah, she lied to him. But he needed her to tell him the truth. He could help.

Of course, he might love her, but it didn't mean he would forgive her for lying.

Hell, he hadn't even forgiven his best friend.

14

PEPPER SHIVERED from the cold whirling around her and from the panic eating her alive as she approached the doors to the sheriff's office.

She liked the sheriff. What would he think of her after she confessed? Would he kick her out of town? Well, he could try, but it wouldn't stop her from completing her mission.

Pulling open the door, she didn't offer a smile—as usual —to Charlotte, who sat at her desk with an unapproachable look.

"You're late."

Yep, she was.

A first for her. She had never been late to work in her life.

Charlotte perused her from top to bottom, a lone brow arching. "You're not wearing your uniform."

How astute of her. She was wearing her pink winter coat and a pair of old faded blue jeans, her favorite pair. The moment she got off the phone with her boss, she had grabbed her keys and left. Not much else had been rattling around her brain.

She should've changed. That was an oversight she missed.

"Is the sheriff in?"

Charlotte didn't even flinch at her rude behavior. "He's in his office."

Without another word, Pepper headed toward the man who would either despise her or understand she was only doing her job.

Logan was a decent guy. He'd been kind and patient with her since the moment she arrived, even when she wasn't always the friendliest. Maybe he'd understand. Maybe he wouldn't go too hard on her.

Knocking on the doorframe, she waited for Logan to look up and wave her in before entering. She closed the door behind her.

"Good morning, Pepper. Is everything okay? You're late." He also eyed her up and down as Charlotte had. "You're not in uniform."

His eyes shimmered with panic before disappearing as if he had to force himself to remain calm.

Her heart started to beat erratically. She fisted her hands to hide the trembles she could feel inhibiting her body.

"Can we talk?" That didn't come out as confident as she would have liked, but it was a step in the right direction.

Now that she was standing in front of him, she had a strong feeling he would hate her. He'd get where she was coming from with having to hide her identity, but he wouldn't like that he had been deceived.

He gestured toward the chair in front of his desk as a look of confusion and concern swept across his features. "What's going on?"

Trying to hide the fact she was shaking like a leaf, she took a seat, gripping the armrests. Realizing how that might look, she relaxed her hands even as the nervous energy coursed through her veins. Wow. She was never nervous. Her job was the one thing she excelled at.

It was all she lived for.

Her life, besides work, was nonexistent. How sad and pitiful she truly was.

"There's clearly something on your mind. You're not in uniform. Just tell me what's going on."

The lingering concern flickering in his eyes gave her a small dose of courage.

"It's Pepper." Inhaling deeply and letting out the breath slowly as she watched the confusion intensify on his face. Of course, her name was Pepper. It was her last name he didn't know. "My name is Pepper...Chapman."

He leaned forward, his brows puckering. "I don't understand. Please explain a lot more than what you're giving me right now."

Well, she got one small portion of her lies out. The rest shouldn't be too much harder.

"I work for the FBI. I've been undercover here as Pepper Wilson."

He sat back in his chair and ran a hand down his face. "Wow. Okay."

Now that she had confessed, she felt a bit lighter like a huge load had shifted. She still felt part of that heavy weight holding her down. The part that needed justice for her sister. But with the sheriff finally knowing who she was—because she had hated lying to the man—some of that stress was gone.

Logan hung his head, running his hand across his face again. "Just what I need. To lose another deputy." He met her gaze. "Why are you here undercover? Are you investigating my department?"

"I'm sorry for deceiving you. This has nothing to do with your department." She tossed her head around as a lame laugh escaped. "Well, it kind of did, but not really. Before I came, I didn't know if I could trust anyone here, but now I know. I highly respect you and know you are a good man who is good at his job."

"That did not answer my question. It only raises a lot more questions." He sat up straighter, leaning forward. "I want some damn clear answers right now."

She could feel the sweat gather in her armpits. The terror racing up and down her spine hadn't rescinded. The jittery nerves always attacked her when she talked—or even thought—about her sister.

She swallowed hard. "My sister was murdered a month ago."

Logan sat up even straighter, his entire posture stiff, his eyes narrowing into deep contemplation. "What does that have to do with my town? We haven't had any recent murders."

"It all stems around the Cheetahs gang. I didn't know if you worked for them or not. I don't think you're a dirty cop."

He groaned and slapped his desk hard. "Like hell I am."

She flinched when he hit his desk.

"Keep talking...please."

And this was why she knew he was a good man. Even though he was pissed she lied, he couldn't stop from being polite. "You won't like my answer."

A dry laugh echoed between them. "I'm not liking anything you're saying right now."

"I work in the violent crimes unit in the New York division. I didn't get along with my sister. We were never close, which is so odd because we're twins. You'd think we would be. We grew up in Florida. I couldn't wait to get the hell out of there. She never left." She sighed as she looked down at her lap, then back up at his expressionless gaze. "I'm pretty sure she started dating some guy in the Cheetahs."

A muscle in his jaw ticked.

"I don't have proof. It's not like she ever told me. We never talked. We rarely saw each other."

Folding his hands, she could see the strain in his entire posture, as if he was trying like hell to keep his emotions in check. "Have they found her killer?"

"No."

"So, you think someone in the Cheetahs killed her?"

She nodded. "I know one of them did." She sighed and rubbed her hands across her jeans. "I wasn't informed right away that my sister had died. She had nothing in her apartment to suggest she had a sister." A strangled laugh echoed between them. "That's how much we didn't get along. She didn't even tell people she had a twin sister. I didn't even get a chance to make the identification. They used her fingerprints, which were in the system for a disorderly conduct charge. I didn't even have any idea she was arrested before. That's how much I didn't know my sister."

God, she hated talking about this. But the expression in Logan's eyes had started to dissipate from anger and turned into compassion. It helped her to continue.

"Another agent in Miami from narcotics heard about the murder, saw the picture of the body, and told me. I wonder how long it would've taken me to find out if not for him. We were in the academy together. She might not have ever talked about having a sister, but I did...sometimes. We look a lot alike, too. Our parents died a few years ago. My mom had a heart attack, and my dad...well, he had a gambling problem and owed the wrong people."

She hung her head, hating to divulge her family history that was just sad and pitiful, but it all had to be said. "I'm pretty sure my mom died of a broken heart when my dad died so...violently. She loved him despite all his transgressions. We have no other family. So, my sister had no next of kin. I spoke to the detective on the case once I found out. He wasn't very helpful. I got the impression he was hiding something. I had the wonderful task of cleaning out her apartment and getting rid of her stuff. It was actually hard to be in her apartment. I went from bawling my eyes out to swearing up a storm, cursing the dead. I was so pissed at her for dying."

"I'm truly sorry for your loss, Pepper."

Wow. That was unexpected. Here she was, confessing to lying and making a fool out of him, and he still has the kindness to offer his condolences. This was why he was a good man, why she could trust him, that he wasn't dirty.

"I was in the bathroom when I heard voices. There were two of them. The door was open a crack, so I was able to get a good look at them. They were looking for something in the living room. I don't know what he grabbed, but I guess I wasn't focused on what he was doing. I was more tuned into what he was saying." Her voice broke as the tears threatened to spill. She hated thinking about this. "He was laughing with his buddy about what a good lay she was. How he was sad he killed her because he'd miss her between the sheets. He didn't sound like he had an ounce of remorse for what he had done. I was too shocked that I let them leave. I didn't even try to stop him."

Logan looked focused and ready for action. "So, you

know exactly who killed your sister? Have they not caught him yet?"

"No, I never told the detective working her case. I told you, there was something off about him and I didn't trust him. I always trust my gut. I spoke to my friend in the Miami division, Agent Rollins, who gave me tons of information on the gang. He also told me to be careful who I trust with any information. Lots of cases get thrown out because they have a lot of cops in their pockets. I flew back to New York and went straight to my boss about everything. I wanted to work the case myself. He told me no, of course, because she's my sister, it's a conflict of interest. Agent Rollins has been keeping me updated on her case, which isn't going anywhere. He's also been keeping me updated on the Cheetahs and the one man I know who killed her."

She leaned forward, the words getting easier to say. "He's here in Lucky. Somewhere. One of Agent Rollins's informants swears he is. I saw the ad for a deputy position and knew I needed to be here to find him. My boss finally agreed." She shrugged. "With a lot of pushing from me."

"So, that's why you're in my town? Because your sister's murderer is here. And you couldn't just tell me this as an FBI agent from the beginning? You had to lie and deceive me because you thought I might be a dirty sheriff, working with that despicable gang."

He sounded hurt. She felt bad for lying, but she had to do what she had to do. She trusted her friend Agent Rollins when he said to be careful who to trust. She had no choice but to come in undercover at first.

"I am sorry for lying, but I was only doing my job. I hope you and Seth can forgive me, but I would do it all the same way."

"Wait, what? My brother knows everything?" Logan

suddenly stood up, the hurt intensified as well as the anger increasing.

She flinched and curled into her seat.

Whoops. She hadn't meant to say that last part. She was more sorry about lying to Seth than she was to Logan.

15

SETH FOLLOWED Danny inside the sheriff's office, smiling and waving hello at Charlotte, even though he didn't feel like it. For now, he had to pretend like his world wasn't falling down around him.

He was worried about Pepper. Worried about what he should do. Should he tell his brother? He didn't like lying.

And she had lied about so much to him. Everything he thought he knew was a lie. Although, she never shared much personal information with him. They always kept it light and carefree. Now he knew why.

But before he could track down Pepper, he had to take care of this problem. Danny and Deke had met him at the hospital, where he relayed everything Stacy told him. Deke had stayed back with Stacy while he and Danny made their way to the sheriff's office to update Logan.

Hopefully, they'd find this Brett guy soon and Evan along with him. He only hoped it wouldn't be Evan's lifeless body they found.

Danny knocked on the door but didn't wait for Logan to answer before he whipped it open and stepped inside.

Seth chuckled but followed him. His laughter died on his lips when he saw Pepper sitting in front of his brother's desk.

Logan looked pissed, standing like a fierce warrior about to go into battle. His fury intensified when he made eye contact with him.

"Everything okay, Logan?" Danny asked cautiously as he glanced around the room.

"Everything is not okay," Logan answered with barely controlled patience as he rounded his desk and took a few steps in Seth's direction. "How long have you known about Pepper?"

Shit.

She told his brother everything. A small weight lifted off his shoulders knowing he didn't have to confess. He had been so torn whether to keep her secret or tell his brother.

Seth looked at her. She met his gaze, her expression blank.

He met Logan's irate gaze. "I found out this morning."

Danny cleared his throat. "What am I missing? Can it wait? Because we finally have a lead in locating Evan and I want to find him."

"What?" Logan jerked his attention toward Danny. "What are you talking about?"

Danny nodded in Seth's direction. "Seth went to the hospital this morning and spoke with Stacy. She finally told him everything she knows. Which isn't a whole lot. Evan never told her what those guys wanted with him, but she recognized the guy who shot her. He frequented the diner. His first name is Brett. That's all she knew, but I'm assuming it's Brett Nelson, one of the Cheetahs' top gang members. This all stems around that gang. Deke's sitting with Stacy right now for protection. I think we need to move her to another location. Maybe a hospital in the Cities. She's not safe here right now."

"Not the Cities."

Seth saw Pepper stand up, her posture stiff as she finally joined the conversation.

Logan also turned in her direction. "The Cheetahs gang has control there, too. That's what you're thinking?"

"Of course, they do. They're everywhere. You can move Stacy, but I wouldn't know where would be the safest."

"I'm lost. What's going on?" Danny interjected.

Logan glanced from Pepper to Seth to Danny, then back to Pepper. "I've learned a lot this morning, Danny. This is Pepper Chapman. She works for the FBI in New York. She's been here undercover trying to find her sister's murderer. But, of course, she couldn't tell us that because she thought we were all dirty cops. Did I get that all correct, Pepper?"

She looked at Logan, her brow arched. "I didn't think you were all dirty, but I had no way of knowing without checking it out first. You might not approve of how I went about my job, but I'm good at my job."

Danny's eyebrows rose in surprise. Seth didn't know how to feel. On one hand, he was grateful his brother knew so he didn't have to withhold the truth from him, but, on the other hand, he hated it. His brother looked pissed and hurt. He felt the same way. Part of him still understood why she had to lie, he just didn't like it.

"Somehow, this news doesn't surprise me," Danny said with an awkward chuckle. "Do you know who killed her?"

"The same name you said. Brett Nelson." A shiver wracked her body, yet she held Danny's gaze.

Why was she suddenly forthcoming with information? She didn't want to tell him anything this morning.

"She doesn't have proof," Logan said.

"I heard him say it," Pepper said. "And as soon as I find him, I'll get him to confess again, but me hearing it in her apartment should be enough for an arrest."

"Well, we know he at least shot Stacy." Danny nodded at Pepper. "We can arrest him for that and get him to confess about your sister as well. This guy is a bad dude. What I don't understand is how you're here undercover when it involves your sister. It's a conflict of interest."

"I can be very persuasive," Pepper said with a gentle smirk. "My boss also knows I'm good at what I do and that I can handle it."

Logan ran a hand down his face. "We've been having a hard time tracking down any of the heavy hitters in the Cheetahs gang. Where do we even begin to find this guy?"

"Mr. Barten has to be involved somehow," Seth said quietly, not sure if he should even voice his opinion. He wasn't a cop, but he knew Mr. Barten was bad news.

Danny nodded in agreement. "They have to be holed up somewhere on his property."

"I have a crazy idea. It might work to get Brett to come out of hiding," Pepper said with an eager glint in her eyes Seth had never seen before.

"I'm all ears," Danny said before Logan could respond.

Seth wasn't sure he wanted to hear what she had to say by the excitement lingering in her eyes.

Although Danny answered her, she waited for Logan to say something. He finally nodded. "Go ahead. What idea do you have?"

"The last time we visited Mr. Barten, I stood to the side and didn't say a word. You didn't even tell him my name. I know everyone knows me as Pepper Wilson around here, but I'll tell Mr. Barten I'm Deputy Pepper Chapman."

Logan's brows lowered, confused and worried. "What are you getting at? Because if it's what I think, absolutely not."

Pepper's stance straightened, her features stoic and impenetrable. "If I tell Mr. Barten my name is Pepper Chapman and I'm looking to talk to Brett about my sister Lillian, he'll come to me. He won't be able to resist."

Oh, hell no. She was not going to put herself up as bait.

"Not happening," Seth said as he took a few steps toward her. "No way in hell."

Logan looked at him, the light dawning in his eyes as if he realized how Seth felt about her. Then Logan looked at Pepper. "I have to agree with my brother. It's not happening. He's dangerous. He killed your sister, Pepper. He almost killed Stacy, and we don't know, but Evan could also be dead. He'll kill you. I can't have that on my conscience."

"I'm a trained federal agent. I can take care of myself, Sheriff."

Logan grinned, despite the situation. "I have no doubt you can, but I can't put you in danger."

"I came here to arrest the man who killed my sister. I came here willing to do whatever I need to do." She stepped closer to Logan. "I can do this. I know I can. And you guys will be there to make sure nothing happens."

"Something could go wrong." Logan groaned and brushed a hand across his face.

"We can either get a warrant and check how many thousands of acres of Mr. Barten's land to locate this jackass." Danny sighed. "Or we can flush him out. It's a good plan, Logan."

Logan swung a hand in her direction. "This man killed her sister. One look at her and he might go off. I just…" His expression softened as he looked at Pepper. "You might not be one of my deputies for real, but right now you are, and I can't risk you getting hurt. I wouldn't want any of my people walking into that kind of situation."

"I've never been close with my sister, Sheriff. I regret a lot of things, especially not telling her I love her despite the fact I acted like I didn't. I need to do this." Pepper sighed. "I don't want to have to go over your head because I do respect you, but I will if I have to."

Danny looked at her, then at Logan. "It's worth a shot. We can do this. We'll be there to protect her. It could work."

"Could, Danny," Seth said through gritted teeth. "You said *could*. Not that it will. It's not happening."

Danny's eyes softened as he laid a hand on his shoulder. "I can see Pepper means something to you, Seth, but you're going to have to push those emotions aside and look at the bigger picture. He needs to be caught."

"And if it was Kat who had to do this? Would you look at the bigger picture?" Seth retorted.

Danny pressed his lips together, then nodded stiffly. "I wouldn't be able to stop your sister if it was her idea. You know that. But I would do anything to keep her safe."

"Fine. I'll go with her."

Logan looked at him as if he had spouted off he was moving to join the circus or something equally as crazy. "You're not a cop. That's not happening, Seth."

"Mr. Barten knows I'm best friends with Evan. It won't look odd if I go with her. I was with her the last time, too. If you two show up, he'll be suspicious. We'll both go. She'll ask to see Brett, and I'll plead that I want to know my friend is okay."

"This is crazy," Logan said as he turned around, running a hand through his hair.

"It is kind of out of left field, but it could work."

Logan twisted back around, glaring at Danny. "But it's

not a hundred percent guarantee it will work. I won't risk my brother's life like that. I won't even risk Pepper's. How can you be agreeing to this?"

Danny shrugged. "I know what it feels like to feel hopeless and desperate. I lived in pain and torment for three months when Aubrey was missing. I would've done anything to get her back. Anything. I can understand why Pepper did what she thought she had to. The Cheetahs are no gang to be messing with. But look at it this way, Logan. She came clean. She told you the truth. Let's get this son of a bitch. It's a good plan. It could—will—work. I have faith it will."

"Thank you, Agent O'Rourke," Pepper said in a soft, tender voice. The pain etched in each syllable made Seth want to pull her into his arms. At the same time, he wanted to spank her ass for lying.

His emotions were so confused and mixed up. But the one thing he knew, he did not want her walking into the situation she was suggesting. At least, not without him by her side.

"Fine." Logan nodded, although his expression said he wasn't happy with the decision. "Fine. We'll go with this plan."

"And I'll be there, too," Seth said before grabbing Pepper's hand and dragging her out of the office.

Neither Logan nor Danny stopped him. Pepper didn't resist either as he pulled her to the supply closet and shut the door.

Without giving her a chance to speak, he kissed her.

16

His kiss was like hot molten lava. Scorching to the touch. She could feel his anger in each twist of his lips, yet it wasn't brutal. He didn't hurt her.

She grabbed the front of his jacket, squeezing her hands into tight fists, loving the moment, but also dreading when it would end. She never expected to have his sweet, adoring lips on her mouth again.

And she didn't deserve it. Not after all of her lies.

The pain radiated everywhere and settled in her heart, twisting and turning, like a barbed wire was decimating the treacherous organ until it was nothing more than a mangled piece of meat.

Her gripped intensified, then she pushed him away, feeling the loss of his lips immediately.

The only sounds that could be heard were the heavy breaths echoing back and forth between them. The closet was pitch black. It was almost soothing in a way. To hear him so close to her. To know one jerk in her direction and she could have his mouth back on hers. The darkness made everything seem not so bad. Because she didn't have to see the anger and pain in his eyes. Not like she had felt it in his lips.

Then bright light illuminated the tiny space.

His eyes glittered with agony. She couldn't read much else in his expression.

Letting go of his jacket, she stepped back out of his reach.

"What was that for?"

That was a dumb question. Did it matter? Not really. She would soak the moment up to relive it down the road while she withered away in her lonely, desolate life. When she thought about it, she had no life. She worked, ate, slept, and then repeated. Over and over. Every day. That's all her life consisted of.

Seth shrugged. "I couldn't help myself." Then he took a step closer. She found herself immediately retreating a step. His expression fell deeper into sorrow. "I don't like this plan, Pepper."

"You want to find your friend Evan." She swallowed, knowing this was the best way to achieve their goals. "I want justice."

"He could kill you on sight. The guy sounds unstable. I can't risk it."

"It sounds like you care. I thought you hated me."

Seth advanced. She retreated until her back was up against a shelf and she had nowhere to go. His hands settled on her hips, his eyes lit up with fire.

"I don't want to care about you after you lied to me." His lips brushed hers. "But I do care. I'm pissed. I'm hurt. And the thought of losing you tears me up inside. I've never felt this way before, Pepper. I don't know how to manage my feelings. I want to hate you and walk away. Right now, I can't. Tomorrow, I might be able to."

Oh, such honesty. Raw and real. No man had ever shared himself with her like Seth was. The thought he could change his mind tomorrow and say "good riddance" splintered her heart like a jawbreaker smashing into a million pieces.

"If I could turn back time...I wish I could've been honest with you from the start. I'm so sorry, Seth. I had to do what I had to do. I wasn't thinking about anyone but myself."

His grip on her hips tightened. "I know a thing or two about only thinking about myself. In the last few months, I've been selfish. I get it. I've never lied to the ones I love, though."

Love?

Was he insinuating something?

Probably not. He cared about her, despite her actions, but he'd never fall in love. Hell, tomorrow he could despise her and stop talking to her altogether.

"I didn't have a happy carefree childhood like you had, Seth. I'm not saying it's a good excuse, but it's a part of who I am." She glanced away. "I lie to myself all the time. That I'm happy. That I can keep doing the same things over and over and it doesn't matter. I didn't lie to hurt you. It had nothing to do with you. I wanted to do something right by my sister for once in my life. I was doing my job."

A tender hand brushed her cheek. "Pepper..."

She looked at him.

One of his hands combed through her hair; she hadn't put it in a ponytail. She had let it air dry, the slight curls still visible. So very unlike her. She always wore it in a ponytail, straightening it before twisting it up tightly.

"I love your hair down. It's so soft and beautiful." He suddenly kissed her hard, his lips almost bruising. Then just as swiftly, his touch turned soft and light as a feather. "We stick together at all times. I'll do the talking." His lips hovered near hers, barely talking above a whisper.

"I'm the deputy, so I'll do the talking. Trust me."

"I care about you, Pepper." His lips brushed hers once again. "But I'm not sure I'll ever trust you again."

He stepped back, held eye contact for a brief second as if waiting for her to argue with the devastating bomb he dropped. But she wouldn't argue. She didn't deserve his trust. It hurt like hell, though, to hear the words come out of his mouth.

She averted his gaze, unable to handle the agony within his glimmering sea-green eyes.

"Well, you'll have to dig deep for a small amount of trust in this mission. Because I'm taking the lead."

Then she walked out of the room.

"WHAT ARE WE DOING, DANNY?" Logan asked as he ran a hand over his face. He had to stop doing that. It was such a bad habit. But life had been so stressful the past few months, he couldn't stop himself.

"What we need to do." Danny propped his leg over his knee as he sat in front of Logan's desk. "The Cheetahs gang has been causing too much trouble. Hell, all the trouble we've dealt with in the past few months has been because of them. It's time to take that organization down. We can start with Brett Nelson. It's a crazy plan that Pepper suggested, but it'll work."

"She's been lying the entire time." This time he swept a hand through his hair.

"She also found Stacy and saved her life. I can make some calls to see what kind of agent she is. Whether we can trust her. But based on working with her, I think she's good at her job. She's got this."

Logan eyed Danny, wondering when he had become such a softie. He was normally the softie around these parts. "Really?"

Danny shrugged. "What can I say? I like her. I got a good sense about her. I understand her not trusting the local law enforcement and coming here undercover. I haven't heard good things about the Cheetahs."

"I don't know, Danny." Logan jerked a hand in the direction of the door, shocked Seth had dragged Pepper out of the room and shocked he had let him. "And Seth...what about him? I think there's a lot going on between them, and I don't know if I like it. Seth has a terrible time dealing with his emotions. This is not going to end well."

"Seth is a big boy. He needs to learn to deal with his shit the proper way." Danny shrugged again. "You can't help who you fall in love with. You, of all people, should know that."

Yeah, he knew that. Falling for Aubrey had happened so swiftly, he didn't even see it coming. Now, he didn't know what he'd do if he ever lost her. He'd be lost himself.

Danny leaned forward. "She's FBI, Logan. I'm sure she's dealt with all kinds of dangerous situations. She's got this."

"Can we trust her?" Logan leaned forward as well, his brows puckering. "Can we honestly trust her, Danny? What happens when she comes face-to-face with Brett? This man killed her sister. She shouldn't be working this case at all. She could kill him."

"One less bad guy we have to lock up, and she'll face the consequences if she does. I don't think she will. I wanted to kill Wayne Barten so badly. I could've. He had a gun on you. I would've been in my right to shoot him dead. But I didn't.

Because I knew it wouldn't change anything. I see the same in her eyes. She won't do it."

"You and she are different. I don't hold that same belief."

"We're not that different." Danny chuckled. "Do you think I played everything by the book when Aubrey was missing? Hell, no. I did things I will never tell you because it's not something I'm proud of. I only wanted my sister back. Yet, it didn't matter what I did; I still didn't find her on my own. Sometimes we do crazy things when it involves people we care about. Is it right? No. Is it rational? No. It just is."

A grin inched up. "Now I want to know what you did. How much did you skirt the line?"

Danny chuckled. "Like I said, I will never tell you."

Logan slumped back into his chair. "I'm surprised you're on her side. I didn't expect that."

"I like to keep you on your toes."

Logan laughed with Danny. Then he frowned. "What are those two doing? If we're doing this, we should do it. And what about Stacy?"

"I'll call Deke and update him on the situation. For now, I'll have him stay by her side. Let's not move her. As far as everyone else goes, Pepper is still Deputy Wilson, not Chapman. Not even Charlotte should know. The less people know, the better."

Logan winced. "Charlotte will chew me a new one when she finds out."

"Yeah, well, it's better this way. Trust me on that."

"I trust you, Danny. We may not always get along, but I trust you."

Danny nodded. "Same."

The door to his office opened and Pepper walked in. Her

cheeks were red and her eyes were a mixture of pain and confusion. Logan felt the same way.

He couldn't believe he'd been duped. That he hadn't done his job correctly vetting the new deputy position. He'd just been so desperate to fill the position, fill the ache of his best friend leaving, he rushed through it all. He grabbed the first application, happy with a recommendation from an old friend because it had been easier. Of course, his old friend probably had done a favor for the FBI to make it all seem legitimate. If the FBI wanted someone in his department, they would've done whatever they needed to do to get it done.

When this was all over, he would have to address the Derek situation. He'd have to come to terms with the fact he lost his best friend—and that he'd have to find another new deputy.

But right now, he had a bad guy to catch, and he wasn't sure this was the best way to do it. Something was bound to go wrong. It didn't matter she was a trained FBI agent. He didn't like putting one of his people—because she was still a deputy—in harm's way.

"I need to go home and grab my uniform and do my hair." Pepper sounded like the old person he knew. Confident. Self-assured. Ready to get down to business. Yet, he saw a lingering fear in the deep depths of her eyes.

Would she be able to pull it off? Could she handle facing her sister's killer?

"Where's Seth?" he asked as he stood up. "I'm not sure I want him going with."

He didn't want Pepper to get hurt, but he didn't want to see his brother get hurt either. And he could. Seth had no background in law enforcement. Letting him tag along with Pepper's scheme was wrong, especially since he suspected

Seth cared about Pepper. Things always went sideways when the wrong emotions were involved.

"I'm right here," Seth said, walking into the room. He stood close to Pepper. His face also looked flushed. "And I'm going with."

Oh, yeah. His brother cared a lot about Pepper.

This plan was not going to work.

Not with Seth involved.

Danny stood up. "You and Seth go home so you can change. Then head to Mr. Barten's residence. We'll set up watch. You won't know we're there, but we'll be there." Danny looked at him. "Sound good, Logan? Let's do this."

No, it did not sound good.

But apparently, he was the only one who didn't like the plan.

"Yeah, okay. Let's do this."

———

PEPPER SMOOTHED the front of her uniform down. Not that it was out of place, nor even a wrinkle in sight. It just made her feel better. She didn't mind wearing the uniform—or working in this small town as a deputy. It had been a nice change of pace from the hustle and bustle of the city.

New York was full of life and vibrancy and many different characters. She had enjoyed it when she first moved there, working as a new recruit in the bureau. It was just part of her life.

But this town...

Experiencing a new way of life...

She liked it. She liked the peace and quiet. She liked the fresh open air and not being crowded as you walked down the street. It would be a little nicer if people actually liked her, but that was her fault. For not trying. For not being a little nicer herself. She just didn't know how to *people*.

Maybe she could learn, adapt.

What the hell was she thinking? As soon as she was finished with this case, she'd be on a plane back to New York. Back to her old life of grinding out case after case after case.

A knock sounded behind her. Turning around, she eyed Seth warily. He looked distraught.

"I was just...making sure you're okay. You were taking a while."

Or maybe it wasn't anger in his eyes, but passion. An intense burning passion that didn't make him feel good, but upset him that he had to feel that way.

He said so himself. He cared about her, but he would never trust her. Which meant he was mad at himself for even caring, for feeling an ounce of anything for her.

She would take what she could get. For one brief moment, her world had been bright and wonderful. She wanted to live in that moment over and over.

Because once this mission was completed, her life would be misery and despair once again, even more so because she had found love and lost it.

He took one step inside the room. "Pepper? You don't have to do this. I don't think you should."

"I can handle it. This is what I do for a living, Seth. I deal with bad guys."

"You looked lost there. Like you were in your own little world. Are you sure you can do this?"

Oh, she would do this or die trying. She would not let an evil monster like Brett Nelson win.

"I got this." Then she turned toward the mirror hanging on the wall and smoothed a hand across her hair. Not a strand was out of place. She had straightened it and pulled it back into the tight ponytail she had worn since the day she arrived in town.

She felt like herself once again.

"Let's go."

She brushed past Seth without waiting for a response. Donning her department-issued jacket, she stepped outside and headed for her patrol vehicle. She wasn't waiting around for Seth. He was either going to be one step behind her or left behind.

Especially since, if she didn't keep the momentum going, she might cave in and not go through with this crazy plan. What would happen when she was face-to-face with her sister's killer? She had frozen like a statue when she heard him confess. She didn't do a damn thing to stop him when he walked out of the apartment. That had been her chance. And she let it slip away. Would she do the same thing once again?

Seth jerked her out of her torrential thoughts when he opened the passenger side door at the same time she opened hers.

The drive to Mr. Barten's residence was silent.

What more could they say?

She could try apologizing again, but she didn't think Seth cared to hear it. How many times could she tell him she'd only been doing her job?

The tires made crunching sounds as she pulled into Mr. Barten's roughly plowed driveway. A twitch at the bay window curtain told her Mr. Barten knew he had company.

Before she could change her mind, she shut the car off and stepped outside. The wind whipped her face, but the only coldness that slapped her was the thought Seth would never forgive her. And she'd never forgive herself for hurting him as she had.

Mr. Barten cracked open his door and peeked out his head. She figured there had to be a weapon hiding behind the door. Honestly, at this point, she wasn't afraid of dying. Nothing could hurt worse than the broken heart she had.

"Good morning, Mr. Barten," she said briskly as she walked up the few porch steps, Seth right by her side.

"This is harassment. Git off my property." Mr. Barten looked at Seth and spit.

Seth didn't flinch, but his brows puckered. "I'm worried about Evan. Have you not heard from him at all?"

"That worthless piece of shit knows better than to call me."

Poor Evan. She had never met the guy, but she felt sorry for him. That he had to grow up with this despicable man as a father.

Her father might've had a problem gambling, losing money left and right, but he had never been cruel and hateful as this man in front of her.

"I never introduced myself the last time we were here. I'm Deputy Pepper Chapman."

"Don't care." Mr. Barten's eyes narrowed. "You got a warrant for something? If not, git off my property."

"I think we have a mutual friend—Brett Nelson." She paused, noting the way Mr. Barten's nostrils flared with recognition, but gave no other indication he knew the guy. "I'd like to talk to him."

"Don't know what you're talking about." Mr. Barten shifted behind the half-closed door and then the sound of a shotgun being pumped echoed between them. "I said to git off my property."

Oh, the man was threatening her. He definitely had a weapon behind the door.

Not good.

Agent O'Rourke had said he and Logan would have their back and she trusted him. She trusted both of them.

She rushed toward the door and pushed it open, grabbing him by the front of the shirt before he could even blink. She twisted the shotgun out of his hand and reached behind her, assuming Seth would have her back. And he did. He took the shotgun from her. Then she backed Mr. Barten up until he was flush against the wall with nowhere to go.

It all happened in a matter of seconds. Fluid and precise. Because she was damn good at her job.

"Let's get one thing straight, Mr. Barten." She grabbed his shirt tighter, her eyes displaying the barely repressed fury waiting to unleash. "Nobody threatens me with a gun. Especially an old, cranky asshole like you. Now, I said we had a mutual friend. I'd like to speak to him. Do you want to answer me differently this time?"

Mr. Barten looked just as pissed, but with a slight hesitation lingering in his eyes. Like he understood she meant business.

"Maybe I heard of him."

"And maybe you can tell him I'd like to talk to him....about my sister, Lillian. That's all you need to tell him." She smiled a sweet, innocent smile. Mr. Barten knew, however, there was nothing sweet behind it because she still had him pressed up against the wall in a firm grip.

"Yeah, maybe."

She leaned closer. "And Evan? Have you talked to your son lately?"

"Got nothing to say to that piece of shit."

It sounded like Mr. Barten told her no. But that wasn't

how he answered, which made her believe that he might not have talked to Evan, but he had seen him.

Was he still alive? What did the Cheetahs want with him?

She let go of Mr. Barten and took a step back. "Great chat. Don't make me come back and visit."

Then she turned around and walked out of the house without looking at Seth once. If she did, she might lose her composure.

Seth followed quickly behind her.

They said nothing to each other as she started the car and backed out of the driveway.

"Wow, that was…"

She glanced at Seth when he paused.

He met her quick gaze. "I've never seen anyone talk to Mr. Barten that way. Not even my brother."

She wasn't sure what to make of his comment. He didn't like how she acted or…he did?

Well, he was finally seeing the real her. All the nasty, coldhearted parts.

Because her sister Lillian had said many times she was nothing but a coldhearted bitch.

And maybe she wasn't wrong.

17

Seth grabbed a mug and poured the coffee to the rim. It was a good thing his back was to everyone in the break room because the shakes in his hand would've been very obvious.

He still couldn't get Pepper out of his mind and the way she had grabbed Mr. Barten and shoved him inside the house. So many things could've gone wrong. Mr. Barten could've gotten a better grip on his shotgun and shot her.

God, he hoped they didn't have to do something like that again. He couldn't bear to see her get hurt. Of course, he knew that's what she did for a living. She was an FBI agent. He had even worked with her around Lucky as a deputy.

But he had never seen her act that way. So forceful. So in control.

It had scared him. It had been the first eye-opener of the dangers she faced in law enforcement.

He turned around, wondering when the conversation would start. He and Pepper had returned to the sheriff's office fifteen minutes ago, and Danny and Logan had arrived shortly after. Now here they were all in one room, and it was oddly quiet.

Danny cleared his throat. "So, that went well."

Logan uncrossed his arms and started to raise his hand, as if he was going to run it down his face, and stopped. "It was unexpected, that's for sure." He leveled a hard glare at Pepper. "That was reckless. What were you thinking?"

She didn't cower at his brother's irate expression. "I was thinking that I had to make sure he relayed the proper information to Brett."

Logan obviously couldn't hold it back because he ran a hand down his face. "Well, I didn't like it. He could've shot you. He could've shot my brother."

"I think he knows where Evan is," Seth interjected, hoping to ease the tension starting to rise between Pepper and his brother.

"Did he say so?" Danny asked.

"No, but when I asked him if he had talked to Evan, his answer was worded in a way that said he hadn't exactly talked to him, but that he's seen him," Pepper replied. "I agree with Seth. He probably knows where Evan is. He's probably somewhere on his property, wherever Brett is holed up."

"Okay," Logan said, "so, when do we think Brett will make an appearance?"

Pepper shrugged. "He's not going to show up while I'm in this building. Unless he's super brazen."

"I agree with that assessment." Danny walked over to the coffeepot. "You need to go back on patrol. Do what you would normally do on any given day."

Seth set his mug down on the table in front of him. "But you can't be alone."

He'd ride with her if he had to. There was no way he'd allow Pepper to get hurt.

"And it'll look suspicious if someone follows you

around," Logan said with a groan. "This was a terrible plan. Because Danny is right. You should be doing what you normally do, which is patrol by yourself. But that's not safe with a dangerous guy like Brett that we've now sicced on you."

"I can handle it. I can protect myself."

"I'm sure your sister thought the same thing until she couldn't...dating a drug dealer," Logan said.

Seth took a step, tempted to round the table and hit his brother for saying something so harsh and brutal. "That was out of line, Logan. Even for you."

Logan looked at him, his gaze troubled. He nodded and brushed a hand down his face. "You're right. I apologize, Pepper. I shouldn't have said that."

"But it's true. Lillian always thought she could handle any situation, just like I do." She shrugged. "Maybe he...he gets the drop on me. I accept that. But I have to try."

What the hell was she saying? That she was okay dying?

Well, he wasn't okay with it.

"I won't let you get hurt." Seth rounded the table and grabbed her by the shoulders. "Do you hear me? He will not hurt you."

"How will you stop him? You can't be by my side twenty-four seven, Seth. And I can protect myself. You're not even a cop."

"I can and I will."

Her eyes bled with pain. "You don't even care about me."

He pulled her closer, his lips close to hers. "I said I cared. I just don't..."

"Trust me," she finished on a whisper. "If you don't trust me, you can't care. It doesn't work both ways."

She grabbed his arms and pushed him away. He didn't fight her. He let her step back and out of his reach.

Maybe she had a point. But he did care. He loved her. His heart raced when he thought about her. His stomach roiled with agony when he thought about losing her. His mind shattered into chaos when he thought he wouldn't be able to make more memories with her.

Oh, he cared.

But trust…

His heart wasn't sure it could handle another brutal blow to his trust. With anyone.

"Well, it wouldn't look completely odd if Seth was with her today. He's been with her quite often in the past week or so helping to find Evan," Danny said quietly, as if unsure he should break the silence.

"No." Logan sounded firm in his decision. "He hasn't been with her in the past few days searching."

"Yeah, but I went with her to Mr. Barten's house," Seth countered.

"No." Logan eyed him as if prepared to fight if it came down to it. "You're too emotional when it comes to Pepper. Things go wrong when you're not in the right frame of mind. And you're not a deputy."

He swore he'd never hit his brother again, but he was about to break that promise to himself.

"She's not driving around alone."

"She can drive with me. Or Bolt. Or Danny." Logan took a step forward, getting closer to him. "You don't have to like it, but you have to accept it. Go to work, Seth. You did your part today, and that's all you'll be doing."

Seth took a step toward him. "Do you want me to hit you again?"

"Sure." Logan cracked a smile. "Go ahead and hit me. I'll lock your ass up and then I won't have to worry about you getting hurt. I'm already worried about keeping Pepper safe.

I don't want to have to worry about you, too. Danny and I got this."

Seth looked at Danny, who shrugged, then he glanced at Pepper, who wouldn't make eye contact. Maybe he loved her, but she didn't seem to share the sentiment. Not when she couldn't even look him in the eye when all he was doing was trying to protect her.

"Fine." Seth grabbed his jacket slung across a chair. "I'll go to work." He stopped right in front of Logan, lowering his voice so Pepper couldn't hear. "And if she gets hurt, I'll never forgive you."

"I would never forgive myself."

Yeah, that sounded like his brother. Always wanting to be the hero and keep people safe, no matter the cost.

Damn. His emotions were too chaotic right now. He was tempted to hit his brother just because. He wanted to kiss Pepper breathless in case he never got the chance again. He wanted to leave town and wait for this all to fix itself without him around.

He was so damn lost and confused about how to feel, but his brother was right. Mistakes happened when you weren't in the right frame of mind.

He walked out of the room and didn't look back once.

———

"Don't hurt my brother."

Pepper looked away from the doorway that Seth stormed out of and looked at Logan. She hated the pain in his voice.

"It's the last thing I want to do." Although, she knew she had already hurt him by lying.

"Did something happen between you two?"

She might sympathize with Logan about not wanting to hurt Seth, but what happened between them was none of his damn business.

"Anything going on between Seth and me is just that. Between us."

Logan took a step closer. "He's my brother."

"And he's a big boy who can speak for himself. You want answers, ask him yourself. But I won't be discussing anything with you."

Not exactly the best way to apologize for her deceit, but she would not discuss her relationship with Seth—or lack thereof—with him.

"Unless there's anything else, I'm going to do my job."

Logan stared at her for a moment, his eyes betraying he wanted to continue arguing, yet he didn't say a word. Then he ran a hand down his face. "You can't drive by yourself."

"I can and I will. I'm used to working alone. I work better alone." She didn't make eye contact with him or Danny at that admission. It was embarrassing. It showed how little she got along with others. "And Brett isn't going to approach me with other people around."

"I don't like it," Logan said quietly, the distress clear in his voice.

"It is what it is," she replied with a shrug.

She wasn't afraid of dying. In her line of work, death could happen at any time. She had seen and dealt with a lot of cruel and evil people. It was just life. It was just her job. She accepted it for what it was. If she could make the world a safer place by arresting one bad guy at a time, then she was A-Okay with whatever consequences came along with that. Including getting hurt in the process.

She'd never been shot before, but she had taken a few

scrapes with a knife. She had the scar on her stomach and right thigh to prove it.

Danny cleared this throat. "I made some inquiries when you went home to change."

She nodded, not surprised. She didn't expect him or Sheriff Caldwell to take her word for it that she was FBI.

Danny looked at Logan after sharing a knowing look with her. "She's a good agent. She knows what she's doing. Bolt's aware of what's going on. We won't get Brett if we don't give her a chance to draw him out."

"I don't feel right about this, Danny." Logan sighed and ran another hand down his face. "But fine." Then he met her gaze with his eyes blazing with concern, worry, and determination. "You will call and check in every hour. If I don't hear from you, I'll assume there's a problem. Keep within town limits and don't isolate yourself too much. Danny, Bolt, and I will be keeping an eye on you."

She nodded again, okay with those terms. "And tonight?"

She was completely fine with going home alone and staying alone. But with as much fuss as the sheriff was putting up right now, she didn't think he'd allow that. Would he allow Seth to be there as her protector? Not that she needed one.

But he had been coming over every night since she arrived in town.

Would he tonight?

Maybe he wouldn't. He left upset. He didn't trust her. She had lied to him.

"Someone will have an eye on your house. If he makes a move, you will have backup." Logan said it with such ferocity, she didn't doubt he'd keep her safe.

He took his job as seriously as she took hers.

"And call and check in every hour tonight as well?"

Logan nodded. "Absolutely."

"Then I guess we're done here."

She waited for Logan or even Danny to say something else, and when they didn't, she left the room. Then the building.

As soon as she shut her car door, she let out a deep breath and forced herself to keep it together. She would not break down. Not here. Not at home. Not until she was done with this case and out of this small town.

But it was so hard to keep her emotions tucked in and out of sight. She wanted to burst into tears at how terrible everything had turned.

Seth knew the truth and would never trust her again. She always knew it was inevitable to keep the lie going and for something between them to work out. But deep in the back of her mind, she thought maybe she could've confessed at the right time in the right way where he would've understood.

The sheriff didn't appear to respect her anymore. Sure, she knew he knew she would get the job done. But she lied to him as well. She insinuated he couldn't be trusted and that hurt his pride and feelings. It hadn't been personal. She was only trying to keep herself safe until she could make an informed decision.

Oh, well.

It happened. Her cover was blown and the world around her hadn't fallen apart. Well, the case wasn't falling apart. Her personal life... That was pure hell.

Because for the first time, she had fallen in love.

And gotten her heart broken.

18

PEPPER PULLED into her driveway and parked the car. She stared at the tiny house she was renting, wondering how much longer she'd be staying there.

Night was falling and Brett would make his move soon. They'd arrest him for attempted murder against Stacy, and then interrogate him until he confessed to her sister's murder. She had no other brilliant plan other than that. Of course, they could charge him with her sister's murder based on her testimony—overhearing him confess. But to make the charges stick, she needed him to legally confess and write it down.

That was asking for a lot, especially from a man who didn't hesitate to shoot an innocent woman. And for what reason? Why had he shot Stacy?

Walking briskly to her front door, she unlocked it and swiftly made entry. Not because she was frightened and afraid someone would get the jump on her, but it was cold as shit outside.

She was used to cold weather. New York weather wasn't

something to laugh at, but Minnesota... New York didn't seem to hold a candle to this brutal coldness.

As she changed into a pair of sweatpants and a T-shirt, she wondered who was outside on watch first. Maybe the sheriff. He seemed overly concerned about her safety. She had called him every hour on the hour to check in as he ordered. It was never a very long phone call. She figured he didn't have much to say to her, and anything he probably wanted to say wouldn't be nice, and the sheriff was nice to a fault.

Well, it didn't matter who was outside watching her house. She felt confident in herself to not let Brett hurt her. She knew he was coming. Her sister probably never saw the attack coming. At least, she assumed so. It had been months since they talked. She didn't know anything about her or what she had been up to or how she'd been feeling.

And now she'd never have the chance. Because of one man.

Walking into the kitchen, she glanced at the clock before grabbing a glass from the cupboard. It was nearing the time Seth showed up with a snack and a handsome smile.

Would he still show up like usual?

Pouring some filtered water from the fridge into her glass, she tried to let all thoughts of Seth out of her mind and took a drink.

Thirty minutes went by and nothing. She didn't hear a sound from outside other than the howling wind. The cold swirling around said it might snow tonight. Her weather app also gave that prediction, and she wasn't looking forward to any kind of snow.

Walking around her house for the first ten minutes, filled with anxious energy, she finally decided to take a seat on the couch, but she didn't turn on the TV. She sat in silence, just waiting.

The waiting was bound to drive her insane.

Waiting for Brett to make an appearance.

Waiting to get out of this small town.

Waiting to find peace with losing her sister.

Waiting for the guilt to disappear.

Waiting for Seth to show.

It looked like she had a lot of waiting to do in every aspect of her life.

Grabbing her phone sitting beside her, she dialed the same number she'd been calling all day.

"How's it going?"

What a silly question. But maybe the sheriff meant it in a way to keep the conversation light and carefree. Because it was going like shit.

"Fine. Still waiting for him to show up."

She meant Brett, of course, as she said that, but part of her also meant Seth. It didn't appear he'd be visiting her like he usually did. Why was she surprised? She shouldn't be.

"Danny and Bolt will be taking turns watching your house for the night. I still want you to call me every hour."

"Okay."

She was tempted to ask why he wasn't taking a turn to watch her house. He had been so leery of the plan from the start. She figured he'd be the first one out there to set up watch.

"Pepper..." He let out a heavy breath but didn't say anything else.

"I'll be fine, Sheriff. No need to worry about me."

She assumed that's why he hesitated. The man worried too much.

"I'll worry until this guy is behind bars. But I just wanted to say..." He paused. "I wanted to apologize if I offended you earlier today. You have to be hurting losing your sister the way you did. I will do everything in my power to help you find the justice she deserves."

Wow.

After all her lies and deceiving this man and the people in this town, she couldn't believe what she was hearing. And this was why she knew right away she could trust him. She should've taken that gut instinct and told him right away why she was in town.

She didn't deserve his kindness.

"I appreciate it, Sheriff. I am sorry for lying to you."

"I know. Sometimes we have to do things that hurt but are necessary. I understand." He hesitated again. "I know you said it's not my business, but I have to say it again. Please don't hurt my brother. He's been through a lot, and I'm not sure he's in a good place to start any kind of relationship."

This time, she didn't take offense like she had the first time. She could hear the worry and pain in his voice. The last thing she wanted to do was hurt Seth.

"I'm sure pursuing any kind of relationship with me is the last thing Seth wants. You don't need to worry about me hurting him."

She could almost feel the sheriff running his hand down his face through the phone.

"It sounds like I need to talk to my brother and tell him not to hurt you."

A low chuckle slipped before she could stop herself. "I'll be fine. But thank you for your kind words."

"Of course." He cleared his throat. "Call me in an hour."

She agreed she would and hung up.

Then she went back to staring at her blank TV and listening to the deafening silence surrounding her.

A PAIR of warm hands circled his waist. Then a soft kiss touched his neck.

"That was nice of you, Logan."

He tossed his phone on the bed and grabbed Aubrey's hands. "I've had time to think about it and I realize I was a little harsh with her this morning." He twisted in her arms and kissed the top of her head. "I imagine I would do some pretty crazy things myself if Kat or Seth were hurt—or killed. I understand now. The Cheetahs are...a ruthless gang."

Aubrey shivered and rested her head against his chest. "She could get hurt after what she did today. You should be helping to keep her safe, too. I'll be...be fine."

Logan hugged her tightly, hating the fear that slipped out. Even if she wouldn't have let her terror show, he wouldn't have left her side for anything. She still didn't like it when the sun went down and he wasn't by her side. She liked to pretend and tell him she'd be okay, but he knew she wasn't ready.

So, yeah. It was up to Danny and Bolt to keep a watch on Pepper. And if—or when—something went down and Brett made a move, he'd worry about who'd stay with Aubrey while he took care of business. But for now, he wasn't leaving her side.

"You know I'm not leaving you. Not at night."

Her breath hitched as if she were holding back tears. "I hate that the dark still frightens me."

"It'll take time, honey. It's okay. I'm here and nothing can hurt you."

He didn't feel the same faith in that with Pepper, though.

He should've never agreed to this crazy plan.

SETH KEPT his eyes peeled as he pulled into Pepper's driveway. He didn't notice any cars in the vicinity. Not even a clue who was watching Pepper's house to keep her safe. He trusted his brother to do his job—so who was out there?

Well, at least, whoever it was who had the first watch was doing their job well and staying out of sight.

He wasn't even sure why he was here. He told himself over the course of the day to keep his distance. Nothing good would come from letting Pepper deeper inside his heart.

Too late.

She was already deep inside his soul. He loved her. He worried about her.

He also wasn't sure he could trust her.

What a dilemma. The same dilemma he dealt with all day. Did he keep his distance or not?

Slamming his car door shut, he knew he wouldn't be able to keep his distance, not while this madman was on the loose. Not until they found Evan and everything went back to normal. Then he could push her away and never look back.

Maybe.

He knocked on her door and wrapped his arms tight around his body. Damn, it was cold out.

The door opened a few seconds later.

Pepper looked tired, but oh, so beautiful. Her hair was

still in a ponytail, her makeup off. She offered a halfhearted smile before gesturing for him to enter.

She watched as he took off his jacket and hung it up, but she didn't make eye contact. "I didn't think you were going to show up."

"I didn't know if I would either."

He didn't miss the flash of hurt in her eyes, but he had to be honest. He expected honesty and trust from her; he needed to dish out the same.

"I can't say what will happen when this is all over, but until this guy is caught, I can't sit back and wait on the sidelines."

"Does your brother know you're here?" She finally looked him in the eyes.

He couldn't decipher what she was thinking. It's as if she had erected a wall after displaying that brief moment of emotion.

"No." He shrugged. "And it wouldn't matter. My brother has no control over me. If I want to be here, I'll be here."

She tilted her head. "And if I don't want you here?"

He flinched, unprepared to hear that. Yeah, he had walked away from her earlier as if upset. But not necessarily at her. At himself. For letting his emotions confuse him and lead him astray. He wanted to trust her. He truly did because he loved her. But a part of him didn't know if he could.

"Do you want me to leave?"

He hated asking. And as much as he didn't want to leave, if she said yes, he would.

No emotions could be deciphered in her gaze or written on her face. She had mastered keeping her expressions to herself. He hated it. He wanted to know what she was thinking.

"Yes, I do."

Wow.

He hadn't been expecting that.

It hurt.

It almost hurt more than finding out she lied to him. Because even though she had lied, he thought there had been something between them.

Apparently, that had been a lie, too.

It was only sex.

Pressing his lips together hard to hold back any kind of retort, he turned around and grabbed his jacket.

This was the last thing he expected when he decided to finally show up. He never thought she'd actually turn him away.

He turned back toward her with his jacket on. He had to hold back the anger in his tone, especially since she wasn't even looking at him.

"I wish I didn't care about you. This just makes it hurt worse. I thought..." He stopped speaking, mad at himself for confessing what he just had.

Well, he knew better now.

Flinging open the door, he stepped outside and slammed it shut. The brutal temperatures didn't penetrate as the pain from her rejection sliced him inside.

He couldn't wait for this entire debacle to be done with. He didn't want anything bad to happen to her, but he didn't want her in this town anymore. The sooner she left, the better.

19

Pepper walked inside the building and tried to offer a friendly smile, hoping to bridge the gap she had originally created with Charlotte.

No such luck.

The woman still hated her. Oh, boy, she hated her. Especially since she had broken Seth Caldwell's heart. That was beyond unforgivable.

But necessary.

She hadn't wanted to turn him away two days ago.

It had broken her to pieces to lie to him as she had—again. The last thing she had wanted was for him to leave, especially since she had been sitting in the dark in her living room, the TV off, waiting for him to come. And when he finally did, she acted like she didn't care one bit.

Of course, it was such a lie. She cared too much.

For his safety, he couldn't be there. What would've happened if Brett showed up while he was there and hurt him? She never would've been able to live with herself.

But Brett continued to shock them all.

Two days and nothing. Not a peep from the man who killed her sister.

Two days of living in pain and torture and not seeing Seth once. She couldn't wait to get out of this horrible town.

"Good morning, Charlotte." There. She'd force the woman to speak to her.

Although Mr. Barten hadn't shared with anyone that her real name was Pepper Chapman, the sheriff had decided to clue in Charlotte as well as his sister Kat and his fiancée Aubrey. They needed to know why they were on high alert with her safety.

Other than them, everybody else in town still knew her as Deputy Wilson. It was surprising her secret hadn't gotten out yet.

"You're late."

That was a lovely good morning returned. Pepper chuckled. Because she was only a minute late walking through the door. But for her, that was a rarity. She was never late. Not even by a minute.

Since Charlotte learned the truth, she couldn't decide if the woman hated her from her behavior when she first arrived, or because she worked for the FBI. It was a mystery.

"I'm sorry we got off on the wrong foot. I never meant to offend you or hurt you."

Pepper exhaled lightly, feeling a bit freer for finally apologizing. She should've done that two days ago.

Charlotte cocked her head to the side, her eyes narrowing. Then her brows smoothed out and her frown tilted upwards. Just a fraction.

"Apology accepted." Then a teasing glint entered her eyes. "You're still late."

Pepper smiled. "It was a trying morning with the hair dryer."

More like, her mind wandered to Seth and how much she hurt him, but that wasn't something she wanted to get into.

"Logan, Danny, and Deke are in the break room. You should probably be there."

Pepper nodded and walked away. She found all three near the coffeepot, fueling up for the day. She needed a cup, too. She could've used a Frappuccino, a vice she couldn't stop, but considering she knew Bolt had been watching her house all night long and had followed her to the station before heading home for some shut-eye, she didn't delay by making a stop at the gas station.

"Morning," she said brightly as she headed for the coffeepot herself. Logan said hello as he walked around the table with his mug. Danny smiled and moved to the side and Deke started to pour her a cup.

She smiled and nodded as he handed her a hot, steamy mug of coffee.

"So, we're having an impromptu meeting?" She blew on the black liquid before taking a sip.

Logan made eye contact with Danny and Deke before training his eyes on her. "It's been two days. I expected Brett to make a move by now."

"Honestly, so did I." She didn't understand why he hadn't yet. "Maybe he knows it's a trap. He's not an idiot."

"Well, we can't keep doing what we're doing. We need to start being proactive, not reactive." Danny took a large sip, then leaned against the counter.

"Thoughts?" She didn't think they had all been here long enough to enact a plan without her, but she could be wrong.

"Unfortunately, no. Nothing legal, anyway." Logan ran a hand down his face.

She didn't know what that meant. What illegal things was the sheriff thinking? Because she had an idea that he wouldn't like. It bordered on illegal.

"Mr. Barten knows where he is. He probably even knows where Evan is. He's the key," Deke said as he leaned against the counter right next to Danny.

"And he's not talking," Danny replied.

"Cranky old bastard," Logan muttered.

"I'm new in town," she said as if it wasn't obvious. Logan's brow rose. She forged on. "I sent out a bread crumb to Brett, and he didn't take the bait. My sister was murdered."

She hated saying that out loud. She hated even thinking about it. But the guilt—besides the pain from Seth—was eating her alive that she never made amends with her sister.

Logan set his mug on the table between them. "What are you getting at, Pepper?"

"I'm not usually one to sit idly around while I'm working a case. I don't make many friends in the agency. Most people don't like working with me because I don't stop to coddle people and their feelings."

"Sounds like Danny," Deke said with a chuckle, nudging Danny in the shoulder, who gave him an evil eye.

"Yeah, and this goofball evens me out. You don't have a partner? Not one person you work with?" Danny asked.

"No." Short and concise. There was no need to go into how she rubbed people wrong. All. The. Time.

But that wasn't the point she was trying to make.

"I don't break the law." She shrugged as her eyes turned down toward her coffee.

Logan cleared his throat. "Well, you better not."

She looked up. "I'm new in town."

His eyes narrowed. "You already said that."

Go broke or go home.

Her father loved to say that...usually right before he gambled away all their money.

"I could take a break at your cabin and maybe explore the area. And...let's say...I happen to accidentally enter Mr. Barten's land without realizing it and come across anything odd, then I do."

There. She said it. What she had been thinking about the last two days.

The best way to find Brett—and Evan—was to get access to Mr. Barten's land, which he would never provide, and they didn't have enough for a search warrant either. So, they'd have to do it without permission. Not the brightest idea, but it was the only way to find some answers.

She'd be more than willing to do it herself. She could always claim she had no idea she still wasn't on Caldwell's property.

"That's your idea. Accidentally enter his land and perhaps stumble upon something." Logan groaned as he ran a hand down his face. "Anything you found wouldn't hold up in court. You know that, right?"

"They don't need to know I was there. But wouldn't it be a good idea to know if Evan is alive?" At least it would give Seth a peace of mind. She knew how it felt to live with the guilt. She didn't want him to have to live with it, too. "While I want Brett to pay for killing my sister, Evan is our priority. It's been over a week since he disappeared with a gunshot wound."

"I think I liked it better when you lied to me, Deputy Chapman." Logan shook his head. "The answer is no."

PEPPER LOOKED up from her phone when a shadow fell across her. Her face brightened when Danny slid inside the booth across from her. Her lips fell a fraction when Kat slid in right after.

So much for a nice, quiet lunch.

Was she about to be ganged up on by two people instead of just Kat like last time?

She had enough of a beating this morning, going back and forth with the sheriff. He wouldn't budge from his stance on the matter.

She was not—under any circumstances—to enter Mr. Barten's land. She couldn't be sure, but she thought the sheriff might do something crazy like arrest her if she did. Stepping on his toes was the last thing she wanted to do.

But she wanted to do something. They couldn't keep sitting around waiting—like Danny said. They needed to be proactive, not reactive.

"Do you mind if we join you?" Danny asked as he grabbed two menus sitting behind the salt and pepper shakers near the window of the booth.

A little late to be asking, but she decided to nod her head. She liked Danny. Kat, on the other hand, not so much.

"Hello, Kat."

She might not like the woman, but Pepper liked her boyfriend and she could attempt to be cordial. It wouldn't kill her.

"Hi."

The one word was clipped and sounded forced. But, hey, it was better than being ignored. She let them study the menus in silence. Callie took their orders. Kat handed her menu back to Danny for him to put them back where he found them. Her eyes zoomed to her ring finger—on her left hand.

The shiny diamond twinkled merrily as the sun hit it perfectly. A princess-cut, sleek and small, but looked perfect on her dainty hand.

Kat must've felt her gaze because she pulled her hand toward her and dipped it under the table.

They stared at one another.

Would it be like this the entire time with her? The animosity? The hatred? The awkwardness?

Did it really matter? As soon as this case was done, she was leaving. Getting as far away from this town as she could.

"Congratulations." Pepper smiled briefly at Kat before turning her full attention to Danny, who had a beaming smile adorned across his face. "I had no idea."

He shrugged. "I bought it yesterday. Too many days too late. But thanks. We're excited."

He shifted in the booth as if he were grabbing one of Kat's hands. Kat suddenly smiled and looked at Danny with adoration and love.

Oh, to have that someday.

A lonesome sigh almost escaped.

She'd never have that. Dating was almost non-existent for her. When she did date, the men couldn't handle her hectic work schedule and her domineering attitude.

Seth had never seemed put off by her attitude.

But he didn't like her lying.

Wiping him from her mind—at least trying to—she widened her smile to hide the sudden ache that wanted to consume her.

"I'm very happy for you."

Kat slowly turned her way, her eyes narrowing. She didn't look like she was about to lay into her and decimate her into a thousand tiny pieces. She looked more thoughtful as if trying to decipher a puzzle that was giving her a headache.

"You sound sincere..." Kat let her words trail off as if the rest of her words were stolen.

Tracing around the bottom of her water glass, one shoulder tilted up slightly. "I like Danny. I am happy for him. He's been very nice to me since the moment we met." She met Kat's confused gaze. "I know you don't like me, but that doesn't mean I wish any ill will toward you."

"I..." Kat swallowed before finally displaying a kind smile in her direction. "I'm sorry. Danny told me about your sister. I'm sorry for your loss. It must've been hard. It still must be with her killer out there."

This was one reason she hated everyone knowing about her sister. The condolences. The constant reminder of her failures. Of her guilt that she'd never be able to assuage.

When she didn't respond—honestly too overwhelmed to find the right words—Kat continued. "We're having an impromptu party tonight to celebrate our engagement and that we're having a baby. Way too many days too late, but so much has been going on we didn't have a chance to tell people until now. Would you like to join us?"

A baby?

They were pregnant, too.

Join them?

Who was this woman, and where did the other vindictive, mean one go?

Her emotions that had been jumping and dancing moments before started to spiral out of control. Her stomach churned. Her throat clogged. Her hands circled around her glass started to tighten.

She couldn't lose it. Not here. Not in a diner filled with people who didn't even know the real her.

Swamping all those emotions deep inside to be unleashed later when she was home and alone, she smiled.

"Congratulations again. A baby. How exciting. You both must be over the moon."

Danny pulled Kat's hand up and kissed it, his smile wide and infectious. It made her smile brighten. An honest one. A real one. Not one she had to force out. His happiness made her hope and wish and ache for her own happiness where a man looked at her with such love and devotion.

Then Danny looked at her. "You're more than welcome to join us. It'll be at Logan's house. You can meet my sister Aubrey. Deke will be there. So will Bolt and Charlotte."

So, in other words, they needed her to come. Because if she didn't, then Bolt couldn't. Someone needed to have eyes on her at all times.

Had Kat's apology even been sincere? Was this a ploy to make it appear like they wanted to include her but in reality, they were forced to due to the circumstances?

Danny never mentioned Seth would be there. But she couldn't imagine Seth missing the celebration for his sister.

"Of course. I'll be there."

It was easier to accept than look like a bitch ruining the party by not allowing Bolt to show up.

Kat's eyes softened as if she knew what Pepper was thinking, but she didn't say anything.

Their food arrived shortly after, and the conversation shifted to small talk. When they were done eating, Kat excused herself to use the restroom. Pepper started to gather her things to leave.

"We honestly want you there," Danny said quietly. "I saw your expression when I mentioned Bolt. I like you, too, Pepper. You fit in around here. Even if it doesn't feel like it. Logan needs to be challenged at times. I'm not saying trespassing on Mr. Barten's land is the way to go, but it's better than any other idea we've had."

She stood up and slung on her jacket. "I appreciate your kindness, Danny. But I'll never fit in here. I've never fit in anywhere. Not even in my own family."

Then she walked away before she blurted out things she couldn't take back.

20

THE DOOR SLAMMED HARD, yet Seth didn't lose his stride as he made his way to the bathroom. He was running late.

Work had been crazy and hectic, more calls than he had anticipated. But most of the calls to fix things had been nothing more than a chance for people to gossip. News of Kat and Danny's engagement and pregnancy had spread like wildfire. Everyone wanted details. As her brother, they assumed he had them all.

He had nothing to give them but a bill and a good day's work.

Slinging off his shoes, dirt and snow dripping to the bathroom floor, he mentally chastised himself for not taking them off at the front door. Oh, well. He'd clean it up later. He didn't have much time to spare. The rest of his clothes joined his shoes on the floor.

Everyone, including his entire family and their few close friends, was meeting at Logan's at six to celebrate.

It was 5:50 pm. He was definitely going to be late.

But did it matter?

He knew *she* would be there.

What would he say? How would he react?

Two days had gone by and he still couldn't get the rejection and the pain to dissipate. The hot water rained down, soothing his sore muscles and relaxing him. He had worked himself to the bone for the past two days. Every time his mind conjured a flash of Pepper's face, it threatened to bring him down a rabbit hole he wasn't sure he'd escape. So, he picked up every possible job he could. He even worked late into the night in his own house, continuing to refinish his kitchen cabinets. He sanded until his hands ached, his arms felt like mud, and he couldn't keep his eyes open a moment longer. Then he fell into bed, dirty and sweaty until he woke up for another day of backbreaking work.

He should wash his bedsheets.

Stepping out of the shower, he dried off and decided he'd change his bedsheets before he left. Because what happened if he came home and forgot to and slid into a dirty bed. He didn't want that to happen.

Walking to his room naked, he grabbed a new pair of boxers, a pair of jeans, and a shirt, dressing quickly. Instead of glancing at the clock and how late he was going to be, he headed for the hall closet.

Grabbing clean sheets, he shucked the old sheets off his bed and proceeded to replace them. One corner of the bed gave him a hard time, but he finally managed to pull and stretch it until it fit comfortably over the edge.

There.

Much better.

Now, when he came home, he'd crawl into a nice, clean bed. There was nothing better than going to bed with smooth, clean sheets.

His eyes glided to the clock.

6:15.

He was officially late.

Right now, all he was doing was procrastinating. Delaying the inevitable.

His hair. He couldn't forget to do his hair.

Heading to the bathroom, he picked up his dirty clothes and threw them into the hamper, deposited his dirty boots near the front door, and washed his hands. He grabbed his comb and smoothed back his brown locks, then added a touch of gel to hold it in place. He finger-combed it several times before he was satisfied it looked perfect.

Once done, he entered the kitchen, his eyes gliding to the microwave clock.

6:25.

Shit. Now he was acting like a jackass. Why couldn't he ever man up and act like an adult? Face his problems like every other person.

But seeing Pepper...

He didn't know what he might say—or even do.

He wasn't even sure why he was so confused. She lied to him. To everyone. Sure, he understood the reasoning behind her lie. She was only doing her job to find her sister's killer. That didn't mean he had to like it. That didn't mean he trusted her.

Sighing, he slumped against the counter as he watched the microwave clock tick another number.

Or maybe he was finding an excuse to protect himself. When had he ever tried to let a woman completely in? Even with Stacy, he had kept it light, fun, and carefree. Maybe that's why they never worked because he didn't give it a chance to work.

But what did it matter with Pepper? She had effectively dismissed him from her life two days ago.

"Stop being a pansy, Seth."

Pep talk done, he straightened and headed for the front door. He'd apologize profusely and promise to give Danny and Kat an extra gift or two for their wedding and the baby.

Engaged and pregnant!

He still couldn't believe it. He knew an engagement would've come sooner rather than later, but the pregnancy had been a surprise. By the look in Kat's eyes when she stopped by his job site to tell him the news, she and Danny had been surprised as well. A good surprise.

Maybe this would help everyone move on and feel happy for once because there had been too many sad and depressing moments to last him a lifetime.

Putting on his favorite pair of sneakers, red and white pumps that comforted his feet no matter how many times he wore them, he grabbed his jacket.

He started to reach for the door handle when he stopped.

His keys.

What did he do with keys?

Pants pocket.

With long strides, he headed back to the bathroom to dig through his hamper. Boy, he was really going to be late now. Hopefully, he didn't get too much flack—and anger—from his family.

He found his keys and walked out of the bathroom. He took two steps before a loud bang sounded on his back door.

What the hell?

As he passed the hallway closet, he grabbed his broom and continued toward the backdoor centered in the kitchen.

Not much of a weapon, but it would have to do.

With night already descended and no light illuminating

the porch, he couldn't make out who stood on the other side of the door.

Another loud bang occurred.

But it didn't sound like a friendly knock.

Gripping the broom tighter, he exhaled slowly as he approached the door.

Suddenly, a face appeared in one of the glass panes.

The broom fell from his fingers.

Oh, he was definitely going to be more than fashionably late to the party.

PEPPER TRIED to stop glancing at the clock in the living room, but it was difficult, especially when it stared at her where she was sitting on the couch.

6:35.

Seth still hadn't arrived.

She had seen Logan on his phone, presumably calling him, but she wasn't brave enough to ask. Was he really not going to show up because of her? It seemed unimaginable. She wasn't that important. He couldn't care that much about her.

Unless she hurt his feelings when she asked him to leave two days ago.

"Would you like some more pop or something else to drink?"

Pepper glanced to her left as Aubrey took a seat next to her and shook her head. "No, thank you. This is fine."

She had accepted a small cup of pop when she first arrived, declining any alcohol. She had noticed Bolt did as well. Danny had a beer in one hand, as did Logan. It looked like when she left here, so would Bolt, his turn—again—to watch her throughout the night.

This was starting to get ridiculous. They couldn't keep this up. Maybe she should do some sleuthing on her own, regardless if it upset the sheriff. She was sick of waiting.

"It's nice to finally meet you. Do you like it in Lucky?" Aubrey asked, her hands rested in her lap, yet she kept twisting them.

Was Pepper making her nervous? She had also noticed how Aubrey kept frequently looking at the big bay window, which was covered by a curtain. But why did she keep looking in that direction? Was she worried about Seth? Should she be? Perhaps something happened to him on his way here. Was that why he hadn't arrived yet?

"Pepper?"

She flinched when Aubrey lightly touched her arm. Oh, her mind had wandered. More like, zoomed to disastrous territory.

"It's lovely to meet you, too. Lucky is a...nice town."

Well, that didn't sound convincing at all. Except she didn't know how to describe Lucky. It was small. People loved to gossip and get into your business. You couldn't hide from your problems unless you stayed tucked inside your own home. She had seen Seth a few times in passing. They never stopped to chat with each other. They didn't even smile. She was positive everyone noticed their behavior and animosity.

Maybe Lucky wasn't so nice after all.

She couldn't wait to escape and never return.

Of course, she'd be leaving her heart behind to a man who would never forgive her for lying. Well, maybe he would forgive, but he'd never forget.

"I'm sorry about your sister." Aubrey turned her head

away, staring at her lap. "Logan understands why you held information from him." Then she looked at her. "He's a good man. He worries too much about...a lot of things. I sense some tension. It's hard not to notice, considering you're in the living room and everyone else is more in the kitchen."

Pepper hadn't meant to distance herself from everyone. Nor did she want to be the cause of tension or Ms. Debbie Downer at the party.

She was just so exhausted. Not from the day itself, but in general. Every day she woke up hoping for a lead, hoping to put the past behind her. Hoping to find some peace to live out the rest of her life without the guilt and shame hanging over her head.

Every day, nothing changed.

If anything, it continued to get worse, especially with what happened between her and Seth.

"This is a great party. You're a wonderful hostess. I'm sorry if I'm bringing down the mood."

It *was* lovely. Aubrey, at least she assumed since it was her home, had hung up decorations. A mixture of bride-to-be paraphernalia and baby-on-the-way goodies displayed merrily. There was a cake sitting on the counter waiting to be devoured, coated with chocolate icing. Pepper hoped it was chocolate under the icing, too. She was a chocoholic when she allowed herself to indulge. A nice set of champagne glasses sat to the side with a bottle of champagne and sparkling grape juice. She assumed they'd share cheers and have a toast as soon as Seth arrived.

His late arrival was holding up the meal as well. The wonderful aroma of what she was told was beer roast filled the entire house. Her mouth watered every time a whiff of it hit her nostrils.

"You're not bringing down the mood. I want to make

sure you're enjoying yourself. I don't want you to think you're not welcome."

Technically, she wasn't. She had only been invited so Bolt could come. She knew this. Kat and Danny didn't come right out and say it, but she read between the lines.

"Thank you, Aubrey."

She'd leave it at that. Because hurting Aubrey's feelings was the last thing she wanted to do.

"Mmm, girl, that smells so delicious," Kat said as she plopped down in the recliner closer to her, yet looked at Aubrey as she did. "I'm starving."

"It's been in the crockpot all day. I'm sure the meat is tender and ready. Just waiting on Seth."

An awkward silence settled between the three as Aubrey's words floated around.

Because they all knew why he hadn't arrived yet— because of her.

"Where is he?" Kat fiddled with her phone. "I've texted him once and Logan called him. He's not answering. It's so annoying."

Aubrey glanced at her and offered a tiny smile. "I'm sure he's running late because he had to work late. I got out of school twenty minutes late today because everyone had to stop me to talk about *you*. You are the talk of the town."

Kat rolled her eyes. "It's ridiculous. It's not a big deal."

Aubrey squealed with delight. "Not a big deal? You're nuts, Kat. It's amazing. I'm going to be an aunt and a sister. I can't wait. I seriously can't believe you two kept this from us for as long as you did."

Kat chuckled. "It was, like, only a week that we kept it to ourselves."

"A week too long," Aubrey said in a teasing, whiny voice.

Aubrey and Kat laughed together and Pepper couldn't

hold back her laughter either. She enjoyed this friendly squabble they were having. She never had that with her sister. Neither Kat nor Aubrey had a sister, but they were soon to become sisters within a matter of months. She was jealous.

Like that, her mood dipped. How sad she never had moments like this with her sister.

"You know I don't like the attention, Aubrey. If that's the reason he's late, I understand, but he doesn't need to ignore my texts." By Kat's tone of voice, her mood had dipped right along with hers.

Pepper looked over at Kat and found her staring at her. She didn't know what to say, or even what expression to offer. So, she simply stared and waited. This was a prime example of why she never got along with others. She was socially awkward at times.

"Did people bug you about details today, too?" Kat finally asked with a small laugh.

Some of the tension dissipated at her attempt to lighten the mood.

Pepper produced a grin. "A few. I honestly had nothing juicy to report. Other than your ring is beyond gorgeous."

Aubrey grabbed her shoulder and squeezed, the excitement spread across her face. "Right. It's so gorgeous. I'm shocked, actually. Danny can be so clueless when it comes to women. He's so not the romantic type."

"He has his moments," Kat said with a crafty smile.

Charlotte suddenly appeared and sat down right next to her on the couch. "I couldn't handle the talk over by the men. They shifted to sports and..." Charlotte shook her head as her eyes sparkled with fury for a brief moment "And yeah."

Kat giggled. "That was so anti-climactic. And yeah?"

"What are we talking about over here?" Charlotte asked, completely ignoring Kat's attempt to dig out what was bothering her.

Pepper was curious, but not enough to come out and say anything like Kat had.

"How romantic Danny can be on occasion." Kat leaned closer toward Charlotte, her voice lowering. "Does your sudden demeanor mean Deke upset you?"

Charlotte flipped her hair behind her shoulder as she rolled her eyes. "Why would that man upset me? He's barely a blip on my radar."

"He's a good man, Charlotte," Aubrey said quietly, her cheeks turning a light shade of red.

Interesting. Pepper had never noticed anything brewing between Charlotte and Deke. Although, in all fairness, she tried to keep her distance from the woman since it appeared Charlotte hated her.

Right now, it felt like she was part of the group and friends with these women, the way they were all seated close together, whispering about the men.

It felt nice.

It felt like she belonged.

Like she fit in for once.

Of course, she was simply lying to herself if she believed it could ever be real. They were only being nice because they had to.

"I'm not talking about him." Charlotte pressed her lips together as if forcing herself not to say another word.

"It's called sexual tension." Kat snickered as she glanced from Charlotte to Deke, who stood in the kitchen between Danny and Logan.

"Ugh, knock it off, Kat." Charlotte swung her gaze to

Pepper, her brow rising sharply. "How's the sexual tension between you and Seth?"

Whoa!

Not cool.

Maybe they weren't pretending to like her. At least, not Charlotte.

Aubrey gasped. Kat cleared her throat. She could only stare at her like a deer in headlights.

Realizing she had tensed up, she relaxed her shoulders and grinned. "Gosh, if it were any of your damn business, I'd tell you. But it's not."

This was another reason she didn't have many friends. She couldn't hold back her words. She always said what came to mind. She was not a fan favorite in high school. Or college. Or the FBI academy.

Charlotte slumped against the cushion, exhaling a slow breath. "I'm sorry, Pepper. I shouldn't take my frustration out on you. That man just—" A strangled breath escaped as she closed her eyes.

"Just ties you up in knots and makes you question everything?" Pepper tentatively finished her sentence, wondering why she even uttered a word.

Except, that's how Seth made her feel. Every time she thought about him, her emotions went haywire and in a million different directions.

Charlotte's eyes slowly opened. The pain and heartache that reflected in her dark chocolate eyes probably mirrored her own. "You care about Seth, don't you?"

She wanted to glance away. She wanted to jump up off the couch and storm out of the house. She wanted to keep going until she was as far away from this town as she could possibly be.

Silence perforated the air. She could almost sense each woman holding their breath waiting for her answer.

Her emotions she tried like hell to keep in all the time. All day. Every day. Even when she was alone. They started to crack. Her bottom lip wobbled. She could feel the tears threatening to flow. How had this conversation centered on her? This party was supposed to be about Kat and Danny.

A lone tear broke free. She swiped it away before anyone could see.

All three women saw it anyway.

Aubrey touched her shoulder in comfort.

Charlotte's expression softened.

Even Kat sighed with understanding.

"I don't just care..." Her voice broke. "I love him. And he won't ever trust me because I lied."

21

Seth rushed to the door, unlocked it, and grabbed Evan around the shoulder, guiding him inside.

"Dude, we have...where have...are you...?" Seth couldn't even formulate the right words.

He never expected in a million years for Evan to knock on his door after being missing for an entire week.

Evan gripped his arm tightly as Seth helped him through the kitchen to the small dining room table. Evan slumped down on the chair, squeezing his arm before finally letting it go.

His hair was flying in different directions, dirty and greasy. Smudges of dirt coated his cheeks. He wore a white T-shirt that wasn't so white anymore. Near the shoulder, he assumed where he was shot, was dark red, as if his wound had opened and started bleeding. Traces of blood were on his pants as well. He had no jacket. He knew Evan had to be freezing because his body had felt like an icicle as he helped him inside.

Seth pulled out a chair and sat down, facing him.

"You look like you need to go to the hospital."

Evan lifted his head, almost as if it took a huge effort to do so. The pain in his eyes tore him up inside. The terror he saw as well increased his own.

Evan was afraid.

"I shouldn't have come here." Evan lowered his eyes. "Stacy's...dead. I shouldn't have come here. I'm sorry, Seth."

Seth touched his arm on his good shoulder's side. "She's alive, man. We found her in time. She's in the hospital. What happened? You need to tell me what's going on."

His gaze shot up when Seth mentioned Stacy. "You're sure? Because I saw him..." Evan's voice cracked. "I saw him shoot her. I'm such a coward. I ran." He choked back a sob. "I ran, Seth."

"She's safe. She told us the name of who shot her. There's a cop we trust sitting with her as we speak. We know what happened has to do with the Cheetahs. You have to tell me what's going on. Where have you been?"

"Trying to survive." Evan shivered. "I managed to get away. I didn't know where to go. So, I went where they probably didn't expect me to. On my dad's land. I've been holed up there at his cabin, but they showed up today. I couldn't stay at the cabin any longer."

"You need medical attention." His wound could be infected. He probably hadn't had much to eat or drink in the past week.

His friend had come this far. Seth couldn't lose him now. They needed to talk about their issues and make amends. Maybe even try to rekindle their friendship. Because in the past week, worrying and wondering about his friend gave him the clarity he finally needed.

What was in the past was in the past. Life was too short for him to hold a grudge.

"If they find me, they'll finish the job. I can't."

Seth sighed and ran a hand down his face. Just like his brother would've.

What would Logan do?

"Then I'll call Logan."

Because Seth had no idea what Logan would do and this kind of stuff was his specialty.

Evan shook his head. "I should've never come. I can't drag you and your family into this mess."

"Dude, my brother is the sheriff. He is the one person we need to call." Seth touched his good arm again, squeezing softly. "I'm glad you came here."

"Are you?"

Seth pulled his arm away and frowned, ashamed how he had been acting. "I can't imagine what you went through this past week, but I know what I went through. Lots of guilt for not meeting you for a drink. Hating myself for never making amends. You're my best friend, and I've been acting like a complete jackass to you. I'm sorry."

"I don't deserve your apology. I did lie to you, Seth. I didn't tell you about Wayne when you asked." Evan sighed, shifting in his seat, wincing as if it hurt to move. "I didn't tell you that these dudes approached me to run drugs through the garage. They said my brothers did it and so could I. That any son of Stanley Barten had no choice but to work for them. I didn't tell you how they threatened Stacy and the people I cared about if I didn't do what they said. I ignored them. I told them to get lost." Evan paused as he tried to compose himself. "And they were true to their word and killed Barry. It's all my fault."

"It's not your fault, man. They're dangerous people. This isn't on you."

Evan glanced around, trembling. Seth couldn't be sure it

was because he had more to say or his body was going into some sort of shock. He needed to get Evan to a hospital.

"I need to call Logan."

Seth wasn't even sure why he didn't stand up and grab his phone. Something he realized he still had in his pants pocket in the hamper. But for some reason, he wanted Evan's approval. He didn't want to fight with his friend anymore. Never again.

"I can't get it out of my mind. The way they hit Barry in the head and then dropped the car on him." Evan's eyes filled with tears. "I panicked. I didn't think you'd answer, so I didn't bother to call you. I called Stacy instead. Now I can't get the image out of my head of them shooting her, too. I struggled and fought with myself for almost a week about whether I should come here. The last thing I want to see is my best friend get hurt, too. I should—"

Seth gripped his arm. "That's what best friends are for." Evan gripped his arm back. "I acted like an ass, but I am your best friend. We'll solve this problem together. Clean slate. Right now. What happened in the past, stays there."

Evan nodded, his lips trembling, but their grip on each other didn't lessen. "I'm scared, man."

"Me, too."

"Okay, call your brother. I know we can trust him. I should've called him right away. I was just...my family...I was ashamed."

"They were never your family. We are. The Caldwells. We're your family."

Evan nodded again as a slow smile appeared.

Seth squeezed his arm one more time before letting go and standing up. "I have to grab my phone. I left it in my other pants pocket. I'm losing my mind tonight."

"Sounds like there's a story there." Evan's grin widened.

"You have no idea. It's quite a story."

And he couldn't wait to tell his best friend all about it. Maybe Evan could offer some advice on how to proceed with Pepper. Because when it came to his emotions and feelings, he didn't know how to respond properly. Take his best friend, for example. He was in trouble—deep trouble—and he didn't think he'd answer so he didn't call. Stacy almost died. He almost died. All because he had acted like a child over something he should've forgiven Evan for and moved on from months ago.

He grabbed his phone from the bathroom and met Evan back in the dining room. He was about to hit dial on his brother's number when a loud knock sounded on his front door this time.

Evan looked over his shoulder. "You expecting company?"

"No, everyone's at Logan's. We're celebrating Kat and Danny's engagement and they're expecting a baby." Seth shared a look with him. "Did they see you leave the cabin?"

"I didn't think so. I dove out the back door as soon as I heard the cars pull up in the front. I'm exhausted. It took forever to get to your house on foot."

Another knock sounded. This time a voice joined it.

"I know you're in there. Your car is in the driveway. Open this door before I open it for you. You're acting ridiculous."

A slow smile spread across his face as he shared another look with Evan.

Evan grinned. "That must be the story you need to tell me about."

Yep.

That was his story on the other side of the door.

For some reason, Pepper came looking for him.

SHE HAD no idea what she was doing. Winging it. For the first time in her life. She always had a plan. She would dissect it, look at it at every angle, think of every variable that could go wrong and then enacted it.

Not now.

Not in this moment.

She had almost completely broken down in front of people she shouldn't even let see a moment of weakness. But she had managed to control herself, hold back the dam of tears. Then, because she couldn't believe she confessed what she had to them, she stood up and fled the house.

She didn't stop to say goodbye. With her jacket in one hand and her purse in the other, she walked out.

Nobody—especially the women—had said a word. Yeah, it shocked her, too, what had come out of her mouth. Admitting she loved Seth in front of his sister and two other people very close to him had been the biggest mistake she could've ever made.

Her phone had vibrated as she drove away. It had been the sheriff. Maybe he even stepped outside to stop her, but she hadn't looked in her rearview mirror to see.

He didn't have to worry about her anymore. None of them did. Because she was going to get Brett on her own by trespassing on property she shouldn't, arrest him, and then ditch town.

She had to get out of this town as fast as she could.

But first, she needed to give Seth a piece of her mind. How dare he not show up to his sister's engagement party. Maybe he didn't want to see her, but that was no excuse to hurt his sister in such a way, and it made her look like the bad guy.

Banging on his door for the third time, she wondered how she'd get inside. She had never attempted to pick a lock before, but she figured she'd start with that before breaking a window or something. If he thought she'd leave peacefully and just let it go, the man was sorely mistaken.

She was about to knock for a fourth time—wondering where she'd find something to pick the lock—when it opened.

Seth grinned at her like she hadn't just been banging and hollering and causing a scene in his neighborhood. Although, one house about a block away didn't make it a *neighborhood*. His house was on the outskirts of town like hers, just the opposite side.

"Hi, Pepper."

Her eyes narrowed. "Hi, Pepper? That's what you're going to say to me after ditching your sister's party and making me look like the bad guy?"

Damn it. She hadn't meant for that to slip out, but she was pissed.

Pissed at him for not forgiving her.

Pissed at herself for lying to him and not telling him the truth before sleeping with him.

Pissed that she confessed she loved him to those three women before confessing to him.

Well, she didn't think she'd have the nerve to tell him she loved him. She wouldn't be able to survive the rejection.

His grin fell, and the agony she felt deep in her bones reflected in his translucent green eyes.

"I...was delaying my departure, but it's not the real reason I haven't shown up yet." He gestured for her to step inside. "Come see for yourself."

He made sure to give her a wide berth as she walked inside the house. Her eyes zoomed to the dining room sitting off to the side. She had sensed another person immediately.

Based on the few pictures she had seen of him, she knew it was Evan Barten. So many questions rattled to the forefront of her brain, but none came out. She was too shocked to do anything but stand there and stare.

He looked worn out and tired. Dirty from head to toe, blood spots lingering everywhere. He looked like he needed medical attention.

The door shut quietly behind her. Then a soft hand touched her back, urging her forward. His touch, even though she couldn't feel it through her thick coat, sent a rush of crackling energy zipping through her veins.

She walked fast enough so his hand would fall away. The last thing she needed was to be distracted by his touch.

"You're Evan Barten. We've been looking for you."

He swallowed, his Adam's apple bobbing, then nodded.

Seth cleared his throat as if that would clear the sudden tension filling the space. "Evan, this is Deputy Pepper Chapman. She replaced Derek."

She whipped her gaze to Seth. "Why haven't you called your brother?"

"I was about to." Then Seth's eyes narrowed into tiny slits. "Why are you by yourself? It's not safe."

"Oh, and you suddenly care."

Ugh. What was she doing? Left and right she was showing her vulnerability.

"Damn it, Pepper, I care. I said I cared," Seth replied with a frustrated groan as he dragged a hand through his damp hair.

"I forgot. You just don't trust me. It can't be both, though." Her phone started to ring once again.

She walked away from Seth before she continued to express all her turbulent feelings. Then she hit answer.

"Hello, Sheriff."

"Why'd you run off like that? It's not safe."

Wow. It was like déjà vu. First, Seth. Now, the sheriff.

"I am a big girl, Sheriff. I can handle myself. I left because..." She swallowed past a large lump in her throat. "Because I did."

She wasn't about to get into the real reasons she left with him. Because A, he was the sheriff and it wasn't his business. Because B, he was brothers with Seth. And because C, Seth was standing right behind her.

"Where are you? I don't care if you think you can handle everything by yourself. You're in my town, on my crew, and you'll do as I say."

Amazing. The sheriff had never laid into her like that before. Sure, he had gotten a little testy and aggravated, but never this forceful with his words.

"I'm at Seth's. You should join us. I'm sorry the party is about to be ruined. Evan showed up."

There was a moment of silence before Logan replied. She even sensed he ran a hand down his face. "I'll be right there. Make sure he doesn't leave."

Well, he might think she wasn't capable of protecting herself, but he had faith in her abilities to hold a man in custody.

She ended the call and slipped her phone back into her pocket. Turning around, Seth was still standing near Evan, and Evan had a worried look on his face.

"Sheriff Caldwell is on his way." She said it briskly and with an enraged tone.

Because she was pissed. That anger and fury she had driven here with had yet to dissipate.

Evan shivered. "Am I under arrest?"

Seth laid a hand on his shoulder. "No, dude."

"That's not necessarily true. He might be arrested."

Crossing his arms, Seth's brow rose as he met her gaze. "For what? He didn't do anything but try to stay alive."

"He fled a crime scene. Two of them." She tilted her head and curled her lips up. Not because she found anything amusing, but because she needed to keep her emotions in check. Commence fake-it-till-you-make-it. "He can share a jail cell with Stacy on obstruction charges."

"Wait, Stacy was arrested?" Evan asked, swiveling his attention back and forth between them.

"Don't mind her, Evan. She's like this with everyone. Hardass, know-it-all. When, really, she's just deflecting, hiding what she's really feeling."

She laughed, tempted to close the distance and slap him hard across the face. "I'm deflecting? From the man who doesn't own up to anything. You whine and posture and pretend you're the victim. When are you going to face your issues?"

"I was. I just talked it out with Evan. We're good."

Mock clapping, she rolled her eyes. "Good for you, big boy. Problems magically solved. Life can go back to normal for you."

But they could never go back to normal for her. She'd never get to make amends with her sister like Seth just had with Evan.

Seth uncrossed his arms, letting them drop to his sides. "Did something happen at the party?"

Besides the part where she nearly broke down in front of his family and friends. No, nothing happened.

She crossed her arms to mimic him. "See, deflecting."

Seth sighed, the fight in his eyes fading. "Maybe we

should table this argument for another time. Do you want to hear what Evan has to say about what happened?"

Shifting her attention from Seth to Evan, she produced the fiercest, sternest look she owned. "Talk. Now."

Evan sat up straighter.

And started to speak.

22

Seth opened the door for Logan, Danny, Bolt, and Deke, who had all come when Pepper told Logan the news about Evan showing up.

"She left." Seth walked away from the open door, running his hands through his hair and squeezing hard.

He had left the room for a moment—less than a minute—to grab a first aid kit for Evan because his shoulder had started to bleed, and she had left before he could stop her.

He didn't like the reasons floating around his head of why she left. What she planned to do.

They all circled the table, but no one took a seat. Logan was the first to speak.

"What do you mean, she left?"

"I mean, she left, Logan." How much clearer did he need to get? "Evan told her what he knew and then she up and left. Which is strange since she threatened to lock him up for obstruction."

Danny chuckled. "That woman doesn't pull any punches."

Logan directed his attention to Evan. "Tell us everything."

Evan glanced at each man before speaking. Seth listened closely again, even though it was his third time hearing the events that took place. His story matched, so he didn't believe Evan was lying. He shouldn't. This was his best friend. Sure, he lied to him in the past, but he was sort of starting to understand why he had. Shame and guilt could do so many things to a person. It's not as if Evan had wanted to lie.

Just like Pepper hadn't wanted to lie. She had been forced to because of her job. For her safety.

"So, they wanted you to run drugs through Lucky, you refused, they threatened the people you cared about and then they showed they meant business." Logan nodded as if understanding why Evan ran and was scared to come forward.

Logan sighed, his hand making a path down his face. "Did you mention where the cabin was located where you were hiding?"

Evan shook his head. "No, I just told these two that's where I'd been for the past week. I know my dad's one of them. I was surprised when I found it empty. I was surprised it took them that long to look for me there."

"That was a good spot. Hiding right under your enemy's nose," Deke said. "Pepper's been on edge. We all have been waiting for Brett to make a move. She's a go-getter, not someone who idly sits and waits for something to happen. She did her homework. She knows where that cabin is located."

"Yeah, which is what worries me." Logan slapped the table hard. "She went to that cabin alone. Why else would she leave?"

Seth groaned, hating to air his problems with everyone, but it wasn't like they didn't know the tension between him and Pepper. "She might've left...because of me. Maybe she went home."

"Did you argue?" Logan asked.

"We exchanged some heated words."

Evan chuckled.

Seth rolled his eyes and started to chuckle with him. "Okay, yes, we argued."

"How many men showed up at the cabin?" Logan asked Evan.

"I didn't stick around to look, Logan. I'm sorry. I heard the car pull up and I just ran out the back door."

"Okay, we divide and conquer. Seth, you go with Evan and Danny to the hospital." Logan made eye contact with Danny. "Don't leave Evan alone for a second because we have no idea where these guys are and what they might do. You stay by his side every second."

"Got it." Danny nodded.

Logan pointed to Deke. "Head to Pepper's house and see if she went home. If so, stay with her. Call me with an update." Then he looked at Bolt. "We'll drive out to Mr. Barten's cabin and see who we're dealing with. With Evan's accounts, I'd say we have enough probable cause to step on his property."

Each man nodded and agreed to Logan's instructions.

Seth did, too.

Mostly.

He wanted to be there for his friend. He honestly did.

But he also wanted to see Pepper. And say what? Hell, he had no idea, but he didn't like how she left without saying goodbye. He didn't like the arguing and tension between them. He didn't like how terrified he was at the thought of her getting hurt. He definitely didn't like the thought of her leaving him for good.

"STAY ALERT. We don't know how many are inside or what they might do." Logan said quietly, almost in a whisper, as he pulled in front of the cabin and put the vehicle in park. He wasn't even sure why he whispered. Fear. Concern. Gut instinct something was about to go wrong.

Although, maybe no one else was inside. Deke had called a few minutes ago informing him Pepper wasn't at home.

Oh, he knew where she was.

He parked right next to her vehicle. No other vehicles but theirs were sitting outside.

So, they all showed up out of the blue and then left right away. Maybe they had stopped to grab something. But what?

They exited the car and shut the doors quietly.

Before they could step up the few porch steps, the front door opened and Pepper walked outside.

"They're gone." Brisk and to the point. Just like always.

No apology. No remorse. No respect.

Maybe Logan would be better off with her gone and out of town, no matter how much it would hurt Seth to see her leave.

"This was unacceptable. You might be willing to put your life on the line like this, but this is my town. You don't do dumb shit like this without my say. Something could've gone wrong."

Logan normally held in his anger. He was the softie around these parts. Charlotte told him so all the time. The fear and worry kicking him in his gut made the harsh words spew out of him.

Pepper didn't even flinch.

"But nothing went wrong."

Logan held up his thumb and forefinger, his lips tight. "I'm this close to kicking you out of my town right now. I don't give a shit if you work for the FBI." Then he strode past her and stopped in the doorway and looked at Bolt. "Let's check the cabin out."

Bolt nodded and then offered a smile in her direction. "Pepper."

"Deputy Bolten."

Bolt frowned, then followed Logan inside.

They both took their time looking around while Pepper waited outside. Logan didn't even care. He was so pissed off it was better she kept her distance for the time being.

"Nothing suspicious, I see. No drugs hiding anywhere. Signs Evan was here. Dirty rags in the trash can, probably from his shoulder wound. There's also some blood on the floor by the door, probably from him, too," Bolt said.

"I agree. No signs that those men Evan heard pull up were even here. Mr. Barten is going to file harassment charges against the department for showing up on his land," Logan replied with a tired chuckle.

Bolt cleared his throat and glanced at the front door. "Did you notice anything odd about Pepper? She seemed... different."

"Where have you been, Bolt? That's how she always is." Logan gestured toward the door. "Let's get out of here. We'll regroup at the hospital. I want you stationed outside of Pepper's house. If she so much as opens the door for an ounce of fresh air, you call me."

"You got it, Sheriff."

At least one of his deputies wasn't going to ignore orders.

They found Pepper still on the porch steps. "I told you they were gone. I could've also told you I found nothing inside."

"Go home, Deputy Chapman. I don't want to see you until tomorrow morning—in my office." Because they were going to have a long chat.

He understood she wanted to find her sister's killer. But her reckless actions and her attitude tonight had crossed a line. She would be leaving his town tomorrow whether she liked it or not.

SETH STEPPED inside the sheriff's office and smiled at Charlotte, who was sitting behind her desk. He didn't feel like smiling, but why give anyone ammunition to question him how he was feeling. He'd just pretend everything was hunky-dory when his life was going down the drain.

Last night had been filled with emotions galore. He was ecstatic Evan was alive and well. Happy that they had bridged the gap between their friendship. Sure, they had some more things to work out. It might take a while to get their easy camaraderie back to the way it was, but Seth knew they would. But he had also felt empty and hurt. It felt like he had lost Pepper—for good—last night. Like she wasn't even willing to fight for them.

Of course, why would she? He told her point-blank he could never forgive her for lying. Which, in and of itself, was a lie.

He forgave Evan.

He could forgive her, too.

Because he loved her, and losing her would be like losing a part of himself.

Charlotte stood up with a gentle smile. "You know you can't fool me, right?"

His smile turned upside. Yeah, he knew. Why pretend?

"How's Evan?"

"He's good." He managed to produce a small grin. "He looked good this morning. Thankfully, no serious infection developed from his gunshot wound. It was a through and through, so he was lucky. Both he and Stacy were very lucky."

Thank God for that.

"She's speaking with Logan right now." Charlotte's expression softened as if she were getting ready to coddle him as his mother used to when he had a terrible nightmare.

"Okay. I didn't ask about Pepper."

"You didn't have to. You deserve a good woman, Seth." She sighed. "I'm not sure Pepper is that woman. That's all I'm going to say."

Good thing, too. Seth wasn't in the mood to act like a petulant child and hurt Charlotte's feelings. But that's exactly what he wanted to do. He was trying to change. Be a better man. No time like the present to work on it.

"Have a good day, Charlotte."

"You, too."

He walked slowly down the corridor toward his brother's office. The door was open and their voices were filtering out. He stepped to the side instead of making his presence known.

"Your behavior last night was unacceptable. I can't have someone like that in my department." His brother paused. "I spoke to your boss this morning. You need to pack your stuff and leave. Today."

Seth inhaled hard, his fists clenching.

No.

What was Logan doing?

How would he make amends with Pepper if she was forced to leave?

Damn it, and Charlotte knew what was happening as they spoke.

"That's it? You're making me leave because I was doing my job."

"You were reckless and put yourself in needless danger. I know you want to find your sister's killer, but not this way. You should've waited for us to arrive."

"And my sister's killer? What about him?"

"We'll find him. I promise."

"Excuse me if I don't have faith in your promise." Seth heard a chair scrape as if she had stood up. "Go to hell, Sheriff. And screw your little town."

What was she doing?

Seth flinched when she walked out of the office and she stopped, turning to him.

The first thing he noticed was the coldness in her eyes. Nothing, no emotion glimmered back.

"Don't leave, Pepper. Not like this. I'll talk to Logan. We need to talk. We can work this out. Me and you."

Damn, he sounded like a pansy. That came out more pleading than he cared to admit.

Instead of giving him one of her smiles he adored, she laughed. Almost like a cackle.

"Me and you? Oh, Seth," she reached out and patted his cheek mockingly. "You're nothing more than a sad, little child. Don't kid yourself. I won't even think of you when I leave."

Who was this woman?

This wasn't the Pepper he knew and fell in love with. Had it all really been a lie between them? Had anything that occurred—especially that night of making love—really been just sex? A way for her to scratch an itch?

He didn't think his heart could hurt worse than when he found out she lied. He was wrong. It suddenly shattered into a million tiny pieces.

Every beautiful thing he thought he loved about her, made him sick to his stomach. Her blonde hair swept up in her tight ponytail; he wanted to cut it off. Her golden hazel eyes that always sparkled with defiance and an air of laughter now displayed nothing but a cruel, heartless woman. He wanted to erase that memory from his mind. Her sweet lips that could curl into a range of different expressions, some telling him what she was thinking and others making him wish he could decipher what was going on in her mind, now looked at him with a coldhearted sneer. The tiny mole close to her lips...

He didn't remember her having a tiny mole on her face. More like a faint freckle. Maybe the sun had brought it out this morning. Although it was cold as shit outside, he didn't know why she'd be standing in the morning sun.

He didn't know anything about her. How mean and hateful she could be.

"Enjoy your life, Pepper."

She produced a wide smile. "Oh, I will."

Then she turned and headed down the hallway. Bolt passed her.

"Pepper."

He waited for her to make her immediate response of,

"Bolt." It was how those two always greeted each other. Except, she ignored him. She said nothing as she kept walking away until she was completely out of his line of sight.

Like that, she was out of his life.

"You okay, Seth?" Bolt asked quietly as if loud words might set him off.

Honestly, he felt numb. Heartbroken didn't even begin to describe how he felt.

"I'm good."

And he would be. He'd survive this like he survived everything. She might've stolen a few moments in his life, but he wouldn't let her steal any more from it.

He would never think of Pepper Chapman again, just as she said to him.

"Pepper seems off. There's something wrong with her."

Of course, it might be hard to forget her if people insisted on talking about her.

"She decided to show the real her. Nothing more than that, Bolt."

Then he stepped inside Logan's office. Bolt followed him.

Logan winced, probably waiting for him to blow up for making Pepper leave.

"You had to do it. I understand." He didn't. He didn't understand anything that just happened.

Logan stood up and rounded his desk. "I'm sorry, Seth. She'll be safer away from here. We'll find Brett. We'll find her sister's killer."

"I still think something's off about her. She's not acting right," Bolt repeated as if that would change anything.

Nothing would change what she said to him.

A hand ran down Logan's face. "I have to admit, I

dismissed it last night when you said something, but she did seem...different...today. The stress is obviously getting to her. It's just you and me for right now, Bolt, until I can find another deputy."

Maybe that was it. Maybe she was still deflecting her feelings. The thought of her sister's killer still out there, able to hurt others.

Or maybe he was an idiot trying to make excuses when she didn't care about him.

"It's going to bug me. I'm telling you, something isn't right," Bolt said again, this time with a little more force. More determination in his voice. "We always say hi in the way we say hi. I say, 'Pepper.' She says, 'Bolt.' It's our thing. Last night she called me Deputy Bolten. This morning, she completely ignored me."

Logan shrugged. "She needs an attitude adjustment, Bolt. What more can I say?" Then Logan frowned. "But you're right, her attitude isn't usually that bad. She was downright evil this morning. Like she couldn't care less that I asked her to leave."

Evil.

That was a good word to describe how she decimated his feelings right outside the door.

Maybe she was hurting so badly, she thought she had to push everyone away. Being a Grade A class bitch would do the job.

No. Seth couldn't let her leave like that.

"I'll try talking to her again."

"What good will that do, Seth?" Logan's expression softened in that brotherly way he did when he knew Seth was hurting. "I heard what she said to you out there. I'm sorry."

"It's not just her not greeting me normal. She looked different today. Last night it was hard to see her face in the dark because she never stepped inside the cabin with us, but in the hallway, she didn't look like herself," Bolt said as if he and Logan weren't talking about something else. Bolt was seriously stuck on his own issue he was trying to solve in his head.

"What are you getting at, Bolt?" Seth asked, exasperated. If he wanted to talk to Pepper, he'd have to hurry. He wouldn't put it past her to pack up quickly and ditch town right away.

Bolt hesitated as they shared a look, then Bolt directed his attention to Logan. "We all looked at those crime scene photos of her sister. They're twins, but they look darn near the same. Except her sister has a mole near her lip."

Shit.

Pepper did today, too.

"She's about to do something stupid, Logan."

No wonder she was pushing everyone away and didn't care Logan was kicking her out of town. She didn't want anyone to stop her.

Logan groaned. "Are you suggesting she's trying to look like her sister? Why?"

"To draw Brett out somehow. I guarantee it."

And she was going to get herself killed in the process.

23

HER HEAD POUNDED.

That was the first thing that registered.

Pepper shivered. Then her body convulsed into trembles, the hair on her arms and legs pebbling from the coldness.

She was half-naked. If she had to guess, she was only wearing her bra and panties.

That was the second thing she registered.

Afraid to open her eyes, but knowing she needed to assess the situation, she dug deep for the strength.

Her eyes opened slowly.

Nothing but pitch-black darkness stared back.

That was the third thing to register.

And her situation was not looking good.

Sitting up a bit more, as she had been slumped, a loud groan escaped as her body screamed with pain. Her hands were tied behind her back. Just the slightest movement set off a wave of pain.

How long had she been out? How long had she been

sitting slumped over, putting awkward pressure on her arms?

Better question, where had they taken her?

Her mind was fuzzy. The pain was overbearing.

She sat, focusing on her breathing, letting everything—every worry and concern—filter out until she felt more centered.

Her arms still ached from being pulled behind her back. Her hands were tied tightly together. The slightest twitch of a finger hurt. The coldness that snaked across her body made the shivers continuously attack her.

But her mind was coming back. Her focus returned.

She remembered listening to Evan's accounts of everything that happened. How it took a few hours to run from his father's cabin to Seth's house. Hours they lost getting Brett into custody. Her only thought at that moment had been to get as far away from Seth as she could and to arrest the man that killed her sister.

So, she left.

Even as she drove away, she knew it had been a terrible idea. She knew the sheriff would be upset. She had done it anyway.

She had cut her lights out as she got closer to the cabin. Giving her position was a rookie mistake. Except, no other cars had been there. The lights in the cabin itself had been out.

They had officially lost their window of opportunity to nab Brett.

She remembered getting out of her car and approaching the cabin. The door had been unlocked when she turned the knob. The moment she had stepped inside, it was like she had been looking in a mirror.

And then someone knocked her over the head.

Lights out.

Her lips wobbled as she fought back tears. She refused to cry. Crying would not solve her dilemma or get her out of this situation.

The situation was dire. Pitch-black, half naked, tied up. Yeah, she was in a world of trouble.

But she had to push through her fear and focus. Use her brain and think of a solution.

Because she would not let her sister win.

Maybe she was losing her mind. The longer she sat in the dark, the more her mind circled the fact she swore her sister had stood right in front of her before she was knocked out.

It was impossible.

She saw the pictures herself.

A terrifying shiver coated her body, making her violently shake to the point she started to tip to the side. Screaming from the pain in her wrists and shoulders, she ignored it and sat back up.

She had to focus.

She might've seen the crime scene photos, but she had never physically looked upon her sister's body. By the time she was notified of her death, an identification had been completed based on her fingerprints.

It was farfetched. It would've taken a few people from the inside to complete, but she was positive her sister had faked her death.

Why?

What was her endgame?

And how in the hell was Pepper going to stop her?

She flinched when a door suddenly opened and a low light flooded the room.

The man she had been searching tirelessly for stood

with a small kerosene lamp and a smile that set her further on edge.

"You're awake finally."

"Where is she?" Pepper wasn't about to mess around. She wanted to speak to her sister. She needed answers.

Brett walked farther into the room, stepping around a box. Pepper took quick stock of the room as he came closer.

The room was tiny. The walls looked to be made of dirt. She fiddled her fingers slowly behind her, surprised she didn't register that before. Of course, she couldn't stop shivering and shaking from the cold that surrounded her. Her body was probably half numb. It took too much energy just to touch the wall as she had to confirm it was dirt.

Where was she?

Boxes lined both sides of the wall, except the one she sat against. She assumed nothing was in the boxes that would help her escape because otherwise, Brett wouldn't have left her in here. And he wasn't a dumb man.

He set the lamp by her leg, his eyes trailing up her body slowly as he crouched near.

Another wave of trembles attacked her, but this time not from the cold. From the disgusting desire that lit up his gaze.

"It's amazing how much you look like her. Face, hair, slender frame." He bit his lip as a crafty smile emerged. "Soft skin."

She forced herself to remain aloof as if his words didn't affect her. She would not let them win and break her this way.

"Where is she?"

He chuckled. "Doing her job." More laughter escaped. "Well, *your* job right now."

"What?"

She couldn't stop herself. She flinched when he leaned even closer, his mouth precariously close to hers.

"Haven't you noticed you lost a few clothes last night? Your sister needed to make it look real."

Last night? Oh, no. Way too many hours had passed. She had been knocked out way too long, which would account why her head still pounded like the devil was knocking on her door.

"She's one coldhearted woman. It wasn't even my idea."

Pepper frowned. "You've lost me. I just want to talk to my sister."

He backed away and stood up. "She won't be coming. She's busy being you right now."

No.

She wouldn't.

They might've never fully connected like sisters do—especially twin sisters—but she wouldn't hurt her like this.

"Like I said, it was all her idea."

"To fake her death? Why?"

Brett laughed as he picked the lamp back up and walked toward the door. "Expanding the business, baby. And with a gorgeous FBI agent like yourself in our pocket, we can do a lot."

Over her dead body.

"I'll never help you."

He laughed again, a loud chortled laugh that echoed against the walls. "You misunderstood me. We don't need you. I have Lillian who is going to be you." He cleared his throat. "We'll be leaving town soon. We'll let this little fiasco that happened settle down and then come back. Evan isn't worth my time right now. We might be a while. I'll check on you then. See how you're doing."

She was too shocked to respond. His words made sense, yet she couldn't fully process what he had said.

Her sister planned to kill her to take her identity.

For a drug business.

He started to close the door. "Oh, and by a while, I mean a few months." Then he winked and closed the door.

The room plunged into darkness.

"Wait!"

The darkness started to swallow her whole.

She was such an idiot. Why had she left's Seth's house by herself?

The door opened again. Brett's evil sneer reflecting in the low lamp made her insides churn with a terror she had never known.

"I'll grant you this one-time scream. But just know, nobody can hear you where you are. Nobody will find you. It's over, Pepper. Just accept it."

"They won't believe her. They'll see it's not me."

She had to cling to that hope.

Because he was right. It was over if no one saw the truth.

"Oh, they have no clue. The sheriff already dismissed her and told her to get out of town for your actions last night." That same cruel, evil smile still burned brightly in the cold, dark room. "And your boyfriend told you to have a nice life. Like I said, it's over."

He started to swing the door closed again, then stopped and set the lamp on a box. "There. I can be nice on occasion."

Then the door closed. A loud click sounded right after.

She was officially locked inside with her hands tied behind her back with no clothes, freezing to death.

But at least she had light. She was grateful for that small favor.

"OKAY, let's think about this rationally," Logan said as he sat against the edge of his desk. "Brett hasn't made a move since she tried to lure him out. What would dressing like her sister accomplish? And why hasn't he made a move?"

Seth blew out a breath. "Maybe she's going back to Mr. Barten's to..." He shrugged, having no idea where he was going with his train of thought. "I don't know. I don't know what to think right now."

"Knock, knock."

All three of them glanced toward the door. Danny entered the office glancing back at all three of them, confused.

"What did I miss? You all look really intense right now."

"Pepper's acting weird. She's sporting a new mole on her face, too," Seth replied.

What was she doing? She had to know they would find her sister's killer.

Her spiteful words and the cruelty in her eyes couldn't be forgotten. He didn't know what to think anymore.

"Okay..." Danny cocked a brow. "I'm not following."

"I thought you were still at the hospital with Evan." Logan stood up.

"I was until they decided to release Stacy this morning. I thought you might be throwing those obstruction charges out..." Danny shrugged. "If so, she needs someone still to protect her. She went to visit Evan. Deke and I figured we didn't need two agents with them if they're in the same room. I thought I'd come here to see what the game plan was."

"We need to call Pepper back here. Or whoever she is,"

Bolt said. The expression on his face said he was about to commit murder.

Seth wasn't sure where his intense anger was coming from. He looked like a volcano ready to explode.

"What?" Danny asked, more confused than before. "What are you talking about?"

Seth was confused by the last comment, too. "Bolt, she's acting weird. She wasn't too pleasant when she left. Do you really think she's going to come back here?"

"Someone explain what's going on," Danny said, using the voice he always used when he was trying to exert his authority.

"Pepper's attitude has been..." Logan ran a hand down his face. "I don't know. We'll talk about Stacy later, but right now, we need to figure out what's going on with Pepper. She acted downright malevolent this morning, especially with Seth. It also looked like she had a mole near her lip. Like her sister. We think she's trying to pretend to be her for some reason, but the reason has us baffled."

"Well, she went to that cabin last night alone, probably wired with too much rage and pain to think clearly." Danny shook his head. "She's still not in a good place. Bolt's right. You need to call her back here."

"I don't think that's Pepper." Bolt's tone was laced with an underlying rage Seth had never heard from him before. Why was he so upset? At them? At her?

But Seth's gut suddenly churned with unease. Especially with how determined Bolt sounded.

"What are you saying, Bolt? It has to be Pepper." Seth didn't like how Bolt's eyes flashed with a moment of terror before the rage reappeared.

"I know I haven't known her for long. None of us do. She's only been here a little over a week. But my gut says that woman is not Pepper." Bolt thrust his attention directly at Logan, taking a step toward him. "You always tell me to trust my gut. My gut says that woman isn't Pepper."

"If it's not Pepper, then the only other person it could be is her sister." Logan rubbed his chin. "And her sister was murdered."

"Is she a triplet?" Danny asked.

It didn't sound like he was joking with that question. Seth knew Pepper had lied about being an FBI agent and coming here under a ruse in the beginning, but he didn't believe she had lied about anything else.

"I don't know, but she's not Pepper," Bolt said with a tight lip.

"If she's not Pepper, then where is Pepper?" Seth hated voicing it. They kept circling 'round and 'round about the fact this woman might not be who she said she was, but nothing about where the real Pepper might be.

Oh, God.

His gut exploded with pain. As if someone had come out of nowhere and stabbed him in the stomach, repeatedly. Over and over.

If Bolt was right...that woman wasn't Pepper.

Which meant Pepper was in trouble.

Logan cleared his throat. "We're getting ahead of ourselves. Let me call her back here. Let's find out for sure, and then we'll go from there."

Logan pulled his phone out. Seth couldn't stand still. He needed to get some of the anxious energy flowing through his veins out. He walked out of the office as Logan told—whoever that woman was—she needed to come back and sign some papers before she left. Hopefully, that dumb excuse would work to get her to come back right away. If not, Seth would go to her and get the answers they needed.

If she wasn't Pepper, then they needed to start looking for the real one.

Where could she be?

Was she already dead?

None of this made sense.

Heading to the break room, he poured a cup of coffee and downed the contents quickly. His tongue burned and ached from rushing. His throat even tingled with the aftereffects of the hot liquid sliding down so fast.

He didn't care.

He deserved the pain.

He should've never let her leave last night. He never should've left the room, except Evan had been bleeding. Of course, how was he supposed to know she'd go off half-cocked and approach the cabin on her own?

That's when Bolt first noticed the difference in her. That's when whatever happened to her had to have gone down. It all had to have happened so quickly, too. His brother and Bolt had left his house shortly after she had.

He poured another cup of coffee, but instead of drinking it, he stared, his eyes zoning out.

A hand touched his shoulder, making him flinch and the coffee to slosh over the rim. He barely felt the pain from the hot liquid.

Turning his gaze up, he met his brother's worried eyes. "You okay?"

"I hate that question." He looked away and shook his head. "I haven't been okay for a while, Logan. You know it. I know it. If something happened to her...if she's...if she's dead, I don't think I'll ever be okay."

Logan squeezed his shoulder. "She's not dead."

"You don't know that."

"I know thinking the worst isn't going to help you. It's

not going to solve the situation." Logan grasped his shoulder in another comforting touch, then removed his hand. "She says she's on her way back. I guess she believed my story that she had a few papers to sign terminating her position as a deputy."

Logan took the cup out of his hand and set it down. Probably a good thing because it would've fallen out of his hand and crashed to the floor. His hand was shaking. His entire body was trembling. He felt like he was on the verge of a meltdown. Just completely losing it—the will to function, the will to speak, the will to even take another breath.

He couldn't lose her.

He barely had her to begin with.

"Come on. Let's wait in my office."

Logan guided him out of the break room. His light touch helped ground him back to reality. Logan was strong all the time. He had to be for Aubrey, who suffered nightmares and sudden setbacks all the time in her recovery. If his brother could be strong day in and day out for the woman he loved, so could he.

Steeling his spine, he let out a slow breath and finished the rest of the walk with determination in each step.

They all waited in his office. Logan sat at his desk as if nothing was wrong. Seth couldn't sit, so he paced back and forth. Danny and Bolt stood to the side so she wouldn't see them as she walked down the corridor toward the office.

It took her thirty minutes to arrive. What had taken her so long?

She noticed him about five feet from the open door. Her expression gave nothing away about what she was thinking. Nothing but emptiness stared back.

As if she had no soul.

Bolt was definitely right.

This wasn't Pepper. This wasn't the woman he loved.

She didn't notice Danny and Bolt until she was halfway to Logan's desk. She hesitated in her steps but kept moving forward when Danny edged his way toward the exit.

"I'm here. Where are the papers?"

Logan offered a smile and gestured at one of the chairs in front of his desk. "Please have a seat. There's a few of them."

She glanced around, then sat. "Why the audience?"

"Oh, we're waiting for Deke to get here." Logan widened his smile. "Does it bother you? Not being a part of the investigation anymore."

"I work for the FBI. I can handle the investigation on my own." A slow smile crept up her face, filled with malice. "So, no, it doesn't bother me."

The more Seth heard her speak, the more his gut screamed this wasn't Pepper. Thank goodness Bolt had been so tenacious to keep speaking about it. How come his gut hadn't screamed at him right away?

Of course, it gave a tiny burp. He noticed the odd mole on her face. But he had brushed it off as an odd freckle.

He wanted to throw up at his own stupidity.

Logan rubbed his chin, then nodded.

"The papers?" She raised her brows as if she couldn't believe she was being so inconvenienced.

Logan stared at her but didn't respond.

She stared back.

Danny shifted restlessly by the door.

Bolt still looked like he had murder in his eyes.

"Where is she?"

It blurted out without thought.

Seth couldn't hold it in any longer. He needed to know Pepper was alive.

The woman who looked so much like her swiveled her head in his direction. He knew right then with the laughter in her eyes she wasn't Pepper. Stone cold evil, the very devil sat in that chair.

"I'm sorry, I don't know what you mean."

Seth stalked her way, stopping less than a foot from her chair. "Pepper. Where is she?"

Her eyes flashed surprise. So quickly, if he hadn't been staring daggers at her, he probably would've missed it. "I'm Pepper, you idiot."

He leaned down right into her face. For the first time, she reacted other than with cool disdain. She flinched and leaned away. "Pepper didn't talk about her sister much. Just that they didn't have a good relationship. That her sister hated her. I'm beginning to understand just how much you truly must hate Pepper. I won't ask again. Where is she? Because. You. Are. Not. Her."

He enunciated each word with such venom, she shrank away another inch.

Then she sat up, making it impossible to lean in so close to her without almost being mouth to mouth. He backed away this time. Her lips curled into a vicious smile. Then a low, evil cackle fell from her lips.

"Oh, I didn't anticipate this. That's too bad. My mistake coming back here." She tilted her head as the malice in her smile increased.

"Is she dead?"

The words almost didn't make it out of his mouth. He had to swallow past the lump in his throat first, and even then, they came out in a strangled croak.

Her evil twin did nothing other than shrug.

"Bolt, take her to lockup."

Logan's voice jolted him out of the trance he'd been in.

He had been staring into the fathomless eyes, looking for a sign of life, of just an ounce of compassion.

"No. No, Logan. She needs to tell us where Pepper is." Seth started to step toward Bolt who already had his hand-cuffs out.

Before he could do anything dumb, like hit Bolt for following orders, Logan stepped in front of him, shielding his view.

Seth pressed his lips together into a thin line. "Move."

"You can hit me, Seth. You can try. We can fight, right here and right now." He leaned in closer and whispered, "Or we can find Pepper."

"But we need her to tell us." He whipped a hand toward the door where Bolt was leading her out. Surprisingly, she didn't fight him.

Seth wasn't even sure why that surprised him. He figured someone with no soul would fight until the death.

Danny suddenly appeared. "She won't talk. Trust me on this, Seth. I heard it in her voice. She's not going to tell us. We'll have to find Pepper on our own."

"How?" he shouted. "We couldn't even find Evan on our own."

Logan ran a trembling hand down his face. "Well, we're done playing by the rules. And we have a missing deputy on our hands. I'd say that gives us free range to search Mr. Barten's property. Because that's where she has to be."

And Seth would tear apart every inch of that property if he had to.

24

ANOTHER SHIVER WRACKED HER BODY, although she felt so numb, she didn't know if the shivers meant she was starting to go into some sort of shock. What were the symptoms of hypothermia? She never had a reason to look them up. If she had to guess, shivering was a symptom.

She was going to die here by freezing to death. That would most likely kill her before dehydration and hunger took her.

How long did it take to die by hypothermia? Was it quick? Was it painful? Would she just slip into unconsciousness and not feel a thing?

Oh, God, she hoped so. She didn't want to feel any pain.

The constant shivering was already making her body ache.

It's as if they had turned the heat off to make her suffer.

But the walls were made of dirt.

So maybe she wasn't in a building.

Without the light, it had been pitch-black. There were no signs of any electricity hooked up. She couldn't believe

Brett had shown her any level of kindness by leaving the kerosene lamp.

Could she be in a bunker like Aubrey had been in when she was abducted? The brief reports she read said the sheriff had it sealed.

So, a different one? How many hidden bunkers did Mr. Barten have on his property?

Maybe that's where they hid their drugs.

She glanced around at all the boxes in the room.

It would be a very smart hiding place. Out of sight. Cops could search all buildings on the property and they'd never find any evidence because it was all underground.

Well, she wasn't dead yet.

Life had taught her many things. One thing it taught her was giving up was not an option. It might hurt to move, the cold seeping into her body taking permanent residence, but she couldn't give up.

She couldn't let her sister win.

Inhaling a deep breath, she mentally prepared herself before trying to scoot her hands behind her back to under her butt to get them to her front. The ropes were tied too tightly, and she couldn't do anything with them behind her back. So just had to dig deep for strength and get them in front of her.

Except the ropes dug deeper into her wrists when she attempted to move and her arms felt like they were being pulled out of their sockets. Maybe they were. Or her body was so numb from the cold it felt like it.

Either way, she had to ignore the pain and forge on.

Screaming, unable to hold it in, she fought with herself as she moved her arms under her butt. Part of her wanted to give up and sit back. The other part kept yelling at her to keep going. *You got this.* Silent tears started to stream down her face as the pain intensified.

Then, like a miracle, her hands slipped until they were directly under her knees. She sat for a moment, resting her head on her raised knees.

She let her breathing even out.

The pain didn't disappear, but it felt better to sit with her hands in front of her rather than behind.

Another intense shiver coated her body. Her teeth started to chatter.

"You got this, Pep. Get your ass moving."

Opening her eyes wide, she lifted her head and finished getting her hands out from underneath her legs. She tinkered with the ropes with her teeth, but the knots weren't budging.

It was a useless endeavor. She had to conserve her energy and only do what was necessary.

She attempted to stand. It took her several tries before her legs would hold, even with support from the wall as she leaned against it with her shoulder.

She took a few steps in place, trying to get the blood pumping through her veins.

Then she headed for the boxes closest to her. They weren't taped shut, the flaps were folded under one another. She could've kissed the gods for something going right.

She opened the first box.

Empty.

Shoving it aside, she opened a second box.

Empty.

No. This wasn't helpful.

Of course, a box full of drugs wouldn't have been helpful either, but nothing in the box dropped her spirits for some reason.

She tackled a few more boxes, her limbs moving a bit freer, albeit still painful, and found each one empty.

"Shit!"

The urge to relax back against a box overwhelmed her, but she forced herself to keep going. She had to find a way out of this room.

The door loomed ahead, her vision zeroing in on it as if it were a tiny insect under a microscope.

She heard the lock click, so she knew it wouldn't open, but she tried anyway.

The handle rattled but didn't budge.

And she had no clue how to pick a lock. Nor did she have anything to pick a lock with. The kerosene lantern burned brightly near her. The handle of the lantern was wire. Slightly thicker than she liked, but it might work.

The door was made of steel and the handle was a lever, not a normal doorknob. But it had a deadbolt lock on the inside, which made her assume she was up against a double-sided lock.

Why had they used a double-sided lock? It made no sense.

Whatever. It didn't matter. All that mattered was getting out of here.

She didn't know how to pick a normal lock. But she was observant. She watched a variety of shows, some being crime shows. They had always used two pieces to pick a lock, so she figured she'd need both sides of the lantern handle.

She hoped it wasn't too thick to slip inside the lock.

Her fingers barely moved when she gripped the lantern. Apparently, she had stood too long staring at the door and the dilemma before her.

Wiggling them a bit, she took a few deep breaths—again —before trying to remove the wire piece from the lantern.

It took a bit of finagling, especially with her hands tied, but she eventually got the wire free. Except it was a long piece. She'd have to break it into two. Bending it in half, a low groan escaped as pain radiated up her arms. She was amazed she could still feel pain. Her body wouldn't stop shivering.

She better start moving her ass faster.

Back and forth. Back and forth. She kept bending the wire back and forth until it finally snapped into two.

Then she stared at the door.

Go time!

Inserting one wire in, she breathed a sigh of relief it fit. Then she inserted the second one.

And stood there.

And stared.

She had no idea what to do.

So she started moving the wire around. Just one of them. They never moved both in shows, just one. So, she had to assume the one wire was meant to hold something in place inside the lock.

Fiddling commenced.

She jerked the wire this way. Then that way. Moving it around as if she knew what the hell she was doing.

Her arms started to ache from holding one position for so long. Her wrists started to burn as the rope continuously rubbed against her skin.

But she kept on going.

The shivers touching her skin every few seconds made her work go slower. So much time passed. She had no clock for a reference, but she knew she had been standing for a very long time.

Then, like another miracle from heaven, she heard a click.

"Holy shit."

Afraid she'd screw something up, she left the wires inside the lock and tried the handle.

The door swung open.

Freedom.

Peeking her head out, she saw nothing but darkness.

Grabbing the lamp by the small circle on top where the wire had been, she walked out of the room. Light flowed in front of her, but in front of that, nothing but darkness.

She had come this far, she couldn't stop now.

Moving slowly, considering she didn't have any shoes on and didn't want to step on anything dangerous, she took each step with care.

Finally, after what felt like miles, she came upon a small set up cobbled stairs. In reality, she probably hadn't walked more than twenty feet. But with the coldness zapping her bones, the constant shivering, and the pain it took to walk, it had felt a lot farther.

She set the lamp down, afraid she'd drop it on the steps, and carefully climbed them.

Only five small steps to freedom.

A steel door hung above her head when she reached the top.

Digging for more strength she didn't think she had, she shoved against it with her shoulder until it swung open and hit the ground.

She inched her head up out of the hole, soaking in the bright sunlight.

Her guess had been correct. They had stashed her in another bunker just like Aubrey had been held in.

Which really sucked.

Because as she looked around the forest surrounding her, she knew she had to stay in the dark pit of hell.

She'd never survive walking through the snow in the low temperatures looking for help in only her bra and panties.

Especially when the shivers wouldn't stop.

So much for freedom.

She closed her eyes from the despair.

SETH MET his brother outside of his patrol vehicle, trembling from the cold wind that hit his face. Bolt stood next to him.

Logan got out and waited until Danny came around the side of the vehicle.

"So, Mr. Barten's house was a dead end. And I'm highly suspicious since he didn't threaten us with a shotgun this time," Logan said as rubbed his hands together.

They had split up in teams to look for Pepper. Logan and Danny had visited Mr. Barten, while Seth and Bolt looked at his cabin again. They had tag-teamed, visiting a few known drug dealers in the area who worked for the Cheetahs in the off chance they'd be dumb enough to stash Pepper there. No such luck. After all the searching, they met in the middle, which happened to be their family cabin.

"Yeah, he seemed cool and collected," Danny added. "We didn't stick around to ask why. We did ask about Pepper and he didn't say a peep. Our other stops were dead ends."

"The cabin was a dead end, too. I didn't think they'd bring her back there, but you never know." Seth huddled his shoulders together to fend off the cold. "None of the other locations panned out either. We're running out of time. I can feel it."

"Does he have any other buildings on his land we don't know about?" Bolt threw out, shivering next to him.

The temperatures had dipped from the day before. The weather app kept saying snow was on the way, but it had yet to hit. Seth felt like a storm was brewing. Or maybe that was his gut telling him a different kind of storm was about to hit.

The grief storm.

They had to find Pepper. And soon.

He felt it in his bones; she didn't have long.

"Just the one cabin." Seth had grown up with Evan, roaming around his dad's land, in addition to his own family's land. He'd know if they had other buildings—or cabins—scattered in the woods.

"He had a hidden bunker no one knew about," Danny said quietly. Probably hating to voice it since it conjured bad memories about the horrors his sister suffered.

"You think there could be more?" Logan asked, rubbing his hands vigorously again. "Lillian hadn't left town, so we can only assume Brett hasn't either. Pepper must still be somewhere. We couldn't find him or his crew anywhere in town. Hiding underground would be the perfect place."

"How in the hell are we supposed to know where the hidden bunkers are?" This was a nightmare Seth didn't foresee. They'd never find Pepper.

"We have no way of knowing," Logan replied softly as he stared at him with remorse. As if he was already giving his condolences.

"Well, the sheriff's department has four-wheelers, as do you. Let's start looking." Danny scanned the woods around them. "If they've been using a hidden bunker, we'll see it. There's a lot of snow on the ground and they'd need to keep the door clear. They might put snow back over it to hide the entrance, but the area will still look disturbed. If it's there, we'll see it."

"That's not much of a plan," Seth snapped. "Searching blindly around for her."

"Where else do you suggest we look?" Danny snapped back. "We looked everywhere we could think of. Just like we had with Evan. It's better than sitting on our asses and doing nothing."

Seth inhaled sharply, then all the anger evaporated, leaving him lost and aching. "I'm...I'm freaking out. We have to find her soon."

"We're trying our best, Seth." Logan nodded with determination. "And we will."

"You have two four-wheelers here." Bolt threw a hand in the direction of the shed. "Why don't you and Seth start looking and I'll drive with Danny to grab the county's four-wheelers. You two start on the east side of Mr. Barten's property and we'll head over to the west side."

Logan didn't seem to mind that Bolt had suddenly issued orders. He nodded and clapped his gloved hands. "Let's get going."

Seth followed his brother to the shed. He hopped on a four-wheeler after grabbing one of the keys in the small drawers sitting on the workbench and headed out of the shed with a short wave to his brother.

They followed side by side until they knew they had entered Mr. Barten's property, then he went one direction and Logan went another.

Seth drove slowly, his eyes peeled for anything amiss.

The cold wind burned his face. He dismissed the pain, willing to go through the gates of hell if it meant Pepper came home alive and well.

He drove on. His eyes alert. His senses on overdrive.

Yet, nothing stuck out.

He couldn't lose faith. Maybe his brother had found something by now. It felt like he had been out in the woods for more than an hour searching. Bolt and Danny had to be out looking as well.

Just as he was about to stop his vehicle and send a text to his brother, something odd caught his eye.

Veering his four-wheeler to the left, his heart jumped out of his chest when he saw a steel door glinting in the harsh sunlight. It might feel like the arctic, but the sun was shining brightly. Thank goodness for that or he would've never seen the reflection of the sun off the door.

He jerked to a stop and nearly shouted Pepper's name when it occurred to him she might not be alone.

Damn it. They might've heard the four-wheeler approach. Too late to fix that mistake. Opening the back compartment, he grabbed a tire iron. They were always prepared for anything around these parts and it was the only viable weapon he had on hand. He also grabbed a flashlight, then carefully made his way to the entrance.

He noticed another set of four-wheeler tracks, but no vehicle.

Maybe they left.

Stopping by the door, he waited a few more seconds, just to see if anyone would come to check out the noise. When nobody did, he started to shove off the snow that he figured they put over to try and hide it. Then he set down the tire iron and flashlight and pulled hard on the handle, having to use all of his strength. It slammed hard to the other side. The snow muffled most of the sound, but the loud clang echoed in the still quietness.

He waited another few beats before deciding it was safe

to enter. Picking up the tire iron and his flashlight, he flicked it on and headed down the few steps.

As soon as he hit the last step, the darkness swallowed him whole.

Sure, he had a flashlight. But it was small compared to the darkness that surrounded him.

No wonder Aubrey hated the dark. No wonder she had nightmares and freaked out anytime Logan wasn't near her when night descended.

Seth had never seen the bunker before this. He could only picture in his mind what she had been through. He would've never guessed this.

Making his way farther into the blackness, he made sure to keep his light close to his feet and not shining far out ahead of him. He didn't want to completely give it away that someone was approaching. He didn't know what he was up against.

But he had a feeling he was the only one here. Those other four-wheeler tracks told him whoever had been here had left.

He inhaled sharply when he came upon a door on his left. Trying the handle, he found it locked. Twisting the lock, he waited for a beat before opening the door. No sound had echoed from inside so he assumed it was okay.

Boxes upon boxes sat in the room.

But no Pepper.

He opened one box because curiosity got the best of him.

His eyes bulged when he saw packages upon packages stacked together. It wasn't in a clear bag so he couldn't say for sure what it was, but he could only assume it was drugs. This was one of their storage facilities. Very smart hiding it here.

Retreating into the hallway, he continued onward. His steps slowed as he approached another door. This time on his right.

Pulling on the handle, he found it locked as the first one. He flipped the lock.

The second he stepped through the threshold and shined his light around, his heart fell from his chest.

"Pepper!"

Rushing to her side where she lay slumped against the wall in nothing more than her bra and panties, he nearly dropped the flashlight in his haste. He did drop the tire iron.

He had passed a kerosene lantern sitting on the boxes near the door, so the flashlight wasn't necessary at the moment.

Why was she half-naked?

"No, no, no, Pepper. Please be alive." Seth cradled her head gently, yet she didn't open her eyes. Her skin was cold as ice.

"Wake up, sweetheart. Please wake up." He bent closer, his lips brushing her forehead. Then he forced himself to lift his fingers to her neck to look for a pulse.

It took a while, considering he was shaking like an earthquake bent on destruction, but he finally felt a weak pulse.

"I need you to wake up. Say something. Stay with me," he whispered. When she didn't respond, he knew he was only wasting time trying to get her to speak.

Whipping off his jacket, he carefully wrapped it around her and zipped it up. He couldn't do anything about her hands tied together since he didn't grab a knife from the four-wheeler. That wasn't a priority anyway. He had to get her to a hospital fast. She was obviously hypothermic.

Picking her up, he cradled her as best as he could with

the flashlight still in one hand, then he walked out of the room. Walking briskly, he made his way outside. The bright sunlight was harsh on his eyes, but he adjusted quickly.

"I got you, sweetheart. You're going to be just fine. I promise."

Probably shouldn't have said that because it could turn out to be a lie.

Her body was so cold, he could feel it through his jacket wrapped around her.

He managed to get seated on the four-wheeler without jostling her too much and cranked the engine. The flashlight slipped from his fingers, but he didn't bother to get off and pick it up.

With her cradled in front of him, he positioned her as well as he could so she wouldn't fall off as they drove.

Just as he was about to take off, racing through the woods, her eyes opened.

"Seth..." A low breath escaped. "I...I'm...ssso..rrr..y."

He kissed her forehead, squeezing her tighter. "Stay with me, Pepper. I got you."

Then he drove off.

25

SETH LEANED his head back against the wall and closed his eyes. He was exhausted and wanted to hold Pepper in his arms until the chaotic energy flowing through his veins slowed down. He wasn't sure it'd ever stop.

But he couldn't.

He had raced through the woods on the four-wheeler, trying to shield her from the brutal wind as best as he could. He had felt her shivering in his arms the entire way. Except for the brief moment she whispered to him a heartbreaking apology, she hadn't uttered a word.

Why was she sorry?

That she was going to die? That she could feel herself slipping away?

He refused to believe it and had pushed the four-wheeler as fast as it would go. When he reached their cabin, he had transferred her to his car as gently as he could and left. He made a brief call to his brother telling him he'd found her and then disconnected. He needed all his attention on saving her.

The ride to the hospital felt like it took hours. He had the heat on blast the entire time. Pepper had shivered, her teeth chattering, yet her eyes remained closed.

They had whisked her away immediately. After overtly threatening a nurse who didn't deserve his harsh treatment, she led him to where Pepper was being treated. Then she pointed a finger for him to sit.

So, he sat.

Where he still sat. Waiting. And waiting.

His brother had arrived, along with Danny and Bolt. Maybe it was because Logan was the sheriff. Maybe it was because he asked nicer than Seth had, but they gave a prognosis on Pepper.

She was on the mild to moderate stages of hypothermia. Her body temperature had been 90 degrees Fahrenheit when he finally got her to the hospital. She had also suffered a head wound, a large gash they had to stitch. He hadn't even noticed the blood matted in her hair.

They were trying to slowly warm her body back up to a normal temperature. It took time. They couldn't do it too fast for the risk of sending her into cardiac arrest. And they wouldn't allow him in the room, so here he sat.

Waiting.

His brother, Danny, and Bolt all left, although Seth had seen it in Logan's eyes he didn't want to leave him alone. He assured him he'd be fine and to go do what he needed to do.

One of those things was arrest Mr. Barten.

Tons of drugs, a whole bunker full, had been found on his property. The old man was finally going down.

Seth didn't feel an ounce of remorse.

He just hoped Mr. Barten didn't do anything stupid, like pull a gun on any of them. His brother was a smart man.

Seth knew he'd walk into the battlefield with a game plan to take him down with minimal fighting.

"Hey. Can I join you?"

Seth opened his eyes and looked at Evan standing in front of him. He nodded and gestured to the open seat next to him.

"You okay?"

He was starting to despise that question. "Were you okay when you thought Stacy died?"

Evan lowered his head, fiddling with his fingers in his lap. "I felt like my world had ended. I felt guilty for dragging her into my mess." He lifted his gaze. "That was a dumb question. You're not okay. I had no idea you were seeing anyone. I am sorry for everything I did. For the gap I created between our friendship."

Seth grinned and patted his back gently, careful not to jar his injured shoulder too much. "In the past, man. Life's too short for me to hold a grudge. I'm sorry, too. I acted like a child and I'm done." Then he frowned as he glanced at the hospital gown he wore. "Where is Deke? Shouldn't he be watching you?"

"He went to help everyone else. I told him to. With the current situation, I imagine Brett is fleeing town and not too concerned about finishing the job with me." Evan chuckled. "I hope so, at least. They said I can be discharged tomorrow. Deke said he'd be back as soon as he could and we'd talk more about my situation."

"Where's Stacy?"

"She went home with her parents earlier. They're taking her out of town for a while. I think it's best for her right now."

Seth agreed. The heat might've died down right now for

them, but it didn't mean it wouldn't start back up. There were too many unknown variables. Too many unanswered questions.

"So..." Evan glanced behind him toward the door. "Deke didn't say much other than he was going to help arrest my dad. Good riddance, I say. He also mentioned that deputy was injured. The one I met last night. What's the story between you two?"

"It's complicated." Seth leaned his head against the wall. "I love her. I know that. That's about the only uncomplicated thing about it all."

"What are you going to do about it?" Evan rubbed his hands on his gown. "I'm here for you...if you want to tell me the whole complicated version. I don't mind."

Twisting his head, he smiled at his best friend. "Well, I've only known her since the day you had to run for your life, and I love her so much I don't even know how it's possible. I barely know her. She lied to me in the beginning. Lied to everyone. For good reasons, I understand that now. She's a twin. Her sister is dating Brett, the man who wants to kill you, and she tried to kill Pepper and steal her identity. That's the shortened version of the complicated story."

Evan's brows lifted as he nodded his head, a goofy grin on his face. "This sounds like it calls for a few beers. Where's a cold one when you need it?"

Seth laughed. "Soon, man. Soon we will grab that beer and catch up." Then his expression fell when his last words penetrated his thoughts a little more clearly. ...A cold one...

Pepper had been so cold to the touch. Like an icicle.

They had reassured him he found her in time. But did he?

Because the longer he sat not seeing her beautiful face,

not holding her tiny hand, not lending the strength she needed, the more he felt like he was losing her.

And if he lost her, he'd lose a large piece of himself.

He would never be okay again.

PEPPER DIDN'T FULLY BECOME aware of what was going on until a loud bang hit the floor. She jerked and groaned as the pain sliced through her body. Then a soft voice filtered through the air.

"You're awake. I'm so sorry I startled you. I dropped my clipboard." A woman in her thirties, if she had to guess, appeared by her side with a tender smile. "I'm Tara. I'm the nurse on duty."

"Nurse?" she croaked. Her throat was dry.

"Do you remember what happened to you?"

Flashes came here and there, but her head hurt to think hard about it.

Tara must've gathered as much from the frown that touched her face. "You were hit in the head pretty hard. We had to stitch up a large gash, about 15 stitches. You were also suffering from hypothermia. We've been slowly raising your body temperature, which I am happy to say is looking much better. We also cleaned and wrapped your wrists that suffered abrasions because your hands were tied together."

Oh, that was all helpful information. It assisted to give her a better picture. She didn't know who hit her on the head, but she remembered the pain and seeing her sister right before she lost consciousness. After that, she couldn't recall a lot other than an intense headache. She remembered being cold, shivering and shaking huddled in the tiny dark room. She remembered trying to get the ropes off and moving her hands from her back to her front.

"Ms. Chapman, are you okay? Are you in pain? How does your head feel?"

Terrible.

Her head felt terrible.

Her body ached.

Her heart was broken.

Was there medicine for that?

"It hurts."

"I'll go get you some pain medication. Usually, we'd release you once your body temperature went back to normal because you only suffered mild—borderline moderate—hypothermia, but you also suffered a concussion. You've been in and out for the last six hours. You'll have to spend the night for observation. If you need anything, you just have to push the button on the remote hanging over the side of your bed."

"Thank you."

Tara started to head to the door, then stopped. "There's a gentleman who has been sitting outside your room since you arrived. He's not family, and without your permission, we couldn't allow him in here. Would you like him to come in? His name is Seth Caldwell."

Oh, yeah, she remembered that, too. The memory was a bit fuzzy, only bits and pieces filtering in, but Seth saved her life.

"Yes, please."

Tara nodded and walked out.

Pepper wasn't sure if she just made the worst mistake of her life. What would Seth say? What would he do?

She had acted irresponsibly last night, leaving Seth's house before the sheriff had arrived. She did this to herself.

The door opened and Seth stepped inside. The relief in his eyes glimmered across the room. She wanted to bottle that expression because she didn't expect it to remain for long.

"Hi." He offered a short grin and rounded the bed to take a seat on the chair, scooting it as close to her bed as he could. "How are you feeling?"

"I'm fine." Such a lie, but she didn't want him to feel sorry for her. She didn't deserve it. She had created this mess.

His brows furrowed, his eyes flickering with indecision before his hand reached across the bed. He grabbed one of her hands and squeezed.

"I don't like lies. So, let's not lie to each other anymore." His lips pressed into a thin line before frowning. "You're not fine. You nearly died."

She looked away from his pain-filled gaze and focused on his soft touch. "My head hurts. My body hurts." Inhaling and exhaling with a slow degree, she dug deep for the last bit of strength she probably would never have again. "My heart hurts. My sister hated me so much, she..." She tried to tug her hand free. When Seth wouldn't budge, she stopped resisting and closed her eyes. "You don't need to be here. Thank you for saving my life, but you can leave."

Her heart, already torn to shreds, disintegrated into nothing when she said that. Because the last thing she wanted was for him to leave. She felt so alone, and his presence helped to fill a void she didn't think she'd ever fill.

"And if I don't want to?" His voice dropped to a whisper. "I lied to you, too, Pepper. I said I would never trust you, but I do. Because if I didn't trust you, I wouldn't love you. Please don't ask me to leave. I waited outside that room for hours, wishing and hoping to see your beautiful face, wishing and praying you wouldn't die, and now that I'm here, I can't lose that."

Her eyes opened and shifted her gaze his way. She saw the truth in his green eyes that sparkled like a polished jade stone.

He loved her?

No, it wasn't possible.

He abhorred liars and she had lied.

Leaning closer to her, a slow smile grew on his handsome face that was sporting a day's growth beard. "Pepper, I can see the confusion on your face. And right now isn't the best time to talk about it, but I'm not lying." He lifted her hand and kissed it. "I love you. Don't make me leave."

Her lips wobbled as her eyes filled with tears. She never thought she could feel such love for another person. Not with the family she had. Hateful sister. Gambling father who barely gave her the time of day. Clueless mother who blindly followed her father.

"I love you, too. I've made so many mistakes. I don't deserve your sweet words."

"We all make mistakes. It's how we fix them that counts."

Her eyes closed again. This time, not because she didn't want to see the ache in his eyes, but because the bright light was starting to make her head pound worse. Where was the nurse with her pain medication?

"You okay? Do you need anything?"

"She said she was going to get me some pain meds," she replied as her eyes remained closed.

"Just rest, Pepper. She'll be back soon." His voice cracked. "I almost lost you. Luck was definitely on my side. You were locked in that room with no clothes. I can't get the pict—" His voice cracked again. "God, I love you."

She wanted to shut her mind off and rest, but his words didn't make sense. Her eyes popped open.

"I got the door unlocked. I picked it with the wire handle from the kerosene lantern."

The agony in his expression softened. "No, sweetheart, I had to unlock that room."

"But I remember standing up and looking through the boxes for something to help me, but they were empty. Then I grabbed the lantern after I noticed it was a lock I could pick. I used the wire and I got the door open. I even looked outside and knew I couldn't venture out there in only my bra and panties."

"Pepper..."

He didn't believe her. How could he not believe her? He just said he loved her.

"I swear, Seth. I'm not lying."

A throat cleared and Tara stepped closer to the bed. Obviously, neither of them heard her open the door.

"I can help. Pepper, you had hypothermia, which lowers your body temperature, but it can also cause confusion and hallucinations. You might have thought you got that door opened, but you didn't. You were also hit hard on the head. You were very disoriented from the combination of both things."

She trembled. "It felt so real."

"The important thing to remember is you're here and you're safe." Tara held up a tiny cup with two pills and a cup of water. "Here, for your pain. It might be best just to rest for now and talk later."

Maybe. Because what she remembered had felt so real. Each detail was ingrained in her memory.

She swallowed the pills with ease and drank the luke-warm water. When she grimaced at the temperature, Tara smiled apologetically. "You can have colder water later. We're still monitoring your temperature."

Then Tara left the room.

She couldn't keep her eyes open, but she grasped his hand in a tight grip. "Don't leave. I'm sorry I asked you to."

"I'll be here by your side until you're released. I promise. You're going to have a hard time getting rid of me."

That didn't sound like a bad thing at all to Pepper.

26

"Are you sure you're up for this?" Seth asked her for what felt like the billionth time.

Of course, she wasn't sure.

Her sister had tried to kill her and take her identity. Who did that? Family was supposed to love and support you. Sure, not all families got along, but to go to this extreme didn't seem fathomable.

"I'm sure," Pepper replied. She *so* wasn't sure.

Seth pulled open the door to the sheriff's department. Pepper stepped through first, feeling a sense of—well, so many emotions. Elation, because she never thought she'd step through these doors again. She had enjoyed working here, even if most of the time she had been lying about who she was. Regret, because it had hurt her to lie to these nice people. But her work always came first. Yeah, and look where that got her. Trepidation, because she was suddenly getting cold feet to look her sister in the eye.

"You don't have to do this." Seth's soft touch to the back of her jacket soothed her. It anchored her to reality.

She didn't have to do this; he was right. She *needed* to do this.

She needed to look her sister in the eye and ask her why. Why did she hate her so much? Why would she try to kill her? Why would she fake her death and let her mourn her passing? Why was she so cruel?

Two days had passed since Seth found her. Two days of ruminating, circling those questions over and over in her mind. She hadn't come to a concrete answer on her own, so here she was, going directly to the source.

They released her from the hospital yesterday afternoon. Her head still ached, a low pounding headache, but overall, she was feeling better. Not disoriented or dizzy anymore. Because the first night she tried to get out of bed to go to the bathroom, she almost fell flat on her face when the dizziness attacked her.

Seth had been her rock, her anchor to the world. She was positive she would've slipped into the darkness if not for him. As he promised, he didn't leave her side once in the hospital. He drove her home and made sure she was comfortable. Even then, he stayed. He spent the night lying by her side holding her, making her feel not so alone where deep inside a lonely little girl lived.

This morning, he made her a light breakfast. When she said she wanted to see her sister, he tried to talk her out of it but had supported her as she got ready and drove her to the sheriff's department.

She could kill two birds with one stone anyway. She had to turn in her gun and badge. Well, her sister had stolen her gun and badge, so metaphorically, she had to turn in her gun and badge. She had to quit. Her job was complete. There was no need to be a deputy anymore. Although she dreaded it, she needed to speak with the sheriff as well.

Logan had come by her room and asked a few questions, but he didn't dig too deep and she didn't offer too many details. She needed to give her whole side of the story and ask about the progress of the case.

Then she'd have to pack up and leave.

Without Seth in her life.

How would she survive? She was barely surviving as it was.

"Hey, this isn't a good idea," Seth whispered as he grabbed her gloved hand.

Maybe he was right, especially since the moment she had stepped through the doors all she had been doing was standing in one spot.

She could feel Charlotte's eyes on her, yet she didn't say a word.

This wasn't who she was. She always maintained control of herself and any situation in front of her. Where was the cool, calm, and collected Pepper?

Inhaling deeply, she squeezed Seth's hand and then made him let go. Taking off her gloves and shoving them in her coat pockets, she looked at him. "I'm okay. I can do this."

He nodded, wrapping a hand behind her neck and pulled her closer, kissing her forehead. He had been keeping the intimacy between them since they left the hospital light. A kiss here, a peck there. Holding hands and snuggling in his embrace. That was it. At the moment, she didn't need more. She just needed to know he was there, in her reach.

Because soon, he wouldn't be.

She'd be leaving soon.

For all his support he'd been giving her, not once had either of them brought up the conversation of her leaving town.

Of course, not something she could think about right now.

Producing a smile she didn't feel, she approached Charlotte's desk. "Good morning, Charlotte. First, I want to apologize for my behavior and if I ever hurt your feelings. Sometimes I get so into the job, I don't think about others around me, and for that, I am sorry."

Before she left, she would make sure she mended all the bridges she had broken.

A sincere smile etched across Charlotte's face. "Apology accepted. I'm glad you're okay. There's fresh coffee in the break room and some doughnuts. Help yourself."

"Thank you. I'd like to see my sister first."

Charlotte shared a look with Seth before looking back at her. "You know where lockup is. She'll be leaving in a few hours, as soon as the agents from the Minneapolis field office arrive."

Which meant she needed to hurry up. Even though he hadn't wanted to, Seth called his brother before they left, informing him they were coming and she wanted to speak to Lillian. Because she was a coward, she didn't ask Logan herself. But, he had given the okay.

So instead of seeing him first, she headed to lockup with Seth right next to her. Part of her didn't want him by her side as she spoke to her sister, the cowardly part of her was grateful for his presence.

Lillian didn't even stand up from the worn cot in the corner. She didn't smile. She didn't frown. She didn't even look like she cared that she stood in front of her and the fate that lay ahead of her.

They stared at one another for the longest time. Even Seth remained silent next to her.

"Why?" Pepper finally managed to say. It came out low,

almost in a whisper. But she said it. She found the courage to speak and ask the one question swirling around her mind since she had woken up in the hospital.

Lillian lifted one side of her shoulder as a tiny smirk emerged. "Why not? Because I could."

Coldhearted. Evil. Her eyes, deep and black, empty. Utterly soulless.

How in the world were they twins?

Then, as if an angel had come down from heaven, her guilt for never making amends, her regret for never treating her kindly, her sadness that they'd never be true sisters, lifted. It soared away.

It's as if all she needed was to look at her sister one last time to see there would be no winning this war. They would never be sisters. They would never make amends. They would never even be friendly with each other.

And that was okay. Pepper could live with it.

"This is the last time we'll ever see each other. This is the last time I'll even think about you. It doesn't make me sad like I thought it would." Pepper tilted her head to the side, more weight flying away. "I forgive you, even though you'll never offer an apology. I still forgive you. Because in the end, it means I forgive myself for all the times I did wrong by you. For all the times I could've reached out instead of pushing you away. You should look at forgiving yourself, too."

Without waiting for a reply, Pepper turned and walked away. Seth followed without a word. Her sister obviously wanted the last word because before the door to the lockup area swung closed, she heard, "When I get out of here, I'll finish the job. You're dead."

Yeah, she could try—if she ever saw the outside of a jail cell. But that wasn't ever likely to happen. She was going down and going down hard.

Seth slipped his hand inside hers and squeezed. "You okay?"

Twisting her gaze in his direction as they headed for Logan's office, she smiled. A real, true honest smile this time. "I'm okay."

This time, he must've believed her because he returned a handsome smile.

Right before they reached Logan's office, she stopped and let go of his hand. "I need to speak to your brother alone. Please."

Seth hesitated but nodded. "I'll be in the lobby."

He walked away and she wanted nothing more than to shout he come back and stand by her side. But she created this mess and she had to face the consequences on her own. She was still shocked Seth had seemed to forgive her so easily for acting so idiotically.

She knocked on the doorframe and stepped inside when Logan waved her in. He stood up and circled his desk.

"You look much better, Pepper. How are you feeling?"

"I still have a slight headache, but overall, much better." She sighed and then a lame chuckle escaped. "I saw Lillian. I'm not even sure why I was so adamant to find her killer anymore."

Logan's expression twisted this way and that as if trying to find the right words. "Well, unfortunately, we can't pick our family." He gestured toward the chair in front of his desk. "We can pick our friends, though."

She took a seat as his last comment swirled around her brain. What did that mean?

He took a seat as well. "We've been busy the last two days. The Cheetahs are embedded deep in a lot of areas. The detective that supposedly handled your sister's murder was arrested for falsifying a police report, among other things. He had to create a fake coroner's report and everything. Every case he's worked is now under investigation as well. The FBI agent that contacted you about her death has also been arrested for his actions. After some digging, I'm sure they'll find the connection to the Cheetahs. Their entire ruse wouldn't have worked without those two. There could even be others involved, but we're not sure at this point."

She nodded but didn't say anything. She had no words. The detective, sure, she could understand him following her sister blindly to do her bidding. But she had thought Agent Rollins was her friend. They went to the academy together. They bonded. That hurt more than she cared to admit.

"We found a ton of drugs in that bunker they were holding you in. A lot." Logan leaned forward as he interlocked his hands. "We arrested Mr. Barten and he won't be getting out anytime soon. That old man has gotten off way too easily every single time I've had to deal with him."

"That's good to hear. I imagine they were also making those drugs on his property, too."

"I definitely agree." Logan ran a hand down his face. "Aubrey was held in a separate bunker. I never imagined there was more than one."

Pepper shivered at the memories of even being in one of those bunkers for the short period she had been.

She understood Aubrey better now. Her constant looking at the window, eyeing the darkness descending. She understood the horror Aubrey lived. The dark terrified her.

It wasn't something she liked too much anymore.

Logan ran another hand down his face. "There's probably a lot more bunkers we don't know about. It's going to take time to find them all. But I have the warrants I need to search every inch of his property. I'll need help, though."

"Oh?"

Was he asking what she thought he was asking? For her to stay?

"I contacted the DEA. This is more up their alley."

Oh.

Not what she was expecting. But it made sense.

"That's good. I'm sure they have tons of information on this gang. They'll be a great source to have."

Logan nodded. "They're sending an agent in the next few days to help us."

"Good. I'm glad to hear that. And what about Stacy and Evan?"

Not that she cared too much. She kind of did. But not really. She was only delaying the inevitable.

"Stacy left town for a while with her parents. Brett ditched town, as far as we know. We haven't seen a sign of him. But the FBI field office in Florida, as well as the DEA, are on high alert for him. Evan is back home and recovering well. He's declined protection, and right now, with Mr. Barten arrested and most of the Cheetahs fleeing town, I'm sure he's okay without it. Barry's son asked Evan to run the garage, and he took him up on it."

"Good. That's good to hear."

If her dumb repeating of "good" wasn't enough indication of how nervous she was, she didn't know what would give it away.

Pepper inhaled, then let it out, knowing she couldn't delay it any longer. "I'm sorry. I acted irresponsibly and recklessly when I left Seth's house without waiting for you or backup. I have no excuse. I want you to know I respect you and it was a pleasure to work for you."

The sheriff already had her gun and badge because her sister took it from her person when she knocked her out at the cabin. She didn't have anything to turn in. She only had her apology and her regret to offer.

"Apology accepted. I don't like to hold grudges. I respect when someone owns their mistakes." Logan opened a desk drawer and pulled out two items. Then he set her badge and gun before her. "I have an opening for a deputy position. Would you like to fill it?"

She glanced at the gun and badge and then back at the sheriff.

Was he serious?

Obviously, because he set the two items before her, and the genuine smile on his face wasn't fake.

What would Seth say?

He said he loved her, but he never asked her to stay in town. Maybe he was just being kind before she left.

Would he want her to stay?

"Pepper? What do you think?"

Think?

She had no idea what to think. She liked to dissect and weigh all options before she made a decision. He couldn't possibly want an answer right this second.

But the eager look in his eyes and the determination twisting his lips said he expected an answer right here and now.

She had no idea what to say.

SETH STOOD up straighter from leaning against Charlotte's desk when Pepper walked into the room. She looked sad.

Not a good sign.

He knew his brother was going to offer her a position because Seth had talked to him about it. He loved this woman. He loved her so much he was willing to move anywhere she went. Except, he loved this small town, too. With time, he thought Pepper might come to love it as well, so he put the bug in his brother's ear. He did need a deputy to fill the vacant spot. Derek wasn't coming back, too butthurt to see that they never wanted him to leave to begin with.

While Pepper had made mistakes, Logan knew she was good at her job and would be a good addition to the department, so he had agreed to ask her to stay.

But the forlorn expression on her face said her decision had not gone in his favor. Would that mean she would be opposed to him moving with her back to New York?

Because he was all in this relationship. He wanted to make it work.

"You okay?"

A forced smile touched her lips. "Let's forgo the 'are you okay' question from now on. I'm fine, Seth."

"Okay." But it wasn't okay because that didn't answer his question.

What did she say to his brother?

"See you around, Charlotte." He tried to keep his attitude light and carefree and not like he was dying inside from the fact she rejected his brother's offer.

Pepper also said goodbye and they headed for his truck. He drove slowly back to her house, silence filling the vehicle. She still didn't say anything when they got inside and removed their jackets and shoes.

"I'll make lunch. Are you hungry?" she asked.

"Yes, but I'll make lunch. You go relax." He nudged her toward the living room, and she didn't argue.

He wasn't sure what to make, but he decided to go with what always made him feel better. Especially since his world felt like it was on the brink of destruction. When he was finished, he told Pepper and waited impatiently for her reaction when she saw the two plates sitting on the table for them.

A grilled cheese sandwich cut into two triangles with ketchup on the side. His favorite comfort food.

"Oh, you pulled out all the stops. You shouldn't have," she said with a chuckle as he pulled out her chair and then scooted it in for her.

"Hey, I know how to impress a lady."

Yet, he didn't feel like he knew how to keep one in his life. Maybe she didn't believe he loved her.

He waited until she took her first bite. A wide smile curved his lips when pure pleasure exploded on her face.

"So delicious. You have magic in your hands."

Oh, that comment just made his mind wander to a territory that he shouldn't even contemplate. Sure, he'd kissed her here and there, but nothing more happened. Of course, she was recovering from a severe concussion and hypothermia, so he had to be gentle with her. But that comment made him want to pick her up and whisk her away to the bedroom to show her how magical his touch could be.

They ate in comfortable silence.

When they both finished, he cleared the plates, washed the dishes and saw Pepper still sitting at the table.

"You—" He cut off his words, considering he was about to ask if she was okay. It was just reflexive. He couldn't help it, especially when the forlorn expression hadn't disappeared. He could still see it reflected in her eyes.

She stood up and touched his cheeks. "I'm fine. You don't have to keep asking."

"You look sad. It couldn't have been easy to see your sister. I understand if—"

"It's not about my sister. Her actions don't surprise me. I didn't lie to her. I forgive her. I have to; otherwise, it'll just eat me alive, and I refuse to let her control my life that way."

Her thumbs rubbed his cheeks before smoothing upward and through his hair. A contented sigh slipped from his lips as her hands rested behind his neck.

"Your brother asked me to stay. He offered me a job."

His heart started to pound. Moment of truth.

His life was either about to get happier or more depressing.

"Did he?" He could feel his body trembling, so she had to feel it, too. "What did you say?"

She bit her lip as her fingers toyed with the bottom of his hair, tickling his neck. "I accepted."

He released a relieved breath. "Thank God."

A tentative smile appeared. "This makes you happy?"

Wrapping his hands around her waist, he picked her up, making her wrap her legs around his waist. "Beyond happy. I love you, Pepper. I don't want you to leave. And if you do want to leave, I'll follow wherever you go."

She hugged him, her lips touching his neck. "I love you, too, Seth. I was so worried you wouldn't want me to stay. But I like it here. I like the people. Now I just need them to like me, too."

"Let them see the real you, and they will. Like I do." He suddenly felt wetness on his neck. "Hey, don't cry. Please, sweetheart."

"Happy tears, I promise. I'm just so happy. I've never felt like I belonged anywhere, and in your arms, I finally feel like I found my home."

"I couldn't agree more. You're my everything I didn't know I needed."

He needed to hold her, but not like this. Walking carefully to her bedroom, he laid her down and joined her, pulling her close.

Kissing her softly on the lips, he whispered, "You and me, always. No more secrets and lies. Only honesty and truth. And the truth is, I think I loved you from the moment I met you. You were the one thing I needed for me to see how childish and irresponsible I was acting. Don't ever stop being you, Pepper. Because the real you is beautiful."

She brushed a hand across his cheek. "I never imagined finding a man like you. I should honestly thank my sister."

He chuckled. "Let's not go that far." Then he kissed her on the lips and proceeded to show her how much he truly loved her.

She might've come to this town for reasons that would haunt her for the rest of her life, but it brought him the woman of his dreams.

Pepper had stolen his heart.

And he didn't want it back. She could keep it until the day he died.

EPILOGUE

CHARLOTTE THREW the empty cupcake container in the trash and then arranged the tray of chocolate cupcakes in the center of the break room table. Of course, they had extra chocolate frosting with blue sprinkles, Bolt's favorite.

Sure, he wasn't the only hero around here who helped save Pepper. Seth had a huge hand in it as well. He did find her. But Bolt was the one who kept pressing the issue, making everyone believe that evil woman was not who she said she was.

It was also Pepper's first day back on the job since everything happened. She had taken a full week off. Charlotte wanted to make her feel welcome.

Of course, when Pepper first arrived, she tried to make her feel welcome with kind words and a friendly smile, but she had rebuffed her kindness. Charlotte understood why she had, but it still hurt. Regardless, she was willing to forgive and forget and try again.

And not only would she be seeing Pepper every day because she worked here officially now, but she was also dating Seth, so she had to work to get along with her. The

Caldwells were like her second family, which made Pepper her family. It only seemed right to make amends with her.

Twisting the tray another quarter degree angle, she smiled and stepped back.

Perfect.

Footsteps nearing the doorway had her looking up.

Ugh.

He was the last person she wanted to see, especially when she was feeling so upbeat and happy about the day. "Good morning, Charlotte," Deke said in that sultry voice of his that always slid down her spine with delicious intent.

She hated the man for that reason alone.

"Do not touch those cupcakes. They're not for you."

A silky brow rose on his handsome face. "I didn't even attempt to take one. Who are they for?"

"Not for you."

She had brought them for everyone, but the immensely bruised part of her soul said he wasn't part of that equation. He couldn't have one of her cupcakes. Not after he broke her heart the way he had.

"What are you doing here?" she snapped. She liked to be forewarned when he was coming around so she could make herself scarce until he left.

Every time she saw him, it made the pain inside her heart intensify to the point it was almost unbearable. Some days, she had to force the tears to stay inside.

"The DEA agent is arriving today. Danny and I wanted to be here." He gestured toward the coffeepot. "I wanted a cup of coffee." Then his expression fell as if he was honestly remorseful for how he had stomped on her heart. "How long are we going to do this, Charlotte? How long are you going to hate me?"

"Until I never have to see your face again. Even then, I'll hate you until I die."

His eyes shattered at her words.

Good.

He could feel an ounce of what she felt.

"Charlotte, I—"

"Good morning." A woman with sleek black hair and the face of an angel walked into the break room. "I'm sorry. I didn't mean to interrupt. The sheriff directed me here and said we'd have a meeting over coffee and cupcakes. I love cupcakes."

Charlotte grabbed the tray and moved it closer to her side. She didn't know why she did because it was rude, and she was never rude to people unless it was necessary.

"Who are you?"

The woman with sparkling hazel eyes, immaculate makeup, and a heart-shaped face that Charlotte assumed most men swooned over laughed. A sweet, delicate laugh that was light and airy, and oh-so-perfect. It made her sick to her stomach.

"I'm sorry. I'm Agent Tiffany Wheeler with the DEA. I'm here to help with the investigation on the Cheetahs." Then she reached out across the table to shake hands.

Darn it. Charlotte should've realized that except Deke's presence was throwing her all out of whack and making her act how she would never act.

She shook hands with the woman and offered a smile. Then Charlotte pushed the tray closer to Agent Wheeler. "Help yourself to a cupcake. Welcome to Lucky."

"Thank you." Then Agent Wheeler turned toward Deke and offered her hand. "Hi. And you are?"

"Agent Sumnter, FBI. Nice to meet you." The sensual smile that lit up his face only aggravated Charlotte further.

He didn't care about her feelings. Openly flirting with this woman. Giving her one of his sexy, signature smiles.

The rat bastard.

She picked up a cupcake and threw it at him. It hit him square in the chest.

Then she smiled when he looked at her with his mouth wide open in shock.

"Enjoy your cupcake, Deke."

Then she walked out of the break room and swore she'd never speak to the man again. No matter the reason.

———

DON'T MISS the next book in this exciting romantic suspense series!

DEADLY MEMORIES

Her past is a deadly puzzle she must solve...before it's too late.

Stumbling into a stranger's isolated cabin, she's terrified—her memories a dangerous blank slate. The only thing her instincts scream is to trust the ruggedly handsome Sheriff Logan Caldwell who found her. With his protective nature and gentle touch, he also makes her feel safer than she has in...well, as long as she can remember.

As shadows of her forgotten past close in, Logan becomes her only ally against an unknown enemy. Every recovered memory brings more fear than answers. As passion ignites between them, one thing becomes clear: if her enemy finds her, she'll meet a fate worse than death.

*With nail-biting suspense and smoldering romance, plunge into the danger and desire with the first book in the **Lucky Town** **series** today!*

For Danny & Kat's story
Dangerous Memories
A Lucky Town Novel, #2

Has the nightmare returned or is this a darker threat?

Agent Danny O'Rourke's greatest wish is for his sister, Aubrey, kidnapped months ago, to finally come home. Though he couldn't save her then, he'll do whatever it takes now to help her heal and bring her back into his life. Except one thing is standing in his way—the Caldwell family.

When a new case links to the Caldwells, he's determined to find answers, even if it means facing off with the alluring Kat Caldwell. Though he tries to hate her, Danny can't deny the intense attraction burning between them.

As the body count rises, Danny has the chilling realization that Kat is the target of this twisted predator's obsession. Haunted by the failures of his past, he'll risk it all to protect her. But one question remains: is the danger they're facing now linked to Aubrey's disappearance...or is an even more sinister force at play?

As Danny follows the clues down a rabbit hole of lies and depravity, there's only one thing he knows for certain: losing Kat is not an option. As their passion flares white-hot, the killer's trails turns deadly cold, and Danny must confront his greatest demon to rescue the woman he loves...before she's taken from him forever.

For Deke & Charlotte's story
Deadly Memories
A Lucky Town Novel, #4

Love is scary...death is terrifying.

Deke Sumnter only has casual sex. Anything beyond that, he's not interested. Until Charlotte. She's smart, sexy, and something he's always craved. But one time was all he could give her. He should've known it wouldn't be enough. Now, she won't even talk to him. He'd take just being friends over the silent treatment.

When trouble starts brewing again in their small town, this time targeting the woman he swears he doesn't love, he won't let anything stop him from protecting her, even if everything inside of him says he needs to stay as far away from her as possible.

Captivating suspense and electric romance unite in this emotional thriller that will leave you breathless. One-click now to start reading today!

FOR BOLT & CHERRY'S STORY
FORGOTTEN MEMORIES
A LUCKY TOWN NOVEL, #5

She isn't looking for trouble...

Despite being a city girl, Cherry Chapman could get used to the small-town life. Not that she's welcome in Lucky. She only wants to meet her half-sister, Pepper, and get to know her, not stir up a hornet's nest. So far, the only person welcoming her is Deputy Bolten, and at times, she feels even he doesn't trust her. The way things are going, she's going to need more than just his kindness. She's going to need his help. But if he doesn't trust her, how can she trust him with the problems that followed her to town?

While the past year has been a rough one, Bolt is trying to move forward. When Cherry comes crashing into their town with her sweet and innocent nature, he can't help but be wary—and attracted to her. The more he gets to know her, the more he wants to help her. He knows something is going on, but no matter how hard he tries, she won't confide in him. He's failed before—getting shot is proof of that—but he vows not to fail again. He'll protect Cherry at all costs, even if that means being on the opposite side of his friends.

*With high tension, suspense, and smoldering romance, dive into the danger and desire with the final book in the **Lucky Town series** today.*

ABOUT THE AUTHOR

I'm a *USA Today* Bestselling Author that loves to write contemporary romance and romantic suspense novels, although I am partial to romantic suspense. I even dabble in paranormal. Honestly, I love anything that has to do with romance. As long as there's a happy ending, I'm a happy camper. And insta-love...yes, please! I love baseball (Go Twins!) and creating awesome crafts. I graduated with a Bachelor's Degree in Criminal Justice, working in that field for several years before I became a stay-at-home mom. I have a few more amazing stories in the works. If you would like to learn more about me and my books, head to my website by scanning the QR code. Thanks for reading!

Scan me

www.ingramcontent.com/pod-product-compliance
Lightning Source LLC
Chambersburg PA
CBHW031105030726
47496CB00002BA/392